PRAISE FOR MELIS:

"With her wonderful characters and resonating emotions, Melissa Foster is a must-read author!"

—*New York Times* bestseller Julie Kenner

"Melissa Foster is synonymous with sexy, swoony, heartfelt romance!"

—*New York Times* bestseller Lauren Blakely

"You can always rely on Melissa Foster to deliver a story that's fresh, emotional, and entertaining."

—*New York Times* bestseller Brenda Novak

"Melissa Foster writes worlds that draw you in, with strong heroes and brave heroines surrounded by a community that makes you want to crawl right on through the page and live there."

—*New York Times* bestseller Julia Kent

"When it comes to contemporary romances with realistic characters, an emotional love story, and smokin'-hot sex, author Melissa Foster always delivers!"

—*The Romance Reviews*

"Foster writes characters that are complex and loyal, and each new story brings further depth and development to a redefined concept of family."

—*RT Book Reviews*

"Melissa Foster definitely knows how to spin a tale and keep you flipping the pages."

—*Book Loving Fairy*

"You can never go wrong with the heroes that Melissa Foster creates. She hasn't made one yet that I haven't fallen in love with."

—*Natalie the Biblioholic*

"Melissa is a very talented author that tells fabulous stories that captivate you and keep your attention from the first page to the last page. Definitely an author that you will want to keep on your go-to list."

—*Between the Coverz*

"Melissa Foster writes the best contemporary romance I have ever read. She does it in bundles, topped it with great plots, hot guys, strong heroines, and sprinkled it with family dynamics—you got yourself an amazing read."

—*Reviews of a Book Maniac*

"[Melissa Foster] has a way with words that endears a family in our hearts, and watching each sibling and friend go on to meet their true love is such a joy!"

—*Thoughts of a Blonde*

CALL HER MINE

MORE BOOKS BY MELISSA FOSTER

LOVE IN BLOOM ROMANCE SERIES

SNOW SISTERS

Sisters in Love
Sisters in Bloom
Sisters in White

THE BRADENS

Lovers at Heart, Reimagined
Destined for Love
Friendship on Fire
Sea of Love
Bursting with Love
Hearts at Play
Taken by Love
Fated for Love
Romancing My Love
Flirting with Love
Dreaming of Love
Crashing into Love
Healed by Love
Surrender My Love
River of Love
Crushing on Love
Whisper of Love
Thrill of Love

THE BRADENS & MONTGOMERYS

Embracing Her Heart
Anything for Love
Trails of Love

Wild, Crazy Hearts
Making You Mine

BRADEN NOVELLAS

Promise My Love
Our New Love
Daring Her Love
Story of Love
Love at Last
A Very Braden Christmas

THE REMINGTONS

Game of Love
Stroke of Love
Flames of Love
Slope of Love
Read, Write, Love
Touched by Love

SEASIDE SUMMERS

Seaside Dreams
Seaside Hearts
Seaside Sunsets
Seaside Secrets
Seaside Nights
Seaside Embrace
Seaside Lovers
Seaside Whispers
Seaside Serenade

BAYSIDE SUMMERS

Bayside Desires
Bayside Passions
Bayside Heat
Bayside Escape
Bayside Romance

THE RYDERS

Seized by Love
Claimed by Love
Chased by Love
Rescued by Love
Swept into Love

SUGAR LAKE

The Real Thing
Only for You
Love Like Ours
Finding My Girl

TRU BLUE & THE WHISKEYS

Tru Blue
Truly, Madly, Whiskey
Driving Whiskey Wild
Wicked Whiskey Love
Mad About Moon
Taming My Whiskey

BILLIONAIRES AFTER DARK SERIES

Wild Boys After Dark

Logan
Heath
Jackson
Cooper

Bad Boys After Dark

Mick
Dylan
Carson
Brett

HARBORSIDE NIGHTS

Catching Cassidy
Discovering Delilah
Tempting Tristan

STAND-ALONE NOVELS

Chasing Amanda (mystery/suspense)
Come Back to Me (mystery/suspense)
Have No Shame (historical fiction/romance)
Love, Lies, & Mystery (three-book bundle)
Megan's Way (literary fiction)
Traces of Kara (psychological thriller)
Where Petals Fall (suspense)

CALL
HER
MINE

Harmony Pointe, Book One

MELISSA
FOSTER

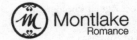
Montlake
Romance

Published by Montlake Romance, Seattle

www.apub.com

Amazon, the Amazon logo, and Montlake Romance are trademarks of Amazon.com, Inc., or its affiliates.

ISBN-13: 9781542007382
ISBN-10: 1542007380

Cover design by Letitia Hasser

Cover photography by Wander Aguiar Photography

Printed in the United States of America

To the Lisas in my life

CHAPTER ONE

AURELIA LOOKED LONGINGLY at the muscular arm circling her waist and the large hand cupping her breast over her shirt and promptly closed her eyes, chastising herself for doing it *again*. *Always a bridesmaid, never a bride* was beginning to ring too true, and it was all Ben Dalton's fault. She'd had a ridiculous crush on her Henry Cavill–lookalike best friend for *far* too long, and it was getting in the way of her life, her thoughts, her *everything*. Every time she went out with a guy, she compared him to Ben, who looked rugged and yummy in jeans that hugged his thick thighs and perfect ass and could rock a suit like he'd strutted off a runway. He even owned a pair of black-framed glasses he sometimes wore for reading, which took him from Superman to Clark Kent in a heartbeat. What woman wasn't turned on by a stud in glasses? But it wasn't just his looks. She quickly bored of every date, waiting for them to be quippy, fun, and unknowingly seductive like Ben. If she wasn't careful, she'd end up the spinster of Sweetwater, New York. *Harmony Pointe,* she corrected herself. Though she'd grown up in Sweetwater and moved back to reopen her grandmother's bookstore and combine it with Ben's sister Willow's business, Sweetie Pie Bakery, Aurelia had recently changed directions. In an effort to stop waking up in Friendsville, she'd bought an adorable bookstore with an apartment above it on the corner of Main Street and West Avenue in the next town over, Harmony Pointe.

She allowed herself another minute to enjoy the feel of Ben's broad chest against her back, his titillating breath warming her neck, and yes, even his morning *wood* pressing into her bottom. The situation would be sexier if the man-child wrapped around her wasn't *also* drooling on her shirt.

That was about all the action she'd ever see from him.

She'd spent the last month swearing she was done doing this with him. But when he'd called her last night and said, "Come on, Rels, hang out with me. I miss you," that was all it had taken. The way he said *Rels* always made her stupid heart melt. She'd been called Aurelia since the day she was born—the day her mother had died—by everyone except Ben. He had coined the nickname *Rels*—or *Relsy* if he was in a particularly sweet mood—and he only seemed to use it when they were alone. It was ridiculous that a secret nickname could make her feel special, but it did. She knew she was important to him. She was the first person he called to share any kind of news, and they were known in their circle of friends as *Ben and Aurelia*—always linked, like Ben and Jerry. Two people who seemed to exist as one perfect combination.

Except she didn't want to be Ben and Jerry.

She wanted to be the perfect combination of man and woman, like Ryan Reynolds and Blake Lively. The type of couple who had wild, crazy sex and woke up naked, tangled in each other's sticky body parts, not clothed on a chaise lounge in the middle of Benjamin Unable-to-Commit Dalton's living room with drool on their shoulders.

She huffed out a breath and peeled his long fingers off her breast, reminding herself this was *exactly* why she'd taken her grandmother Flossie's words to heart after her grandfather had passed away last month. She'd heard stories about couples like her grandparents who had been together for more than fifty years dying within weeks of each other, and she'd been petrified that she'd lose her grandmother, too. As they'd driven back to the Long Island assisted-living facility where her grandparents had lived for the past several years, Aurelia had begged her grandmother to move back to Sweetwater and let her care for her. But her bright-eyed grandmother—the woman who had taught her to tie her shoes *and* speak her mind, the woman who had owned a bookstore in Sweetwater for forty-plus years and instilled a love of all things literary in Aurelia—had said, *This isn't the end of my story, bubbelah. Your grandfather and I could fill a library with books about our love. We had our happily ever after, and we shared a beautiful, spectacular life. But as your grandpa would say, now it's time to start a new adventure—my next chapter.*

Ben murmured, holding Aurelia tighter and pressing his all-too-tempting arousal harder against her jeans, tearing her from the pages of her past—and thrusting her into the going-nowhere scribblings of the present.

She tried to pry his fingers off her again and said, "Time to wake up, Benny boy."

He groaned, tightening his hold.

"Ben!" she snapped, irritated with herself for falling into her old ways so easily. She'd moved into her apartment above the bookstore two weeks ago in an effort to be in before Ben's sister Bridgette's wedding, which had taken place two days ago. That was her deadline for her fresh start, her own *new chapter*.

I sure screwed that up.

Ben startled awake and peered over her shoulder. "Sorry, Rels. I didn't mean to grab your boob again."

Right, you didn't mean to. Thanks for the reminder. "Whatever." She sat up, and he hauled her back against his chest, making her laugh despite herself.

"I love waking up with my best bud by my side," he said. "Even if she is cranky in the morning."

"I'm not cranky." She eyed the bottle of tequila on the table and sighed inwardly. She knew better than to drink with Ben. They laughed and drank and always ended up crashing together—never in the way she wanted, despite the fact that he'd bought her a toothbrush for his house months ago. She wondered how he explained *that* to his one-night stands. She knew he had them, but in truth, she had no idea if they came home with him or if they always did the deed elsewhere. Her stomach sank.

It was time for this to end once and for all. "We can't drink tequila anymore," she said adamantly.

"Okay, next time we'll get Jack and Coke."

"Maybe we need to stop drinking when we watch movies," she said half-heartedly, because she loved their comfy, fun evenings. But being friend-zoned with Ben made her feel pathetic, so she said, "I *do* have a new apartment to inhabit."

"For the record, as glad as I am that you found such a great investment, I hate that you're not right around the corner anymore. And you did it all so fast, Rels. One day you're driving Flossie home, and the next you announce that you're moving to Harmony Pointe."

She'd driven through Harmony Pointe on her way back from taking her grandmother home after her grandfather's funeral, and when she'd stopped at a red light, she'd seen a FOR SALE sign on the door of the corner bookstore, which was called Chapter One. It had felt like a neon sign screaming at her to move on with her life, and she'd made an offer that day.

"Well, apparently all it takes is one call and I'm right back in your living room," she said, trying not to make too much of his comment.

"Because that's what friends do. They keep each other company."

Friends. The greatest buzzkill of all.

He began kneading her shoulders. He had the biggest, strongest hands. *Magic hands.* She'd fantasized about them slipping beneath her clothing, caressing, groping, and teasing until she was wet and wanting—

"See? You need this in the mornings to take the edge off," he said in a low voice, snapping her out of her fantasy.

She turned her head to see his face, and her heart stumbled. Ben hadn't always had the chiseled face of a model. His cheeks had been a little full until he'd hit his twenties, as if his body had refused to give up that last trace of boyishness, especially when he'd smiled. But he'd kept the hint of dimples, and a playful grin never failed to make its way up to his dark eyes. Those seriously sexy eyes could smolder the panties off a woman as easily as they could command a boardroom. She imagined they made him a master negotiator in the bedroom, too. And don't get her started on his lips . . .

"You're all tight again," he said, still rubbing her shoulders.

Reality hit her like a freight train. What was she doing? Her bestie was a venture capitalist and had gotten lucky with investments when he'd first gone to college, and he'd been getting lucky with random women ever since. Except he'd never tried a damn thing with Aurelia, and he'd had plenty of chances.

Then again, she hadn't tried anything with him, either, and she was no wallflower. Aurelia didn't exactly shy away from making moves on men. But with Ben, things were different. *Complicated.* The Daltons were her second family. Ben's four sisters were her best girlfriends, and then there was this sizzling, teasing, almost-but-not-really *thing* between her and Ben. Besties. Drinking buddies. *Ben and Jerry.*

Fuck Ben and Jerry. She wanted to eat whipped cream off his *big cone*, but not at the risk of losing him as her friend or screwing up her relationship with the rest of his family.

Aaaand that was why she had to leave.

Now.

"I've got to go." She tried to pull away, but he dug his fingers into her knotted muscles, releasing tension and drawing a moan from her traitorous lungs.

"Don't run off," he coaxed. "I wasn't kidding. You are my best friend. I trust you with my secrets, and I love who you are."

Hope bubbled up inside her, and she closed her eyes, glad he couldn't see her face. Had their time finally come? "Really?"

"Of course," he said, and she heard the smile in his voice.

That made her feel all sorts of good, and the truth came easily. "I love who you are, too."

He leaned his chin on her shoulder, his hard chest pressing against her back as he said, "I especially love who you are when you're making me breakfast."

"Ugh!" She pushed to her feet, but he snagged her wrist, giving her the puppy-dog eyes she'd never been able to resist. The ones that said, *Please don't leave me.* "Ben," she warned.

"Relsy," he pleaded.

"I am not making you breakfast. I have to go." She yanked her hand away and said, "And I'm busy for the next few weeks. Actually, for a *lifetime,* so . . ." She shoved her feet into her red Converse sneakers and grabbed her purse.

"I seriously have to make my own breakfast?" Ben pushed to his feet and stretched, six-plus feet of hotness towering over her five-two frame. "But you make waffles better than I do."

"I do a lot of things better than you. Don't forget to call Aiden back." Aiden was his business partner. He'd called Ben last night while they were watching a movie and Ben had made her laugh, causing tequila to come out of her nose, which had sent him into hysterics and rendered him unable to answer the call.

"Shit, that's right." He grabbed his phone from the table. "He was supposed to set up a meeting with our legal team."

"For the hotel chain you're buying?"

"Yeah. Hey, take my sweatshirt. It's early. You'll be cold."

He pulled his sweatshirt over his head and tossed it to her, revealing a dusting of chest hair over muscular pecs and a treasure trail that disappeared beneath the waist of his low-slung jeans. His sweatshirt hit her in the chest and landed at her feet, reminding her she was staring.

Ben laughed. "Nice catch, Rels. Remind me not to pick you for my baseball team."

"I don't want to be on your team. You run the bases too slow," she mumbled as she picked up his sweatshirt and tugged it over her head, inhaling his masculine scent. Even his smell made her nipples stand at attention. "I'm out of here."

"How about cereal?" he asked with a wink. "I'll make it."

"Since when did you become so needy?"

A coy grin slid across his face. "I know that once you're in my kitchen, there's no holding back. You won't let me eat crap when you can make something delicious."

"Yeah, you should see me in the bedroom." She felt her eyes bug out. She slammed her mouth closed, unable to believe what she'd said. She stormed through the hallway and out the door, followed by Ben's laughter—and almost tripped over a basket. She leaned back, holding the door open, and hollered, "I think Willow left you muffins. There's a basket on your porch."

"Way to go, Willow," he said as he strode down the hall. "Let's see the goods."

She realized she was staring at his bare chest again and snapped, "I'm taking the biggest muffin," as if it was his fault he had great pecs and abs she wanted to lick, and bite, and—

Down, girl.

He cocked a grin and said, "Take as many as you'd like, but you'll pay for them later."

In my dreams.

Ben loved the playful look in Aurelia's eyes as she tried to come up with a smart-ass response. Her hair was tousled, and her cheeks held the warm glow of sleep. He could tell the moment she gave up on a sassy response, because she raked a hand through her long dark hair, and her eyes drifted from him to the basket. She didn't usually give up that easily, but hey, at least this gave him a few seconds to appreciate her fine ass as she bent over the basket.

"See? You don't need me cooking you breakfast." She gazed over her shoulder at him with a smile that lit up the sky as she lifted the top of the basket and said, "Willow's got you covered."

Ben's heart nearly stopped at the sight of a tiny sleeping baby nestled among blankets in the basket. *"Fuck. Me."*

"I . . . um . . . *Wha*—" She followed his gaze to the baby in the basket and gasped, dropping to her knees beside it. "Holy cow, *Ben*! It's a *baby*!"

He took a step back, as if he couldn't get away fast enough, and said, "Why is it on my porch?"

"I don't know!"

"There's a note. Grab it." He pointed to an envelope tucked into the side of the blanket. "Whose kid is it?" He looked up and down the street. For what, he wasn't sure, but he got a twisted, dark feeling in his gut as Aurelia rose to her feet, the color draining from her face.

She handed him the letter with a shaky hand and said, "She's *yours*."

"What? No, it's *not*." He snagged and scanned the typewritten letter. His heart pounded faster with every word. *Dear Ben, I'm sorry to do this to you, but I didn't know where else to turn. I'm not in a position to care for a baby. I hope you can make room in your life for your daughter.*

"What the fuck?" He looked down at the baby. "I need to call my lawyer and the cops. This is bullshit. Some crazy bitch wants money or something."

Aurelia looked at him like *he* was crazy.

"What?" he snapped.

"I . . ." She swallowed hard and looked down at the baby. "We should get her inside."

"No, we *shouldn't*. We should take it directly to the police station."

She shook her head, her gaze moving between him and the baby in the basket. "Are you *crazy*? If she *is* your baby, do you really want her going into social services? Being cared for by strangers?"

"It's *not* mine, Rels." He grabbed the basket by the handles and said, "Grab the top of the fucking basket. Let's take care of this."

She picked up the top and followed him inside. "*This* is a baby, and pink blankets indicate a girl. *She*, not *it*. What are you going to do?"

"I'm going to get a shirt on, and then we're going to the police station." He set down the basket and took his phone from his pocket. "But first I'm calling my attorney."

"Wait!" She grabbed his wrist, her brows imploring him to listen. "*Don't. Please.* Let's just think for a second."

He scoffed. "*Think?* Aurelia, it isn't mine. Seriously."

"You can't know that for sure. Even the best birth control is only ninety-nine percent effective."

"Christ. Do *you* want this baby? Do you have some weird baby fetish that I don't know about? Because you can have it and deal with the crazy bitch who's going to report that her baby has been abducted. And then you're looking at defending yourself instead of asking for help up front."

She paced, crossing and uncrossing her arms. "Ben," she said pleadingly, "you have to find out if she's yours for sure before you give her up."

"Fuck that." Now *he* was pacing. "I'd *know* if I had a baby."

"How? By osmosis? You travel all the time. God only knows how many women you've screwed."

"I'm careful, Rels. *So* fucking careful." Because the last thing he wanted was a baby by some random hookup.

"But what if she's yours? Take it from a girl who would do anything to know who her father was. *Knowing* is everything."

He closed his eyes, his heart breaking for Aurelia. Her mother had hemorrhaged and died when Aurelia was born and had never revealed the identity of Aurelia's father to anyone. She'd only said that he wanted nothing to do with her or a baby. Aurelia had confided in Ben about how hard that was for her, and she'd been brought to tears a number of times with a longing so deep he'd felt her emptiness as his own.

He looked at the baby again. Its lower lip was quivering, but all he saw was Aurelia as a baby, orphaned at birth. *Damn it.*

The baby started crying, and he said, "You've got to pick it up."

"I don't know anything about babies! I've never even babysat. You have a nephew. *You* pick her up." Aurelia crossed her arms, watching him expectantly. His nephew, Louie, was his younger sister Bridgette's adorable six-year-old son.

Ben might be able to take command in any boardroom, but babies terrified him. They were too fragile, too dependent. He held his hands up in surrender as the baby began wailing. *Loud.* "I never touched Louie until he couldn't break. That baby is *breakable.* She's smaller than a loaf of bread."

"Ugh!" She knelt beside the basket and picked up the wailing baby, cradling it against her stomach.

"Don't drop it!"

She gave him a deadpan stare, then turned a worried gaze to the baby. "She won't stop crying."

"Bounce it." He tried to remember anything he might have heard Bridgette say when Louie was little, but blood rushed through his ears, and his only thought was, *Holy fuck. It can't be mine!*

She bounced the baby in her arms, and the baby's eyes slammed shut, her cries escalating into shaky, shrill sounds that tore at his gut. Ben dropped to his knees beside Aurelia and said, "Do the shoulder thing!"

"Shoulder thing?"

"Put it on your shoulder. Burp it!"

"Burp it?" Aurelia scowled. "You're an idiot. There are diapers in the basket. Look for a bottle."

He dug around beneath the tiny diapers and found a bottle. He must have been looking at it like it was a foreign object, because Aurelia gave an exasperated sigh and snapped, "Shake it!"

He shook the hell out of the bottle as the shrill cries vibrated into long, shaky, gut-wrenching sounds—and then fell silent, like the baby couldn't breathe at all. "She's not breathing! Do something! CPR? What if she's sick? Oh God, Rels! Did we do th—" His words were drowned out by another piercing wail.

"Give me that!" Aurelia snatched the bottle, shifting positions, sitting cross-legged and cradling the baby against her belly. She put the bottle to the baby's lips, and it panted, gulped—*wailed*—and then the tiniest pink lips he'd ever seen wrapped around the nipple. He held his breath as the baby gasped again, whimpered, then suckled the nipple. It kept up the agonizing suck-gasp-whimper-suck pattern so long Ben thought he was going to pass out, before he remembered *he* wasn't breathing.

"Fuuuuck," left his lungs in one long, tortured breath. "First stop Vic Preacher's, before the cops." His buddy Vic was a pediatrician.

"To see if you're the father?"

"To make sure she's not sick, and yeah, that other thing."

"You can't drive her without a car seat."

"Then we'll *walk*, because it'll take too long to go shopping and she could stop breathing again. We know nothing about this kid." Suddenly hit with the realization that this wasn't Aurelia's problem, he said, "You'll come with me, right, Rels?"

"What?" she said absently, staring at the baby with a dreamy expression.

Seeing her look at the baby like that made his gut twist in a different way. The image didn't fit. Aurelia was his good-times girl, the only woman with whom he could talk about anything. She starred in *all* his darkest fantasies, which was torture since he couldn't have her, but she made one hell of a hot fantasy, and he wasn't nearly ready to give that up. His mind shouted, *No! Stop looking at her like that!*

She gazed up at him through those long lashes that drove him crazy and whispered, "She didn't stop breathing. She was just hungry." She looked down at the baby and said, "We suck at babies, Ben, but at least we didn't break her."

CHAPTER TWO

"LET'S GO," BEN said as he came downstairs wearing a tight black T-shirt with the jeans he'd worn last night, looking just as harried as he had when he'd taken the stairs two at a time on the way up. His feet were still bare, his five-o'clock shadow was dark as night, and his thick dark hair looked like he'd pulled a sexy all-nighter, though Aurelia knew better.

It was the morning delivery that had him chasing his tail around his massive house, grabbing his keys, walking back and forth from the kitchen to the living room, and doing everything he could to avoid looking at the sweet little girl in the basket.

"Go *where*?" Aurelia asked softly so as not to wake the baby. She couldn't wrap her head around the idea that the baby might actually be Ben's. Other than in his work, which he nurtured and cared for like it was a living, breathing thing, he avoided anything remotely close to commitment.

His dark brows slanted in annoyance. "The *doctor's*. I said that already. I called Vic and he said to bring her by whenever we could. Let's go."

"Right, with no shoes and no car seat. Ben, she's *sleeping*. Haven't you ever heard the old saying *Let sleeping babies lie?*"

"I think that's *dogs*, and what does it mean, anyway? Don't wake up a dog? Why not?"

"I don't freaking know," she whispered, glancing at the baby in the basket. "But she's finally quiet and I'm not upsetting her again."

"So, *what* . . . ? We're supposed to sit around with this kid until it wakes up? It could sleep for hours." He paced like a caged tiger. "We've got to figure this shit out. Who would leave a kid on a doorstep? We *need* to find the mother. This is bullshit. I have an important meeting next week I need to prepare for, and I need a fucking shower. And now I've got a baby who could stop breathing at any second . . ."

She'd never seen Ben frazzled, and he was talking so fast Aurelia couldn't get a word in edgewise. She went to him, but he continued ranting about laws of abandonment and not being the father.

She grabbed his arms and said, "Benjamin!" in a harsh whisper.

He blinked several times, as if he'd only just realized she was there.

"Take a deep breath, and don't say another word until I get some coffee in you." She picked up the basket.

"Where are you taking that?"

"I'm taking *her* into the kitchen. Let's go." Jesus, *she* was freaking out inside, and *he* was freaking out outside. They were quite a pair. She set the basket on the floor by the kitchen table, and then she pointed to the chair nearest the basket and said, "Sit."

She was surprised when he complied. She began making coffee and said, "While she's sleeping, we need to figure out who the mother is. Then we'll get her checked out by Vic."

His eyes widened. "So you think it's sick, too?"

She rolled her eyes. "Stop calling her *it*." She grasped for a name and went with the first thing that came to mind. "She's *Baby B* for now."

"Baby *B*? Who's Baby A?"

"There is no Baby A. Baby *Ben*, just until—"

"She's *not* my kid, Aurelia," he said through gritted teeth, but his gaze fell to the baby, and though his jaw clenched tight, Aurelia swore his eyes softened a little.

Was he thinking about the possible mothers? Remembering the women he'd slept with? Or was he accepting that he might in fact be a father? She didn't want to think about two of those questions as she handed him a mug of coffee.

"We don't know that, and she can't be *it*, so she's Baby B. Or just *B* for now." She poured herself a cup of coffee, grabbed a notepad and a pen from the drawer where he kept them, and sat at the table. "Okay, focus, Ben. Let's figure this out. How old do you think she is?"

Ben looked like he'd swallowed a frog. "How the hell would I know?"

"Never mind. I'll google it. Geez, when it comes to business you plan and strategize until you're blue in the face. Just try to help me out here, *please*. She can't be very old; she can't hold her head up or anything." She whipped out her phone and searched *how to tell how old a baby is*. Finding only baby-age calculators, she said, "Shit. This doesn't help at all."

"Because you suck at research." He grabbed her phone, thumbed out something, then said, "This site should help. They have milestones by month, starting with month zero. What milestone does a newborn have?"

They huddled over the phone, reading about feedings, baths, and sleep schedules, and agreed that the information didn't help since they had no information on which to base the baby's schedule or weight.

"She can't be more than a month or so, right? She's so tiny. Maybe we should estimate three to six weeks, just to be safe." Aurelia navigated to the calendar on her phone and counted back to figure out when the baby was conceived. "I can't believe I'm actually trying to figure out when you had sex. This is so messed up."

Ben's jaw clenched again, and his eyes turned apologetic. "What do you want me to say? Neither one of us is celibate."

"You have no idea what I am," she said sharply, keeping her eyes trained on the phone. She'd been with her share of men, but it had been forever since she'd had sex, which was only part of the problem with staying overnight at Ben's. When he held her, which was every damn time she stayed over, he *always* ended up wrapped around her like a blanket—and she realized just how much she wanted *more* from him.

But now . . .

She eyed the baby. She might not be the only female who needed more than he was capable of giving.

Or wants to give?

She pushed that painful thought aside and said, "We need to figure out everyone you slept with from late May to early July, just to cover your bases."

"You can't be serious. How am I supposed to remember?"

Her jaw dropped. "Have there been that many women?"

He shrugged, flashing a cocky grin, which pissed her off.

She rolled her eyes and said, "Get out your calendar, *gigolo*."

"My calendar? You think I take notes on who I sleep with?" He laughed. "Let me see *your* calendar."

"I'm not the one who might be supporting a dependent for the next eighteen years. Get your frigging calendar out and see where you were last summer." Her words flew fast and angry.

He navigated to the calendar on his phone, his eyes flicking from the screen to Aurelia every few seconds. "May and June?"

"Mm-hm." She swallowed hard. What if he'd slept with a bunch of the single women she knew? What if he'd slept with a married woman? *He'd never do that. But what if . . . ?* Could she handle that?

"Zane was filming that movie last summer with Remi Divine," he said, and guilt rose in his eyes. Zane was Willow's husband. He was an actor-turned-screenwriter, and he'd had the lead opposite actress Remi Divine in his last movie.

Aurelia's heart sank. She and Remi had become close friends that summer. They texted often and got together whenever Remi's schedule allowed. She was coming to Harmony Pointe to film another movie soon. How awkward would that be, knowing she'd slept with the one man Aurelia wanted but couldn't have?

"Well, we know Remi isn't pregnant," she said without looking at him.

"I didn't sleep with Remi. Not only is she my business partner's sister, but she's not my type."

"A Natalie Portman lookalike isn't your type?" Aurelia met his gaze, and boy did he look pissed. "How am I supposed to know your *type*?"

He looked like he was chewing on nails. "Her name was *Payton*."

Bile rose in her throat. "You slept with that sweet redhead from craft services? Seriously? That's your *type*?" She pressed the tip of the pen to the paper and wrote *Payton*, wondering what Payton had that she didn't. "Last name?"

"No idea."

"Payton *One-Nighter*. Got it." She felt like she'd been stabbed in the gut. "Who else?"

He looked at his calendar. "I was in New York City for business . . ."

"*Sex* business?" she asked, feeling like she might puke.

"Jesus, I can't do this." He pushed to his feet. "I'm not telling you everyone I slept with."

"Fine." She slapped down the pen and stood up. "Do it yourself. It's not exactly my idea of fun, either." She stormed into the living room and grabbed her purse, tears and anger warring for dominance.

"Aurelia, wait." He grabbed her arm, his eyes pleading for help—or understanding—or *something*.

She wrenched her arm free, glowering at him. "You might have a *child*, Ben!" she whispered harshly. "A living, breathing baby. Grow up and figure your shit out."

"And hurt you in the process? Or piss you off?" His dark eyes drilled into her, and he stood so close his stomach brushed against her chest. "No, thank you."

She didn't know what to say. *Yes,* this fucking hurt, and *yes,* it pissed her off, even if she had no right to feel either of those ways, but she couldn't tell him that. She was breathing so hard, it made it difficult to speak, but she managed, "Maybe you should get Zane to help you."

"Zane?" He looked at her like she was crazy.

"How about Talia?" Talia was the oldest of the Dalton siblings, at just over a year older than Ben. He had always been closest to her. They'd even attended the same college, and when Talia's college boyfriend had cheated on her, Ben had gone after him and beaten him up pretty badly. Aurelia knew how hurt Ben had been when Talia had kept her fiancé Derek's job of dancing at a nightclub a secret from him, but Talia resonated quiet strength and meticulous thinking. Ben needed that right now, considering neither he nor Aurelia was capable of *meticulously* doing anything at the moment.

"I don't want my family knowing about this until we know for sure if she's mine," he said. "I don't want to freak them out."

"But it's okay to freak *me* out?" *Great. If that doesn't tell me where I stand, nothing ever will.*

"No! That's why I stopped." He sighed heavily. "I'm sorry . . ."

For what? Freaking me out? Having a baby? Having sex?

"Okay, so no Talia yet," she agreed. "But Zane won't say anything." As she said the words, she realized they probably weren't true. Zane didn't keep secrets from Willow, and Ben's disbelieving expression told her he was thinking the same thing, but he had to know this sucked for her. "The last thing *I* want to do is talk about the people you've slept with."

"Trust me, I don't want to tell you any more than you want to hear it." He took her hand, holding it tight. "But I'm freaking out here, Rels. I'll figure it out on my own if I have to, but I don't want to do the wrong thing to that little girl. Don't leave me alone with her, please? For *her* sake? I don't even know how to hold her."

She looked away from his pleading eyes, and he squeezed her hand, drawing her attention as he said, "I don't think there were a lot of women. *Please?* I trust you with this personal information, and I don't want to do this with anyone else."

She closed her eyes for a second, steeling herself against the jealousy clawing up her neck. He'd been there for her so many times over the past few years—after every shitty breakup, when she'd cried all night after her grandfather had died, and countless other times. She could do this for him, put aside her feelings and be there when he needed her most. "You realize *I'm* freaking out and I can't call *any* of my girlfriends and talk about it because you're related to them, right? I can't even call *Remi*, because chances are she heard about you and Payton." She set down her purse and walked toward the kitchen.

"I know. I'm sorry."

She stopped short, and Ben barreled into her and mumbled, "Sorry."

"You owe me." She stared into his gorgeous, grateful eyes and said, "*Big-time.* It's a good thing I haven't opened the bookstore yet, or you'd be on your own." The grand opening of Chapter One was a few weeks away, but even if the shop had been open, she'd have helped, because he was *Ben*, and he never asked for help with anything.

"I'll do anything you want," he said. "That is, if you don't hate me by the end of the day."

It'd be hard to hate him over a baby as beautiful as the little girl in the basket. Jealousy might be gnawing at her every nerve, but she was a realist above all else, and she knew unplanned pregnancies happened—and not everyone could raise their babies. Having been orphaned at birth drove that reality home. Even though her grandparents had never made her feel like anything but a treasured gift, she knew they'd missed out on a lot by raising her.

As they settled back at the kitchen table, she said, "I'll text Remi and make up an excuse to get Craft Services Girl's last name."

"Thank you."

She picked up the pen, pressing the tip into the paper as she asked, "Who's your New York fuck buddy?"

He uttered a curse. "She's an attorney. Blond, a few years older than me."

"I don't need her *résumé . . .*" *Or visuals, thank you very much.*

"Aida Strong. Listen, I'll just call her. We hook up—"

Her hand shot up, cutting him off. "Don't even go there. I don't want to know." She wrote *Big Apple Fuck Buddy* next to Aida's name, set down the pen, and folded her arms, *wanting* to go there and hating herself for it. This was a mistake. She felt sick.

"Was she all your Thursday night *meetings*?" When he didn't respond, she asked, "Have you been with her in the last few months?"

He nodded, looking regretful. "Not all that recently, but . . ."

"Then it's obviously not her. I think you would have noticed a pregnant belly." She crossed out Aida's name. "It's not going to be a lawyer anyway. Whoever did this has got to know she could get in legal trouble for abandoning a baby."

Ben scrubbed his hand over his chin. "There were only two others that I remember."

"That you *remember* . . . ? Men are such pigs."

He narrowed his eyes. "How many guys were you with last June and July?"

She looked away.

"Come on, Rels. There was that guy you met down by the lake."

"Joey Stewart," she said, remembering the hot football player who had been passing through town. She hadn't slept with him, though he'd wanted her to. But she wasn't into one-night stands, and she definitely didn't want to be a notch in his belt.

"And the asshole you met at the club in Harmony Pointe," he reminded her.

"Who?"

"The blond guy who looked at his phone the whole date."

"Oh my gosh, I forgot about him." She met Ben's stare and said, "How did *you* remember?"

He shifted in his seat with a pinched expression and looked at her list. "Getting back to the last two women, there was a yoga instructor. She lives on the outskirts of town."

"Name?" Aurelia asked, still wondering how he'd remembered her forgettable date.

He shrugged. "Joanie? Jeannie? I don't know. It started with a *J*. She was blond." He leaned back and said, "And *really* flexible."

She glared at him and wrote *Pretzel Girl J*. "Who's the last one? And make it fast because I'm about to puke thinking about you and all these women."

"I was in LA for business. It was the night you went out with that designer you met online."

"Ollie? *Oh*, I liked him."

"Fucking *Ollie*. What kind of name is that?"

"He's from the UK, and he is hot and *very* talented." She was talking about his design skills, but Ben was grinding his teeth, and though she knew he wasn't jealous—he probably felt protective of her, like a brother would of a sister—she couldn't resist goading him. "And that accent." She sighed dreamily, just to drive his discomfort home.

His eyes narrowed. "*Anyway*, she was blond with a *big rack*," he said angrily.

"Of course she was." No wonder he had no interest in her. None of the women he'd slept with were brunette.

"She worked at the hotel I was staying in." Ben crossed his arms.

"Name?"

"Caroline something. I think."

"You *think*?" She wrote *Blond, Caroline, Hotel Hookup* on the paper and set down the pen.

"We were commiserating. You know what they say: the best way to get over one woman is to get *into* another."

"That's not exactly the saying, *and* it implies you were once *hung up* on someone. I don't remember that. Who was she?"

He stared blankly at her, his eyes slightly narrowed.

"God, Ben. *Really?* Then you weren't *that* hung up on whoever she was." When he didn't respond, she said, "Whatever. Are you sure that's it?"

"Pretty sure."

She tapped the pen on the table, thinking about Bridgette's husband, Bodhi's, beautiful blond friend Shira, who had flirted with Ben at the wedding—and every chance she got when she visited from the city. Aurelia didn't blame her, because if Ben wasn't her best guy friend and he looked at her like he looked at other hot women, she'd try to pick him up, too. Jealousy gnawed at her, because she could see Ben being attracted to more than just Shira's looks. She was a brilliant accountant, a badass martial artist, and the president of the Hearts for Heroes foundation, which Bodhi had founded.

"Shira?" slipped out, and she winced.

He looked confused. "What about her? Did she *look* like she'd just had a baby when she was at the wedding?"

She shook her head, and her stomach sank. He didn't say he hadn't slept with her.

"Besides, I didn't have sex with Shira," he snapped.

Relief and embarrassment swept through her.

His troubled eyes held hers as he asked, "Anyone else you want to know about?"

"Hey, don't get mad at *me*. I'm not the one with supersonic sperm." She glared at him and said, "Is that it? Just those four?"

He nodded, his jaw tight.

"Great. Do you happen to have Pretzel Girl's or Malibu Barbie's numbers?"

"Malibu Barbie?"

"Sorry, Hotel Hookup." She glanced at the sleeping baby and felt a little guilty for making fun.

He sighed heavily and said, "*No.* They were one-time things."

"Oh." She felt like she'd swallowed a boulder. "Like Ollie and Joey," she lied, but at least it made her feel a little less pathetic.

"Can you please not talk about *them* right now? I'm under enough stress."

"How do my dates cause *you* stress?"

"Someone's got to worry about you when you're out with strange guys."

"Whatever. They weren't *strange.* Why don't I text Remi now and get that girl's last name?"

"Wait. Before we start nosing around, I have to call my attorney. I'm a wealthy guy, and people know it. I have to protect myself. Give me five minutes." He pushed to his feet and strode into the living room, holding the phone to his ear.

Watching him pace the living room sparked a familiar flutter of desire. Aurelia didn't care how much money he earned. To her he'd always be *Ben*—Willow's older brother, the usually take-charge, sometimes overly serious, other times insanely childish man she'd fallen for years ago—and *Benny boy*, her best friend. The man she'd happily be flexible for. His modesty was just one of the things she loved about him. *Wealthy* was an understatement. Ben had been a multimillionaire by the time he'd graduated from college, long before he and Aiden Aldridge, Remi's older brother, became partners. He'd since earned billionaire status. Not that anyone would know it if they met him on the streets of Sweetwater, looking rugged and badass in jeans and boots—but if he was in the city doing business, they'd surely know it. Then he'd likely be dressed in Armani's best.

And doing Aida Strong.

The air seeped from her lungs.

♥ ♥ ♥

Ben called his attorney, who agreed that he should keep the situation under wraps to prevent crazies from coming out of the woodwork, get a paternity test right away, and *then* contact the local authorities. His attorney had a friend who worked for social services and owed him a favor. If Ben was the father, the child could remain with him and they could fast-track the legal documents, and if he wasn't the baby's father, then she would go into the system and be handled appropriately. In the space of time it took to make that phone call, Ben's head cleared enough for him to think about what Aurelia had said. And she was right to stand up for the baby's welfare. In case that innocent baby girl was his, he was going to do all he could to keep her from going into the system, and he didn't give a rat's ass what he had to deal with in order to accomplish that.

He sat on the couch with his head in his hands, trying to figure out how he could have gotten into this situation. He always used a condom, and he didn't remember a single one breaking. But that didn't matter if the test determined that he was the father. Oddly, none of that was as troubling as his conversation with Aurelia. He'd hated telling her about the women he'd slept with, but he'd never lied to her, and he wasn't about to start. She'd looked disappointed when he said he'd slept with Payton, and when he'd told her about Aida, he'd thought she might get up and leave right then and there. But when he'd mentioned the girl from the hotel, he'd felt another change, a chill in the air. And he was furious with himself. He'd been so pissed thinking about her dates with those other guys, he'd said things he shouldn't have, like about the yoga girl being *flexible*. That was a dick move, but the thought of another man's hands on Aurelia made his blood boil. Now that he'd had a little space to clear his head, the idea that she'd think less of him for his sexual habits wrecked him.

But he'd made his mess, and now he had to face the music. Despite his attorney's suggestion, he couldn't shake the worry that this was some kind of setup, so he called his father's longtime friend police chief Ronald Klein. Ron had known Ben since the day he was born.

"Ben Dalton, to what do I owe this pleasure?" Ron asked jovially.

"Hi, Ron. I've got a hypothetical question." As an afterthought he said, "For a friend."

"A friend, huh? Whatcha got?"

"Let's say a woman left a baby on a doorstep with a note saying the kid was this buddy of mine's. How much trouble is he looking at if he keeps the kid while he has the paternity test done?"

"You in trouble, son?"

"Nope. Just checking it out for a friend."

"Does this *friend* have the money and connections to push a paternity test through quickly? Because there are legalities if he's holding on to a baby that isn't his. *Hypothetically speaking*, that is."

"Yes."

"Then you didn't hear this from me, but hypothetically speaking, I'd haul ass over to the doc's office, get the tests done, lawyer up, and go from there."

After the call Ben sent a text to his assistant, telling him he'd be tied up for the next couple of days and his responses to emails would be delayed. Though Ben had an office in town, he preferred to work from the one in his home.

He pushed to his feet and headed for the kitchen, hesitating in the doorway to watch Aurelia, who was sitting on the floor beside the baby.

Baby B.

That did crazy shit to his stomach.

Aurelia was scrolling through Facebook. She was so beautiful, her lustrous hair falling over her shoulders, her brows knitted in concentration. She was a petite, fearless thing, and seeing the worry in her eyes over that baby—*Baby B*—also did something funky to his gut.

He and Aurelia had a lot of good things between them, but timing had never been one of them. He'd thought he'd have a chance with her after she'd first moved back to town, but she had just come off a bad relationship and had sworn off men. Like an idiot, he'd respected her need for space. And then, between his travel schedule and her random dates, it hadn't ever seemed like the right time to try for something more. Besides, every damn time he made a sexual innuendo, she blew him off.

She looked up as he came to her side. "I found Payton on Facebook—"

"You looked her up? I would've done it."

"Right, well, you were a little busy. Anyway, she has definitely *not* been pregnant recently. She posted pictures of a cruise she took three months ago. I have to admit, the girl rocks a bikini. I'm a little jealous, but if you ever repeat that, I'll kill you."

"You're ten times hotter than Payton could ever dream of being."

She rolled her eyes. "Uh-huh. That's why you slept with her, *obviously.*"

He clenched his jaw to keep from saying, *I slept with her because you kept turning me down.* It was probably a shitty reason, but they'd both had a good time, and Payton hadn't been looking for anything more than a hookup, either.

"I also found your Big Apple fuck buddy. You have a thing for Barbies, don't you?"

"No," he said emphatically.

"Could have fooled me. She's tall, blond, and *hot.*"

"She's smart, funny, and no-strings-attached. Nothing more. Besides, we already knew she wasn't the mother, so why'd you look her up?"

She shrugged, but a whisper of something refuted the detached affect she was trying to portray. "I searched yoga teachers but couldn't find any Barbies. If you know where she lives, you should go there."

"*Go* there?"

"How else will you know if she's the mother? Besides, she's the only local woman you mentioned. Pretzel Girl is probably Baby B's mother."

They both looked at the sleeping baby. Her little hands were fisted, one tucked by her chin, the other beside her head. She had a dusting of light brownish hair and the cutest little nose. She made a suckling motion in her sleep, and he wondered if she was hungry.

"What did your attorney say?" Aurelia asked.

"To get the paternity test and not call the authorities until I know for sure if she's mine."

"And . . . ?"

"I called Chief Klein."

Aurelia's eyes widened. "Of course, because you never listen to anyone about anything."

I listened to you and gave you space. Look where that got me. "I posed a hypothetical question," he clarified. "We've got to get B to Vic and get that test done."

"Okay . . . *Wait.* You called her B." A smile lifted her lips. "Your heart didn't go cold after all."

He glared at her, earning one of her sweet laughs.

"I'm kidding! *Geez.* I'll run to the store and get diapers, formula, and a car seat, and then we'll go."

"What?" Panic bloomed inside him. "You can't leave me alone with her. I've never even changed a diaper."

"Fine. I'll stay; you go. Just be sure to get formula, diapers, wipes, and an infant car seat."

He wished she could go with him. Everything was better when they were together. He hooked his arm around her neck, pulling her against his chest. He'd done that so often, it felt like her *spot*, and damn, she felt great in it. "Thanks, Rels." He pressed a kiss to her temple. "I couldn't do this without you."

He was an idiot for having waited so long to make his move, as he'd realized a few weeks ago. He'd decided he was done with innuendos, done pussyfooting around the woman he wanted, and he'd convinced himself to risk their friendship for a chance at forever. He'd planned the whole thing out, prepared to make his move at Bridgette and Bodhi's wedding reception. Like a fool, he'd had a romantic notion of professing his feelings to her as they slow danced beneath the stars, and since most of his family would be tied up after the wedding, it was the perfect time to finally become a couple. Bridgette and Bodhi would be on their honeymoon, his parents were leaving for a trip to a resort, and Willow and Zane would be caring for Louie and his enormous dog, Dahlia. Talia and Derek had their hands full with home renovations and caring for Derek's father, Jonah, who had Alzheimer's, which left only Piper to distract Aurelia. But Aurelia had shut him down two weeks before the wedding when she'd bought the fucking bookstore and moved to Harmony Pointe in search of a *fresh start*. She'd said she was starting a new chapter in her life. She'd not only friend-zoned him; she'd tried to put him firmly in the past-life album, only he refused to let her go.

He clung to their friendship, because if she didn't want more, at least he'd have that.

Now she gazed up at him with trusting eyes, as if he knew exactly what to get at the store and wouldn't let either her or Baby B down, and he berated himself for the millionth time for letting his chance slip away—because if that baby girl was his, it just might be too late.

CHAPTER THREE

SHOPPING FOR A baby was nothing like shopping for an adult. There were too many choices and too many cute things Ben simply couldn't pass up. Even if Baby B wasn't his, she'd already had a tough go of things, and every little girl deserved to have pretty outfits, soft, cozy blankets, and a few toys. As he stepped inside with his arms loaded up with purchases, he called out, "Honey, I'm home," and kicked the door closed behind him—sparking a bloodcurdling wail from the living room.

Aw, shit.

"Ben! You woke her up," Aurelia scolded as she picked up the crying baby and held her against her shoulder. "Oh, she *stinks*. What'd you do, buy out the store?"

"Sorry, but you try getting out of a baby store without spending a thousand dollars. It's not possible." He dropped the bags, trying to figure out what the brownish stuff was in the basket. He looked at the baby, and the same watery mess stained the back of her outfit. "What *is* that?"

He stepped closer, and the pungent odor of poop hit him like a gust of rancid wind. He gagged, pointing to the baby's back and trying to speak at the same time. But all that came out was dry heaves.

"What?" Aurelia lifted her hand, and the mess was on her forearm, her shirt, and the front of the baby's legs. "*Gross!* Help me!" She held the wailing baby away from her body as if it were a ticking time bomb.

Ben pulled off his shirt, answering Aurelia's perplexed expression with, "I'm not getting that shit on my shirt." He reached for the baby, holding his breath.

She shoved the baby into his hands, and he held her away from his body, trying to get his dry heaves under control. Aurelia tore her shirt over her head—drawing Ben's attention and immediately remedying his gags. He had a screaming baby in his hands and his eyes were riveted to Aurelia's breasts, which were practically popping out of a sexy lace bra.

"*What* are you doing, Rels? This isn't exactly the best time to try to turn me on."

She shot him a death glare, using the shirt to wipe her arms and hands. "It's *all* over me!"

"You keep doing that and you'll have more than poop all over you," he warned, earning another glare. "Get the scissors from the kitchen and cut her clothes off."

Aurelia darted into the kitchen. She returned seconds later and quickly and carefully cut off the baby's poop-covered clothes. Then she ran to the kitchen to throw them away.

Ben looked past the screaming baby at Aurelia as she ran back into the room. "Take her. I don't want to drop her."

"Let me get something to wrap her in so we can change her." She looked around the living room.

"Use my shirt!"

"But you just said you didn't want to get sh—"

"Do it!"

She grabbed his shirt and wrapped it around the baby, who was still screaming bloody murder.

He remembered how the baby had quieted when she'd fed her and said, "I'll get a bottle."

"Ben! *Focus*," she said, bouncing the baby in her arms. "She doesn't need to *eat*. She has *poop* all over her. She needs to be changed."

"Okay. I got diapers." He dug through the bags, found the diapers and wipes, and held them up like prizes. "Got them!"

Aurelia knelt to lay the baby on the floor.

"Wait. That's too hard. She'll hate it." He grabbed the blankets from the basket, holding his breath as he folded the dirty parts inside and then laid them on the floor. "Put her on that."

Aurelia placed her on the blankets, and B's eyes slammed shut with a louder, shriller wail. Her tiny arms shot straight up, hands fisted, and her cry tapered to silence, the same frightening way it had earlier. Ben's heart stopped. *The hell with the poop.* He scooped B into his arms and put her on his chest as another cry sounded. *Thank God.*

"Ben! What are you doing?"

"Change her like this. I don't want her to stop breathing, and she's so unhappy. Just do it, please."

"Then take her in the kitchen in case this stuff drips."

He followed her into the kitchen, holding B against his hammering heart, floored that his skyrocketing pulse wasn't due solely to Aurelia traipsing around in a skimpy bra.

As Aurelia peeled off the diaper, Ben pressed his lips to the baby's head and tried to soothe her. "It's okay. We're going to get that nasty diaper off you. Shh, sweetheart. We've got you. You're okay." As he said the words, he knew they were true. They did have her, and he'd make damn sure she was okay.

"Can you stop bouncing her?" Aurelia asked as she tossed the diaper into the trash.

"I didn't know I was."

He stood stock-still, and Aurelia used what seemed like dozens of baby wipes to clean her up.

"Holding her isn't so hard," he said. "As long as you support her head. She's like a floppy doll. How old are babies before they can hold their heads up?" Her tiny fingers clung to him, and his protective urges surged. He pressed his lips to her head again. "We have to watch out for her, Rels. She's so small, and she has no one else."

He glanced at Aurelia and realized she was staring at him with a soft, unfamiliar gaze. In the next second the unmistakable look of desire darkened her beautiful eyes. The temperature around them spiked, and she quickly shifted her eyes away. *Holy hell.* He wanted *more* of that heat, that *connection.*

Testing the Ben-and-Aurelia waters, he said, "If I'd known baby poop was a turn-on, I'd have rented a baby."

"Shut up. All guys look hotter with their strong arms holding a tiny baby."

"Good to know you like my arms. You should see my—"

She silenced him with another glare, and he chuckled.

"Sorry. I'm making a mental note . . . 'How to get Aurelia naked. Step one, rent a baby. Step two, make its diaper explode.'"

"No wonder you're still single. Turn her around so I can get the front." As he shifted the baby, she said, "We should give her a bath. Did you buy a baby bath?"

"A *what?*"

"Never mind." She lifted the baby's legs as she cleaned her. "There are at least six bags out there. What *did* you buy?"

"I don't know. Things I thought she needed," he said as she tossed the wipes in the trash. He turned the baby toward him again, cradling her bottom and her head as he gently placed her on his chest and shoulder. He realized B had stopped crying and whispered, "Listen. She's not crying."

He kissed B's head again, holding her tiny body against him. Aurelia was looking at him that way again, like he wasn't her *friend* Ben but something more. He wanted to pull her into his arms, too, but he was afraid he might lose his grip on the baby. She went to the sink and washed her hands, but not before he noticed a pink flush creeping up her cheeks.

"We did it, Rels. We've always made a great team."

She busied herself washing her hands as she said, "How about we *team* our way over to the sink for a bath?"

"You want to put her in the *sink*?" He went to her, and when she turned around, he was *right there*. He didn't step back, unwilling to put space between them. Not after that spark he'd seen in her eyes. The flush on her cheeks deepened, probably because she was shirtless and her breast was brushing against the back of his hand, but he'd like to think it was because they were in this crazy situation *together*, and it was hard not to think of each other in a whole different way.

"What are you doing?" she asked a little breathlessly. "You have a better idea than the sink?"

"I've got about a hundred better ideas, but none of them are about the baby," came out before he could stop it. She breathed harder, her breasts brushing temptingly against his skin with every inhalation.

"You're *not* using that child as a wingman." She stepped around him and escaped into his laundry room, returning a moment later wearing one of his clean T-shirts—and looking just as hot as she did in her bra.

Didn't she know what she wore didn't matter?

"We have to bathe her before taking her to see Vic." She put the stopper in the sink and filled it with water.

"You can't just stick her in the sink."

She began opening cabinets. "Where's that big popcorn bowl?"

"Are you insane? You're not putting B in a *bowl*." He stalked out to the living room, retrieved a thin throw pillow, and dropped it in the sink, pressing it beneath the water. "We'll lay her on that."

"You realize you just ruined your pillow."

"I don't care. I'll buy a hundred more if I need them." He lowered the baby from his shoulder and said, "Look at her, Rels. She doesn't know if we're good or bad, rich or poor. All she knows is we're the ones she's with right now. Whether she's mine or not, I want to make sure that while she's with us, she's comfortable, happy, and safe." He looked at Aurelia and said, "Like you."

Aurelia didn't know what was worse, that Ben was finally looking at her the way she'd always dreamed he might or that he might be doing it just so she wouldn't leave him alone with the baby. His words, *Like you*, kept coming back to her, hitting her each time with a new dose of warmth. But he could have meant that as a friend. Lord knew neither one of them was thinking straight right now. They were both so afraid of doing something wrong as they bathed the baby that they hovered over her, their sides mashed together so they could reach her. Water splashed over the edge of the sink because of the pillow, but it actually worked pretty well, keeping the baby's head out of the water and making it easier for them to bathe her.

When they were done, they dressed her in a long-sleeve pink-and-white-striped onesie and a pair of the tiniest pink leggings Aurelia had ever seen, both of which Ben had bought. He'd even remembered to buy socks. She'd known he would come through for the baby.

It took them only twenty-five minutes to figure out the right way to install the car seat and to get her in it properly, which was a miracle considering Ben questioned Aurelia's every move and insisted on reading the directions three times. He drove so slowly to Vic's office she didn't think they'd ever arrive.

They parked around back and used the rear entrance because rumors in Sweetwater traveled faster than spit in the wind. Ben refused to carry the baby in the carrier part of the car seat. *It might break. I'd rather she was in my arms.*

As he carried her in, he said, "I feel like I'm making a drug deal."

Vic was coming down the hall wearing scrubs the same royal-blue color as his eyes. He had short honey-brown hair and ever-present scruff. The handsome physician always looked like he'd just walked off the set of *Grey's Anatomy*, even when he was jogging through town.

He looked at them like he was holding back a joke and pointed to his office as he said, "Go on in. I'll just be another minute or two."

They waited in his office, and Aurelia felt like she could *finally* breathe. Her heart had been racing since they'd found the baby, and over the last few hours Ben had made it beat even harder. She stole a glance at him, looking lovingly down at the baby cradled in his right arm. B looked even smaller against his broad, athletic body. She was whimpering a little, and he lifted her to his shoulder and rubbed her back, looking nothing like the man who had acted like the baby might burn him a few hours ago.

"Shh, peanut," he said softly. "You're okay. I've got you."

Peanut? That language was hardly fair. What woman wouldn't turn to mush seeing a big man like Ben Dalton get all squishy and lovey over a baby like that? He kissed the baby's temple the same way he kissed hers, and her heart melted every single time.

"Seems like you're getting pretty attached."

Ben's brow wrinkled. "Why? Because I'm trying to keep her happy?"

"*Peanut?*"

"Look at her. She's as small as a peanut." The baby started crying, and he stood up and paced with her. "Trust me, I'm not getting attached. The last thing I want is a baby that needs constant attention just to stay alive. I'm on the cusp of one of the biggest deals of my life. Barrister Hotels is an international conglomerate of boutique hotels. It requires my *full* concentration, and once the deal goes through, I'll be traveling internationally for the next several months. I'm nowhere *near* ready for this type of commitment."

Aurelia knew all of that, and it was one of the reasons she'd finally forced herself to move away. But seeing him with B and hearing him talk so affectionately, she'd wondered if *he'd* momentarily lost sight of all of that. It was silly of her to think Ben Businessman Dalton would put anything before business in the long run.

"I'm just doing what anyone else would do in this situation," he said. The baby cried louder. "Shh. It's okay." He touched his lips to the baby's head again, and then he looked at Aurelia and said, "I'm trying to keep my shit together until we figure out the bottom line."

The door opened and Vic breezed in, closing the door behind him as he said, "Good to see you, Ben, Aurelia. Aurelia, I was sorry to hear about your grandfather passing away. How's your grandmother holding up?"

"Thank you. She's doing well," she said, wincing as the baby's cries escalated.

"I see Ben's still adept at making girls cry."

Ben gave him a disapproving, serious look and said, "You have no idea how loud this baby can cry. Thanks for seeing us so quickly."

"And *covertly*," Vic reminded him. "How long has she been crying like that?"

"Just a few minutes," Aurelia said. "She cried earlier, but she'd had a diaper blowout."

"And she cries so hard it seems like she stops breathing," Ben said.

"But she doesn't," Aurelia explained. "Her cries taper off and she goes silent for a second or two, and then she wails again."

"That's common." Vic put his hands on his hips, brows knitted. "When's the last time she ate?"

Ben looked at Aurelia, like she had the answers.

"A few hours ago," Aurelia said. "Actually, she cried then, too. It was shortly after we found her."

"She's probably hungry," Vic said. "When they're this young, they eat every few hours. You'd be smart to carry a bottle and diapers with you at all times." His gaze ran over Ben's tousled hair, thicker-than-usual scruff, and damp T-shirt.

When he glanced at Aurelia, she realized she was still wearing Ben's shirt, which hung halfway down her thighs, and the front was wet from bathing the baby. She picked up the hem of the shirt and tied it in a knot at her hip. "We haven't showered. The morning's been a little crazy." The second the words left her mouth, she regretted them. *We haven't showered* sounded very much like they'd slept together. She quickly added, "We fell asleep watching a movie last night. As *friends*, not . . ."

Ben chuckled.

"No judgment here," Vic said. "Most new parents look disheveled and sleep deprived for the first couple months."

"We're not her parents," Ben reminded him.

"We'll see about paternity soon enough," Vic said. "Where's your baby bag?"

"Oh shoot. I forgot it," she said, and looked at Ben. The guilt in his eyes was palpable, but *she* should have remembered. He'd had his hands full with the baby.

"No worries. You've only had a few hours with a baby. You'll learn these things." He pressed a button on his phone and spoke into it. "Britt, can you bring me a new-parent pack and a bottle of formula, please?"

When he was done, Ben said, "Hopefully we won't need to learn too many baby rules. This is so screwed up."

"There are worse things in life than being handed a beautiful baby girl. She's a lucky one," Vic said. "Her mother cared enough to give her to you, her supposed father. Thousands of infants suffer far worse fates."

Ben's shoulders rounded, and his hands spread over the head and back of the baby, like he was trying to protect her from those *worse fates*.

There was a knock at the door, and Vic blocked whoever it was from coming into the room as he retrieved the things he'd asked for. He thanked her and closed the door. Then he handed a bottle of formula to Ben.

Ben sat down on a chair and said, "I've never fed her. Is there anything I need to know?"

Vic grinned. "Keep her head elevated and watch her. She'll guide you."

Ben looked at Aurelia, as if he could somehow learn from her silent guidance, and she took a little guilty pleasure in being so important to him. The smile that appeared on Ben's handsome face when the baby stopped crying and nursed the bottle made her warm all over, but when that smile reached his eyes and he turned that prideful glow on Aurelia, her knees weakened. She lowered herself to the chair beside him, and without thinking she squeezed his thigh in a silent *Way to go!*

"So, what's this little lady's name?" Vic asked.

Ben flashed a secretive smile at Aurelia and said, "We don't know. We call her Baby B."

"That's cute," Vic said. "Like Beatrice, but shortened?"

"Something like that," Ben said.

Vic handed the bag of supplies to Aurelia and said, "You'll find diapers, wipes, formula, pamphlets, and a few other things you'll need in there. Read the pamphlets. They'll help you over the next few weeks."

"Few *weeks*?" Ben glanced at the baby and asked, "How long does a paternity test take?"

"Depends on the lab. Normally it can take anywhere from a day or two to three months or more."

"Are you fu—" Ben winced and said, "*Freaking* kidding me? I'll pay whatever it takes to get the results fast."

"Duly noted. I figured you'd want to fast-track it, and I've already made a few calls. I'll finalize the arrangements and we should have the results within the week."

As Ben fed the baby, Vic asked a host of questions, most of which they couldn't answer. Then he examined the baby, and he didn't even flinch when the baby pooped as he was examining her, though Ben looked mortified. Vic cleaned her up, cooing and tickling her the whole time. When Vic swabbed the inside of the baby's cheek, Ben kept his face beside hers, soothing her with sweet words. When B cried, Aurelia thought Ben might cry, too, but he scooped her into his arms, clutching her against his chest like he was protecting her from the big, bad doctor.

"Well, Ben, from what I can see, you've got a healthy little girl," Vic said. "I could do blood work, but I don't see a reason to poke her if we don't need to."

"No needles," Ben said, turning and shielding the baby from Vic with his big body, which made Aurelia get all warm and fuzzy inside again.

Vic laughed. "If you *are* her father, you're going to have to get used to needles. Babies get a lot of shots. They're like puppies that way. Anyway, my guess is she's three to six weeks old. It's hard to tell. She should have gotten her first hepatitis B shot in the hospital, *assuming* she was born in a hospital. Since we have no immunization records, we need to discuss how to handle the shots she should have. For obvious reasons, I don't want to repeat immunizations, but we want her protected. Assuming she's had her first shot, she'll be due for a booster within a few weeks, along with a number of other shots. There's a schedule of shots in the bag I gave you."

"We're looking for her mother," Ben said, glancing guiltily at Aurelia.

"You mentioned on the phone that you were tracking down two women? Hopefully you'll find them and figure this out sooner rather than later. We should have the paternity issue worked out quickly enough, but paternity is only a small portion of the equation." Vic leaned against the desk and crossed his arms, setting a serious stare on Ben. "Ben, before I swab you, fatherhood is a major commitment. It takes dedication, and it'll put a serious damper on your *spontaneity*."

Aurelia felt her cheeks burn. She was thankful Vic was looking at Ben and not her.

"Are you sure you're ready for the results?" Vic asked.

"As ready as I can be. I wasn't ready to find her on my porch this morning. If it weren't for Aurelia, I don't know what I would have done."

"You would have sent me a nine-one-one text," Aurelia said with a laugh. "Like you did when that awful woman who works with Talia tried to pick you up at that club." *And I would have come running, just like always.*

One side of Ben's lips tipped up. "That's the truth. You're a good friend."

Vic eyed Aurelia, and she tried to hide the sting from the *f*-word, but based on the pitying look in Vic's eyes, she had a feeling she'd failed miserably.

The rest of the day passed in a blur of feedings and diaper changes. Aurelia had newfound appreciation for parents. She also had a greater appreciation for Ben. He *was* human after all. She'd started to wonder if there was anything he couldn't handle. Now she knew there was one thing that could rattle the calm, cool, and collected man. Throw a baby at him, and he kind of fell apart for a while. She thought about their chaotic, exhausting day and felt the tug of a smile.

Whoever said that all babies did was eat, sleep, and poop got two parts right. But Baby B was *not* a great sleeper. She slept in fits and spurts and was happiest snuggled on Ben's chest.

I would be, too, Aurelia thought.

Every time he put the baby down, she cried, so he picked her up. Watching him try to answer emails with the baby cradled in the crook of one of his arms was pretty funny, but he adjusted quickly. Aurelia had heard enough baby talk from Bridgette to know it wasn't good for the baby to be held all the time, but B had just been abandoned by her mother, and Aurelia figured she deserved the extra love. Besides, she was hardly one to argue with wanting to be in Ben's arms.

They'd navigated some pretty stinky situations today, but at least with the second diaper blowout she hadn't had to cast away her— *Ben's*—shirt, which she was still wearing. They'd bathed the baby again, but neither she nor Ben had found time to shower. Now they were back where they'd started, sprawled out on the chaise lounge. Ben smelled like sweat and baby puke, and *still* her stomach fluttered when he tightened his hold on her or made one of his sleepy, sexy noises. It would be much easier to start fresh in Harmony Pointe and leave her feelings for *Benny boy* behind if he were an asshole. But even that thought felt wrong, because being an asshole wouldn't make him a good father for Baby B, and she'd never want that—even if it kind of felt weird that he might actually be the father to some random woman's baby.

She lay beside him and B, wondering how she'd ended up there. After they'd ordered, and devoured, an entire extra-large pizza, she'd tried to leave so she could go home to shower and check on her renovations, but Ben had flashed those dark, sexy eyes, pleading for her to stay as he pulled her down on the chaise lounge beside him, and she was *toast*. She'd been lying with him and B ever since. Now it was after eleven, the living room was dark, Ben and B were fast asleep, and she could barely stand the smell of herself.

She carefully and quietly pushed up to a sitting position, and as she rose to her feet, Ben grabbed her wrist.

"Don't leave," he whispered.

"I'm just going to shower. I smell like baby puke and poop."

A smile lifted his lips, and he said, "I love how you smell."

She sighed over the honesty in his voice, but she knew better and quickly reined in that hopeful thought. "That's because you're delirious from lack of sleep." She pried his fingers from her wrist and said, "I'm borrowing your flannel pajama pants and another shirt to sleep in."

He pressed a kiss to the baby's head and pulled one of the new blankets he'd bought her over her little body. "You can have anything, as long as you come back and sleep with me."

Her body threw a little celebration at his words, despite knowing he didn't mean it the way she hoped. But after wanting him for so long, and seeing him love up the baby all day, her hormones were in overdrive.

He yawned and patted the spot she'd just vacated, his eyes fluttering closed again as he said, "Hurry back. We'll miss you."

There went the fireworks again.

I'm leaving in the morning.

No ifs, ands, or buts about it.

Today had felt like a month rather than a day. She *had* to get on with her life.

At least that's what she told herself, because *I'm falling harder for him* was too terrifying a thought to ponder.

CHAPTER FOUR

MORNING CAME FOR the *third* time on Tuesday, announced by the hungry cry of the sweet girl draped over Ben's chest.

And it wasn't Baby B.

"Benny," Aurelia whisper-whined. "I changed B *twice* last night. Making breakfast is the least you can do."

B was sleeping soundly on the other side of his chest. Aurelia had slept with one leg over his, her arm stretched across his body, her hand resting on B's back, and she'd woken right up every time the baby made a noise. They'd both gotten up with B and had fallen into an unspoken agreement in which Ben fed her and Aurelia changed her. They'd tried to put her in the basket last night after each feeding, but she'd wailed, as if she feared being abandoned again. Ben had a feeling sleeping with her on his chest wasn't the best idea, and Aurelia had told him as much, but they both agreed that if she wasn't his, she'd have enough discomfort and upheaval in the coming days to last a lifetime. The truth was, he enjoyed holding her while she slept. That way he knew she was safe and he could feel her breathing. But between worrying about the baby and enjoying Aurelia curled around him in ways she never had before, he'd only half slept.

Now, bleary eyed and exhausted, he was surprised to find he was also in a really great mood—and he was in no hurry to move away from Aurelia. "Stay right there," he whispered. "Food can wait."

She lifted her head, giving him a do-you-even-know-me look. Aurelia wasn't one of those women who was afraid to eat, and it was just one of the things he adored about her. She would eat just about anything he put in front of her, but she also exercised and hardly ever sat still. They went jogging together often, and while he could whip her in speed, she could run for *hours*. Actually, there wasn't much she *couldn't* do. She was fearless about life and business, and she was creative in ways he could only dream of being. Her biggest flaw was that she had terrible taste in men, and it was a bone of contention between them. When he pointed out that a guy seemed like a dick or wasn't worthy of her, it only made her more determined to go out with him, which pissed Ben off.

She tried to lean up, and he held her against his chest. "Ben!" she whispered harshly. "I'm *hungry*."

He reached behind her and retrieved one of the huge bags of peanut M&M's he'd bought for her when he'd gone shopping for diapers. He plopped them on his stomach and said, "Eat." They were Aurelia's favorite candy.

She groaned. "I don't want candy. I want *sustenance*." She pushed free of his grip, moving slowly and quietly, her beautiful eyes locked on the baby as she sat up.

Ben instantly mourned the feel of her beside him. "Hey, Rels?" He grabbed the back of her shirt, and she turned with a sleepy smile.

"Yeah?"

Maybe it was because of all they'd just been through, but his love for her swelled, making his chest constrict. There were so many things he wanted to say to her, but this mess he was in, this baby who might be his, wasn't Aurelia's issue to deal with, so he kept those intimate thoughts to himself and said, "Morning looks good on you."

She snort-laughed, then covered her mouth. She hated when she did that, but he thought it was the cutest thing ever. "You're into girls with bags under their eyes?"

I'm into you no matter what you look like.

Her gaze shifted over all the things he'd bought yesterday, which were now scattered around the room. Baby blankets lay across the couch and recliner. Piles of tiny outfits covered the coffee table, and several toys, still in their packaging, littered the floor. There were bags of diapers and packages of baby wipes beside a pile of clean towels, on which they'd changed B last night. The kitchen trash can was beside the towels, and empty bottles sat atop the end table by the chaise lounge.

"I think a hurricane hit your house," she said as she grabbed a handful of M&M's and stuffed them into her mouth. "I'm going to the bakery to get breakfast. I'll bring you back something. But you have to let go of my shirt."

"I think you mean *my* shirt," he said as he released it.

She stood up and put her hands on her hips, turning from side to side. His flannel pajama pants hung off her petite frame, and his shirt hung nearly to her knees. She had no idea that her hands cinching the shirt at her waist made the outline of her breasts and nipples prominent.

"Bet this is a turn-on, huh?" she asked with a teasing smile.

"You have no fucking idea."

"Yeah, right." She rolled her eyes as she pulled off his flannel pants and tugged on her jeans. Even though she was completely covered by his shirt, seeing that flash of bare legs made his cock twitch. He vowed right then and there, if Baby B wasn't his, the hell with Aurelia's fresh start. He was going to tell her how he felt. That determination came with a jolt of unexpected discontent as his eyes shifted to the sweet little girl sleeping on his chest. *Fuck.* He didn't want to wish her away as he had when they'd first found her, at least not with the vehemence he had yesterday.

"I forgot to throw the clothes in the dryer last night," Aurelia said. "I'll throw them in before I leave." She knotted his shirt above her belly button.

Damn. With a flash of her taut stomach, she was even more tempting. He knew *exactly* what he wanted for breakfast, and it sure as hell wasn't at the bakery. He wasn't about to let her leave looking that hot for some other guy to enjoy.

"Aren't you missing something?" he practically growled.

"What?" She sat down to put on her sneakers, and he eyed her bra, sitting on her purse by her feet. She followed his gaze and laughed. "The bakery isn't open yet. Only Willow and Piper will be there, and they've seen me without a bra."

Willow got to the bakery between four thirty and five every morning to prepare for the morning rush, and Ben's sisters and Aurelia often hung out with her before going to work. Now that Aurelia was living in Harmony Pointe, he knew she hardly ever got a chance to hang out with them in the mornings. Talia and her fiancé, Derek, were also living in Harmony Pointe, and Talia no longer joined them, either.

He glanced at the clock on the wall, relieved that it was only six fifteen. "Please don't mention B to them."

"You were serious about that? You know they'd help you. What are you worried about?"

He sat up, holding B against his chest and speaking quietly. "It's too complicated. I feel like a dick for not knowing the name of the woman in LA or the last name of the yoga girl, and the last thing I need is my sisters all over my case. It sucks enough that I had to admit all that to *you*."

A flash of pain washed over her face, and just as quickly it disappeared and she said, "You think they've never hooked up with a guy they didn't put through a thorough interview first?" She smiled and shook her head. "Listen, Benny boy. You may not want to think about your sisters doing that, but girls *do* hook up with guys. We're no different from you."

He scowled. "I don't want to think about them or *you* hooking up with random guys, and before they get excited *or* irritated at the idea of B, I want to be sure she's mine. Is that too much to ask?"

"Of course not. You know I'd never say anything behind your back."

He breathed a sigh of relief. "Thanks, Rels."

"I have to go brush my teeth," she said, heading for the stairs. "I wish I had deodorant."

"Just use mine."

"And get your cooties?" she said as she headed for the stairs.

"I'll give you a hell of a lot more than *cooties*," he mumbled.

He pressed a kiss to B's head and whispered, "She's really something, isn't she, peanut?"

He thought about the two women they needed to locate and how hard it must have been to leave such a tiny baby. How could a woman go through an entire pregnancy, give birth, care for this sweet girl for weeks, and *then* abandon her? He couldn't fathom leaving her. He was getting attached after only one day. She must have been desperate. Or in trouble.

Aurelia came downstairs looking tired, though she was smiling.

"Take my truck. It's parked behind your car in the driveway," he said. "The keys are on the table."

"Okay. I'll help you clean up when I get back. Any special requests from the bakery?"

"You know what I like," he said, and not for the first time—or the millionth—he thought about what it would feel like to say that to her when they were lying naked in his bed, when she was touching her lips to his flesh after he'd torn off her panties with his teeth, teased her until she begged him to make love to her. He wanted to hear her say it as he buried himself deep inside her—

The baby cried, wrenching him from his fantasy.

Reality slammed into him again. Baby B was not Aurelia's, and the chances of her wanting him if he was raising another woman's baby were slim to none.

Aurelia pulled open the back door to the bakery, inhaling the sugary goodness. She felt like she was sleepwalking as she stepped inside. Yesterday had been emotionally and physically exhausting. She wanted to hunker down in a comfy chair with about a dozen doughnuts and talk out all her conflicting emotions with her girlfriends. But considering her closest girlfriends were Ben's sisters and Remi, she was screwed.

"Hey, girl. I've missed you!" Willow said as she pulled a tray of delicious-looking muffins from the oven and set them on the counter, where doughnuts and croissants were already cooling. Her long blond hair was braided in a thick plait over one shoulder, and her jeans and shirt were speckled with flour. "What brings you to Sweetwater so early in the morning?"

Piper eyed her from her perch on the counter, where she sat in her torn work jeans and boots, eating a chocolate croissant. She scarfed down food like she had a hollow leg, but she and her father owned Dalton Contracting, and her job was hard manual labor, which enabled her to eat like a horse and remain a size two. "I think we can *guess* what brought you back. Rough night?"

"You could say that." Aurelia snagged a croissant and slumped into a chair. "I was up practically *all* night."

"Sounds like my type of night." Piper was as unfiltered and direct as her sisters were careful about the things they said.

"It was *exhausting*," Aurelia said.

As Willow transferred the muffins to the cooling rack, she said, "Exhausting can be fun."

"*Exhilarating,*" Piper agreed, taking another bite of her croissant.

"I don't know how people stay up night after night. I haven't been home in *two* days. I mean, look at me." She looked down at her shirt. "I'm wearing *Ben's* shirt."

"*Ben's* shirt?" Willow and Piper said in unison.

"I knew it!" Willow said. "Zane and I have always said that you two were perfect together."

Piper held her hands up. "I do not want to hear about *Ben's* sexual endeavors."

"We are *not* sleeping together," Aurelia snapped.

"Yeah, right. You said you wanted a new chapter in your life." Piper laughed and waved her finger at Aurelia. "One look at you says fuck-fest survivor. I'd call that a hell of a chapter."

"What? No! Ben is not my *new chapter*."

Willow smiled and said, "Staying up for *two* nights in a row? I'd say he's your entire flipping manuscript *and* your epilogue!"

Aurelia groaned. "I'm just helping him with a big project."

"I don't want to hear about my brother's *big project*." Piper slid off the counter, finishing her croissant.

"*Please!* Your brother has never liked me that way."

"Are you blind?" Willow wiped her hands and leaned against the counter. "Ben is your best friend."

"Exactly," Aurelia said.

"He knows everything about you," Willow said. "Good and bad, and he's still your closest male friend."

"Right. Your point?" Aurelia asked.

"He even loves the way you snort-laugh," Piper added. "The dude is totally into you, Aurelia."

Aurelia rolled her eyes. "He's into one-night, no-strings-attached sex, and"—*now he might have a baby*—"yes, he'd probably like to fuck me, but that's as far as it goes."

"I think you're wrong. You spend all of your free time with him," Willow pointed out.

"Because we have fun together, but trust me, he's not what I need. You guys know this about him. I mean, open your eyes. Besides, he's never even asked me out."

"Bullshit." Piper picked up a muffin, tore off a piece, and popped it into her mouth.

Aurelia looked at her like she'd lost her mind. "What are you talking about? I think I'd remember if he asked me out."

"He's always propositioning you," Piper said. "We've all heard it."

"She's right about that," Willow agreed.

"Have you lost your minds? Yes, he has propositioned me for *sex!*"

Piper sauntered over, her blond ponytail swinging behind her. "Not that I want to think of you and Ben in that way, but lots of relationships start with sex. Look at Willow and Zane and Bridgette and Bodhi."

"Well, I want hot, wild sex with my man, but I want more than that," Aurelia insisted. "I want romantic nights—"

"Like the night you and Ben watched the sun set over Sugar Lake when you were celebrating his big investment last fall?" Willow asked. "And when he had my mom make you Mexican wedding soup when you were sick, because it was your favorite?"

"I puked it all up," Aurelia reminded her.

Willow's gaze went soft, and she said, "Still, it was a romantic gesture, and he held your hair back."

"Hey, he called *you* when he sprained his ankle playing basketball. That's not romantic, but come *on*," Piper said. "He could have called *any* of us."

Aurelia's head fell back, and she sighed. "What are you saying? That I should jump in the sack with your brother and *maybe* it'll lead to more?" A little thrill ran through her at the prospect, even if she knew she wouldn't do it.

"Yes!" Willow said at the same time Piper said, *"Gross."*

"You know what? This is crazy." Aurelia bit into her croissant, and with her mouth full of deliciousness, she said, "I'm not having this conversation."

"I wasn't going to tell you this because I have been secretly pulling for you and Ben, and I know if he finds out he'll stop using it," Willow said, "but I think my mom has been infusing the body wash she makes him with one of her love potions."

Their mother, Roxie, made lotions, soaps, fragrances, and a host of other products, which she sold locally and online, and she made special brands for those she deemed in need of a little matchmaking help. Her love potions had become folklore around Sweetwater. People swore by them, and so did all her daughters—except Piper. But according to Talia, Willow, and Bridgette, Piper's belief would change once Roxie created one for *her*.

"What?" Aurelia's eyes flew open so wide they burned. She didn't know if she wholeheartedly believed in Roxie's love potions, but she definitely wouldn't discount them. Their mother seemed to have a sixth sense about who belonged together before the couples even did.

"You can't tell Ben," Willow said conspiratorially. "He'd be pissed."

"You could have warned *me*. You know I stay over there a lot. I've used his body wash dozens of times." She probably shouldn't be so mad, since she'd loved him even before she'd started showering at his house. But she was, because maybe that potion made her love him even more. Maybe that was why she couldn't stop accepting his every request to hang out. *Oh no.* Did that also mean the potion *didn't* work on Ben? Because he wasn't exactly pawing at her.

Piper laughed.

"Sorry," Willow said, but her smile told Aurelia she wasn't really sorry. "What kind of project are you working on with Ben? He hasn't said anything to Zane about a big project other than that hotel take-over. Although Zane's going running with him later this morning, after he drops Louie off at school, so maybe he'll tell him about it then."

Shit. She pulled her phone from her pocket and texted Ben. *911! Zane is coming over to run with you after taking Louie to school. You'd better call him unless you want him to see B!*

Skipping right over Willow's question about the project, she said, "Ben's probably too tired to go running."

Willow began putting ingredients into a bowl. "They're always tired when they start. He'll wake up."

Aurelia's phone vibrated with Ben's response. *Shit. Thanks. I'll call him and cancel. When are you coming back?* She typed, *Soon.* As she sent the message, she thought about what Willow had said about Ben's romantic gestures. He'd brought her a peanut-M&M-covered cupcake on her birthday morning every year for the past . . . well . . . since she went away to college. *Whoa. That is romantic.* He'd also let her cry on his shoulder countless times, sent her texts when he knew she was having a rough day, and stayed with her for three nights after her grandfather passed away. *And he bought me M&M's yesterday when I desperately needed them. He thought about me even though he was frazzled over finding B.*

Maybe she *was* on his mind as more than only a friend.

Or maybe he just wanted his good friend to help him with *Project Baby B.*

Her stomach knotted. She knew B wasn't a *project* for either of them. She'd seen the way Ben had protected her at Vic's office and how his face had crumpled every time she cried, as if her pain were his own. She'd be lying to herself if she tried to pretend that the whole time she'd been at the bakery she hadn't been thinking about *both* Ben and B.

Her phone vibrated again with a text from Ben. *Good. Someone misses you.* Comments like that might drive her mad. She was falling even harder for him, and she was an idiot. He didn't say *he* missed her. For all she knew, what he really meant was that B needed a diaper change.

"Hello? Earth to Aurelia." Piper waved her hand in front of Aurelia's face, startling her.

"Sorry. I'm so tired I must have zoned out."

Piper eyed Aurelia's phone, and Aurelia quickly turned it over. "I asked if you could pry yourself away from my brother's big *project* long enough to meet me at the bookstore to go over a few things before my guys start painting."

Piper and Mr. Dalton owned Dalton Contracting and specialized in custom building. Piper was handling the renovations to the bookstore and to the bakery for the new direction of Aurelia and Willow's partnership. They were going to offer books at the bakery and baked goods at the bookstore.

"Yeah, sure, of course," Aurelia said. "I promised Ben I'd drop off breakfast. Let me just swing by his place and then shower real quick."

"With Ben?" Piper arched a brow.

Aurelia glared at her. "At *home*. Before I go, though, I want to see how Willow's book nook is coming along."

"Oh my gosh, it's *gorgeous*," Willow said as she put dollops of batter on a tray. "I think this was the smartest thing we could have done, utilizing both locations instead of just making the bakery/bookstore here in Sweetwater. And it leaves the apartment above the bakery free. Shira's been tossing around the idea of spending more time here now that Bodhi and his mother have both moved. This way she can stay upstairs if she wants."

Willow put the tray in the oven. As they headed into the bakery to check out the book nook, she asked, "Did you hear about Remi's stalker?"

"What? *No.*"

"Scary shit," Piper said.

"Someone is sending her threatening letters, and they broke into her house. I'm surprised it wasn't on TMZ, but Aiden managed to keep it all under wraps to protect her," Willow explained.

"Oh my gosh. How is Remi handling it? Was she home when they broke in?"

"No, and you know Remi," Willow said. "She thinks everyone is overreacting. She hates the bodyguards Aiden hired, and she feels like if whoever broke in really wanted to hurt her, they would have broken in when she was home. She kind of has a point. I'm just glad she'll be here filming soon. LA is so crazy."

Aurelia thought about Ben's big-boobed LA hookup, and her stomach seized. She'd always known Ben had been with plenty of women, but she'd been thinking about it so much the last twenty-four hours, it made her queasy.

She forced those thoughts away and focused on the bakery, which adjoined Bridgette's flower shop through an arched doorway. Aurelia loved the distressed mint and pink cabinetry and the wide glass displays spanning almost the full width of the store. Behind the register, packages of bakery paraphernalia wrapped with pretty pink and green bows decorated the shelves. They'd cleared the tables at the far end of the room for the new reading nook. The shelves started halfway up the side wall and ran the length of it. Aurelia pictured the shelves displaying books from her store, the enticing covers silently calling out to readers—and even those who didn't yet realize they were readers—because she knew books had special powers to captivate people and sweep them out of their own lives into someplace magical.

"We're going to stain the bookshelves the same color as the hardwood floors," Piper explained.

"This is perfect," Aurelia said in wonder. "Simply *perfect*."

"I found an antique sofa and two end chairs online last night," Willow said. "I'll send you pictures. I think they'll give it the coziness we talked about."

As Willow and Piper discussed the build-out, Aurelia's mind circled back to Ben and B. Had he changed her diaper? What if she needed another bath? He couldn't bathe her alone. He hadn't showered last night because B was sleeping on his chest. She should probably stick around long enough for him to shower before going home.

Half an hour later, as she drove down the cobblestone streets toward Ben's house with a bag of his favorite cheese Danishes and Boston cream pie doughnuts, she was still thinking about everything his sisters had said.

He even loves the way you snort-laugh. The dude is totally into you . . .

Maybe she should just tell Ben how she felt and leave the ball in his court. She was a big girl. She could handle it if he laughed in her face, couldn't she? Or if he said, *Great, let's fuck*? What if all he really wanted was a one-night stand? Or worse, what if his innuendos were jokes and he really didn't like her in that way *at all*?

By the time she reached his house, she was all riled up and confused. She stormed through the front door and through the clean living room—*Clean?* For some reason that only heightened her anxiety. Leave it to master-at-everything Ben to take control of his frigging chaos in the space of a morning and be able to handle fatherhood with ease and grace.

He wasn't in the kitchen or his office. She stalked upstairs, gritting her teeth and practicing her lay-it-on-the-line speech. *Ben, I like you. I might even love you. And you don't have to like me back—or love me—but I wanted you to know.*

I can do this. I can do this, she told herself as she stomped down the hall toward his bedroom. *I am totally doing this!* She felt lighter already. This was exactly what she needed to do.

She walked into the bedroom as he was coming out of the bathroom wearing nothing but a towel and carrying Baby B's basket. His hair was wet, and he hadn't shaved. He always shaved! *Damn it.* His scruff was dark and sexy, and it made him look edgier than usual, which made her all sorts of nervous.

He set down the basket, in which B was fast asleep, and stepped toward her, smiling as he said, "Hey, Rels. I got the place cleaned up."

Her eyes were riveted to the water dripping down the treasure trail on his abs. She opened her mouth to speak, but it was bone dry, and her mind went completely and utterly blank.

"You okay?" he asked.

Her fingers itched to rip off that towel and throw herself into his arms, but she was frozen in place, and he reached out, touching her fingers, sending lightning through her veins. She dropped the bag from the bakery, said, "I can't do this," and practically ran down the stairs and out the front door.

CHAPTER FIVE

AFTER BABY DUTY and breakfast, courtesy of his very confusing best friend, who still hadn't returned his texts from this morning, Ben was finally trying to get himself thinking straight before his conference call with Aiden. Thank God B was sound asleep after two bottles and three diaper changes. Now if he could only focus on work.

He gazed out the window of his home office. He had a six-thousand-square-foot home on seven acres within walking distance of town, tucked away down a long tree-lined driveway, he ran a multibillion-dollar empire, he *might* have a beautiful baby girl, but he couldn't even hold on to the only woman he wanted. His house never felt like a home except when Aurelia was in it, and even then it didn't feel as warm and homey as her apartment did. In Aurelia's apartment, they fell asleep on the couch together most of the time, but even if he fell asleep on the couch and she went into her bedroom, she was still *right there*, just a few steps away. That felt good and right. In his house they slept on the couch, or the chaise lounge, and he would never even think about leaving her to go upstairs to the bedroom. It was too far away.

His mind circled back to Aurelia running out of his bedroom, when she'd said, *I can't do this.* He'd started to go after her, but then he'd remembered the tiny ball and chain relying on him. He hadn't even been able to call out after Aurelia for fear of waking the baby.

He looked down at B sleeping soundly in the basket by his desk and crouched beside her. He should be pissed every time he looked at the baby who was turning his life upside down, but how could anyone be angry at an innocent child? It wasn't her fault he might have screwed up and her mother was too weak to care for her. Or maybe she was in trouble. *Fuck.* He needed to find out, but he was biding his time, wanting to find out the paternity results first, because if B wasn't his, then social services could deal with tracking down her mother.

His chest constricted at that thought, which confused him even more. How could he feel so much for her so fast? He touched the baby's head.

It's just you and me, B.

Baby Ben. Who called a baby something like that? Thinking of how easily Aurelia had come up with the name brought a smile. She hadn't harassed him for possibly having a child. She'd gone into organized-and-efficient Aurelia mode and made a list of possible mothers.

Ben stood up and snagged the list from his desk, reading the names she'd given the women he'd slept with—Hotel Hookup/Malibu Barbie, Big Apple Fuck Buddy, and Pretzel Girl. She was a much better person than he was, because if the tables were turned he'd have called the men she'd slept with something like Dick Weed, Asshole, or Dead Meat. Like that little prick who had sent her running back to Sweetwater in the first place. Kent, the on-again, off-again boyfriend she'd dated when she'd lived in New York City. Hell, he should probably thank the guy, but he had a feeling if he ever came face-to-face with the asshole, he'd make him pay for hurting her.

He pulled out his phone to send her another text, but he'd already sent one apologizing for the situation he was in and thanking her for sticking with him as long as she had. What else could he say? She had a life to live, a business she was setting up, and a new apartment. She had her *fresh start,* and she'd made it pretty clear she didn't want it to include him and the baby. And damn, that pissed him off, because he'd never abandon her in her time of need. He would suck up his jealousy, hurt, and anger and make sure she was okay.

Aw, hell.

He sank into his chair as understanding dawned on him. Maybe *that's* why it was easier for her to leave—because she *wasn't* jealous, hurt, or angry. She didn't have *those* feelings toward him. She just wasn't willing to mess up her *fresh start* by being his copilot while he navigated this new, potentially life-altering terrain.

He pulled out his phone and mumbled, "The hell with that," as he thumbed out another text. His phone rang, and Aiden's name flashed on the screen. *Damn it.* He glanced at the clock and realized it was time for their conference call. Leaving the text to Aurelia unsent, he answered the call.

"Hi, Aiden," he said distractedly.

"How's it going?"

Ben eyed the baby. "A bit crazy, but we're—*I'm*—good."

"What's going on, man? You sure you're okay?"

He sat back, gazing out the window and wrestling with lying to his business partner. *What am I thinking?* Like all the relationships that meant something to Ben, his relationship with Aiden was built on trust, and he wasn't about to mess that up.

"I have a *situation* I'm dealing with right now, but it's fine."

"Situation? Ben, we're on the verge of the biggest takeover of our lives. Talk to me. We can't afford for something to go awry."

Ben stood and paced, picturing his partner's serious eyes. Aiden had a few years on Ben and a lifetime of experience raising his much younger sister, Remi. If Ben could confide in anyone, it was Aiden.

"It's complicated, but I might have a kid. An infant. A *daughter.*" Ben glanced at B and felt himself smiling again.

"A *baby?* What do you mean *might?* Is there some question? Should you call your attorney?"

"Already did. First thing."

"Christ, Ben. A baby? You couldn't have told me this a few months ago, *before* we spent hundreds of thousands of dollars preparing for this takeover?"

"I had no idea then." Ben explained what had happened, and then he said, "I should have the results of the paternity test soon, but don't worry. It's not going to have an impact on business either way."

Aiden scoffed, and then what sounded like an incredulous laugh came through the phone. "Dude, you have no idea what you're talking about. Remi was twelve when our parents died. *Twelve.* She could feed and bathe herself, put herself to bed, and she sure as hell didn't need diapers. I had to table everything in my life except the bare essentials needed to run my business. How are you going to travel with a baby? Maybe we should think about letting Garth take over for a while."

Garth Anziano was one of their directors. He managed several of their investments and had always done a top-notch job. He had a stellar reputation and was trustworthy and loyal. But this deal was happening because *Ben* had brought it to the table. He'd spent the last eighteen months working every angle to make it come to fruition, and there was no way he was going to hand it over to anyone.

"I've got this, Aiden, and I'm not going to let anything stand in my way." *Not even the adorable little peanut in the basket.*

"If this kid is yours, you're going to have a hell of a lot more to think about than this deal, and, Ben, that's okay. Look, you've spent years making things happen. You've got more money than you could spend in several lifetimes. You don't need this particular deal or the international travel required to make it a success added to your portfolio."

Ben pinched the bridge of his nose, trying to keep from losing his cool as he said in a tone that left no room for negotiation, "I am *not* going to hand this off to anyone."

"Okay," Aiden relented. "Then let's get down to business."

Two hours, one bottle, and one diaper change later—thank God for speakerphone—Ben ended the call with Aiden and read the text that had *finally* rolled in from Aurelia. *Sorry to bail. I had to meet Piper at the bookstore.*

"That was an awfully fast escape for just meeting my sister," Ben said to B, who was looking at him like she knew who he was, which he was pretty sure was impossible. "I think it's time we paid our friend *Relsy* a visit."

After showing up at Vic's without proper baby supplies, Ben wasn't taking any chances. He packed *everything* he'd bought for the baby— and the bags of peanut M&M's, because chocolate went a long way with his tormented girl—into his Land Rover and drove to Harmony Pointe.

It was official. There was no place on earth Aurelia felt more at home than in a bookstore. It made sense, since she'd practically grown up in her grandparents' bookstore in Sweetwater, and she'd worked for Pages, the largest bookstore chain on the East Coast, in its flagship store in New York City for the past several years. After her grandfather had suffered a stroke, an attorney named Mick Bad had purchased her grandparents' bookstore. He'd kept it intact and allowed Aurelia to open it every few weeks, when she could find the time to return home from the city. When she moved back to Sweetwater after a nasty breakup, she had intended to buy the store from Mick and combine it with Willow's bakery. But being around Ben all the time had proven much more difficult than she'd anticipated. They'd always had a love-hate relationship, at least in her mind, and she was pretty sure it was because she *loved* being with him and *hated* that he wasn't the type of guy to settle down.

This was where she belonged, surrounded by fictional stories— and hopefully soon by people who loved reading them—*not* playing house with Ben. She had to stop letting her heart lead the way and start thinking with her head again and remember all the reasons she couldn't spend every minute of her free time with Ben. He needed her now because parenting was hard, but what would happen if he found out he wasn't B's father? She knew exactly where that would leave them. He'd go back to his one-night stands, and she'd be his buddy when he wasn't out carousing.

Buying this shop was definitely the right thing to do.

Piper's construction crew was hard at work putting up shelving, repointing the front and rear brick walls, installing the bakery display cabinets, and refinishing the checkout counter. In her grandparents' shop, one thing she'd always loved was that the checkout counter had an area that was just above knee height, so children could set their books down and feel like they were part of the whole bookstore experience. She was having that done in Chapter One. Piper was in and out, managing several jobs at once, but her burly project manager, Kase Force, was always on-site, and he was currently heading Aurelia's way. The guy's arms and legs were as thick as tree trunks. Tattoos snaked out from beneath his short sleeves, and the blue baseball cap he'd worn every day since he'd begun working there was firmly in place, a hint of brown hair poking out in the back. In the week he'd been working there, she hadn't seen him crack a single smile.

He nodded as he approached, his face as stoic as granite. "Do you have a second to go over the schedules?"

"Sure." She followed him to the back, where the floor plans were laid out on a table by the door.

Kase leaned over the blueprints, pointing to each area as he spoke. "The counter and these shelving units should be done by the end of the week. The moldings in the classics and romance areas should be done today."

"And the flooring in the classics section?" She'd asked them to scuff up the hardwood in that area, which Kase had balked at, but she had a vision and she wanted to carry it out.

In addition to renovating, she had plans to make each section feel special. Her friend Everly Love was a talented artist and a green-living specialist who happened to be between jobs. She was helping Aurelia with the shop while she looked for a job in her field, and she was going to paint a mural in the kids' section. The reference and nonfiction area would be set up in classic library style with substantial wooden furniture and leather reading chairs and desks. The romance section would be decorated with elements made out of leather and lace, and the classics area was being outfitted with ornate moldings, worn shelves, and, eventually, antique furniture. When Aurelia worked at Pages, she had done biweekly readings from the classics. She'd had quite a loyal following, and she hoped to inspire the same love for them in Harmony Pointe.

"It'll be done just as you've specified," Kase said. "Can I ask you something?" He didn't wait for an answer. "I know you said you grew up in a bookstore, but according to my sisters, nobody buys paperbacks anymore. You're spending a lot of money on renovations. Aren't you worried about going belly-up?"

Nearly everyone she knew had worried about her buying a floundering bookstore when she could have spent much less money reopening her grandparents' store and combining it with Willow's bakery. She still had a pretty rabid readership in Sweetwater. Residents knew she opened her grandmother's old shop every few weeks, and they waited with bated breath for those openings. Ben was the only person other than Willow and Flossie who had thought her ideas were solid, and because of his business expertise, his blessing had given her the extra confidence she needed to take the plunge and invest her money in the changes she thought would make big differences.

"I'm doing things a little differently than most bookstores. I'm going to have a book borrow section, where for two dollars a customer can borrow a book for two weeks, since the small town library is often understocked. I anticipate most readers will come back and read a book a week, but only time will tell. I'll have specials, when they can borrow for a buck, and when the books get too used, I'll offer scratch-and-dent sales. I'm also going to do monthly readings, where I dress up as characters from books. I used to do it in the city, and I had a huge following there. We always sold a lot of books after my readings, and I'm hoping to eventually find my niche here doing the same type of thing. And from time to time I'll hold book swaps for readers, and I'm hoping to start a monthly book club, so I have ideas . . ."

His brows shot up. "You're going to do all that?"

"That's the plan, once I hire a few employees and we get past the grand opening. Are we still on target for the eatery area?"

"Yes. The painting throughout the store should be done by next week. Then we'll move on to installing the tile in the eatery area. Once you clear out the stockroom, we'll finish up in there, too."

She and Everly had boxed up the shop's inventory for the remodeling. As time allowed, they were working through her current stock, figuring out what needed to be returned to the distributor and what they would keep. Shipments of new books would begin arriving the following Monday, and it would take them some time to go through those. But once they were able to restock the shelves, it would *smell* like a bookstore again.

"It may take some time before we have that area cleared out. Would it be a problem for you to come back a week or two after the rest of the renovations are done?"

The corners of Kase's lips quirked up, softening his granitelike features. "I'll come back as often as you'd like."

The back door of the shop opened, and Aurelia was surprised to see Ben with an enormous duffel bag slung over his shoulder, holding B's carrier in one hand and several big department store bags in the other. His eyes connected with hers, and that killer smile she loved reached his eyes. The image of him in a towel shot into her mind like a flaming bullet, and just like that her heart ricocheted.

So much for leading with my head.

Ben's gaze shifted to Kase, and he threw his shoulders back, lifting his chin the way guys did when they were showing dominance. His killer smile morphed into something possessive and dark.

Kase's blue eyes found hers again, and he said, "Whenever you're ready for me, I'll be here."

Tension billowed around Ben like dense fog as he approached.

"Hey, Ben." Aurelia's brow furrowed and she said, "What are you doing, moving in?"

"Maybe," he said evenly, eyes trained on Kase as he walked away.

She bent down and tickled B's chin. "Hello, sweet girl. Did you have a nice day with Daddy Ben?"

"Did that guy ask you out?" Ben asked.

She stood up and said, "Seriously?"

"Is that why you took off like a bat out of hell this morning? To come back here and see him?"

"Ben, don't be an ass." She walked away, needing to put space between them. She didn't care that there were four men watching them and she probably looked like a bitch with steam coming out of her ears. He had no right to size up the guys she talked to.

He set down the bags and followed her, still holding B's carrier. "What? It's a legitimate question. You're single and hot. Why wouldn't he ask you out?"

She stopped in the middle of the store, crossed her arms, and held his steady gaze. "You're right. I'm *definitely* single. Thanks for the reminder."

He stared at her as if *she'd* said something wrong, his nostrils flaring, jaw clenched so tight it had to hurt.

"*What*, Ben? Do you have something to say? Because I haven't slept in two nights, and I'm not really in the mood to go through an inquisition. I've spent practically all my free time with you since I moved out of the city, and now I'm staying up all night with you and B." Holy shit, the word vomit just kept coming, and the more she said, the angrier she got and the more it tumbled out. "You know what? I *hope* he asks me out. At least then there would be something for you to get all *over-protective* about."

"I'm not being *overprotective*," he seethed, and set the carrier down beside him.

She half laughed, half scoffed. "Oh no? What do you call it? Because I have no idea what you want from me, but if it's a temporary baby mama—"

He hauled her against him and crashed his lips to hers. His fingers pressed into her arms, and his tongue plunged into her mouth, fiercely possessive and utterly intoxicating. One strong arm swept around her, crushing her against his hard frame. The other pushed into her hair, fisting tight, angling her mouth beneath his so he could take the kiss deeper—and *boy*, did he . . .

His kisses were rough and *thorough*, claiming more of her with every swipe of his tongue, like he'd been thinking of *exactly* how he wanted to kiss her for years. And Lord knew *she* had been doing the same. She clung to his arms as heat spread through her body like wildfire, filling up her chest and pooling low in her belly. He eased his efforts, kissing her softer, slower, so tenderly it sent shivers down her spine and goose bumps rose on her flesh. His lips were warm and insistent, and his mouth moved sensually over hers. She felt his arousal against her belly, and when his lips brushed lightly over hers, she realized her whole body was trembling.

"Possessive," he whispered against her lips.

She was breathless and dizzy. *"What?"*

"I'm not being overprotective. I'm being *possessive*." His lips pressed hard and fast against hers again, and then they were gone, and his eyes drilled into hers as he said, "I get that way over things that are mine."

She shook her swooning head, confused by his kiss, his words, and the way he was looking at her, like he wanted to eat her alive—which made her entire body clench with anticipation.

"I have been waiting for the right time, but fuck the right time. Be *mine*, Aurelia," he said demandingly, still holding her body against his. "I'm an asshole for not telling you how I felt sooner. I don't want a temporary *anything*. I want *you* in my life, by my side, constantly."

B whimpered, and they both looked down at her. It was then that Aurelia caught sight of Piper standing a few feet behind Ben, her jaw agape.

"Piper . . ."

Ben's head whipped in the direction of his sister.

Piper was closing the distance between them, peering around Ben's big body with a stunned look in her eyes. "I don't know what I'm more mesmerized by, that fucking-hot kiss or the baby my brother carried in here."

CHAPTER SIX

THE LAST THING Ben wanted to do was let go of Aurelia and deal with Piper when Aurelia was looking at him like she wanted to either fuck him or kill him. It bothered him that he couldn't tell the difference. Her lips were swollen from their kisses and her cheeks were red, he assumed from embarrassment, given that everyone in the damn store was staring at them. He glared at the workers, who respectfully turned away.

Holding Aurelia tightly, he said, "Let's go upstairs and deal with Piper, and then we can deal with us."

"Us?" came out flustered and tentative, like it was a foreign word.

They'd always been an *us*, just in a different context. *Fuck everyone else.* He wasn't going to let this chance to be clear about his feelings slip away. He was done letting anything come between them. He framed her beautiful, flushed face between his hands and looked determinedly into her eyes so there was no mistaking his intentions as he said, "Yes. *Us.* You and me, Aurelia. Everything else, except B, is just noise right now. I know my timing sucks, but this is about us as a couple, and I want that. Got it?"

"In the animal kingdom that kiss was the equivalent of peeing on Aurelia," Piper said. "I think everyone in here *got it.*"

He glared at Piper. Then, refusing to be deterred from the person who mattered most, he shifted his gaze back to Aurelia and said, "Why don't you take B and Piper upstairs. I'll grab the rest of the stuff and be right up."

She nodded, but her fingers dug into his arms like she couldn't let go. That was how he *knew*, without a shadow of a doubt, she was still reeling from their kiss, *not* regretting it.

He couldn't resist pressing his lips to hers again, softer and reassuringly. She returned his efforts, and he felt like a freaking kid at Christmas, reveling in her affection. It was about damn time they took this step. He touched his cheek to hers, whispering for her ears only, "In case you have any doubt, there's going to be a lot more of that coming your way . . . *without* an audience."

A needy sound escaped her lips, and it was enough to make his blood burn even hotter.

"Great." Piper picked up B's carrier and said, "Whatever *that* was rendered her completely useless. Nice move, bro."

She grabbed Aurelia's arm and dragged her toward the door that led up to her apartment. Aurelia looked over her shoulder and bit her lower lip, trying to stop a clearly unstoppable smile.

After they disappeared through the door, Ben had one more thing to tend to. He strode over to his burly competition and extended his hand. "Ben Dalton. You'll be seeing a lot of me around here."

The guy laughed as he shook Ben's hand. "Kase Force, and I did not ask her out. I might have in another day or two. But, dude, the minute she saw you, I knew she wasn't single."

Ben nodded, and then he went to gather his things. He carried the bags up to Aurelia's apartment and set them down inside the door on the knotty hardwood floors. She'd only just moved in, and already it felt like *her*—organized but not oppressive, light and spacious but not empty. The brick walls were painted white. A light gray sofa, which Ben had slept on more than a dozen times in the last year alone, was covered with throw pillows in muted rust, pale green, peach, and dark gray, as were the pale yellow armchairs. Her loft-style apartment was open save for the two bedrooms and the bathroom. The kitchen overlooked Main Street, boasting stainless-steel appliances and four circle-head windows. It was separated from the living room/dining room combination by a large island with four barstools and a built-in reading nook, which cantilevered out about six feet over the sidewalk. The nook had L-shaped bookshelves that ran from floor to ceiling and were already chock-full of books and framed photographs. The books dominated the dining area like hundreds of sentinels watching over the room.

Aurelia organized her books by author, publication date, and series, which she'd been doing since she was a kid. That was just one of Aurelia's bookish quirks. There were pictures of her and her grandparents; pictures of her mother, whom she'd never known; and pictures of Ben and his family, Remi and Aiden, and a few of her other friends. His favorite picture of all was one Aiden had taken at the opening of Remi and Zane's movie. Ben's entire family had gone, and they were all beaming at the camera. Aurelia had stood in front of him, his arms around her middle. Her hands were on top of his, and Aiden had caught her looking up at Ben with what he told himself was adoration and a hint of annoyance, since he'd just whispered, *Let's blow this taco stand and make out in the back of the theater.* In reality, it was probably annoyance with a hint of putting up with him he saw in her eyes.

"So," Piper said, jerking him from his memories. She was sitting on the couch with B in her arms, feeding her a bottle. "About that kiss . . ."

Aurelia was pacing, wearing black skinny jeans and a gray T-shirt he knew by heart. He didn't have to see the print on the front to know it was the one that had a picture of a girl wearing a black floppy hat, with the words STOP THINKING & JUST LET THINGS HAPPEN written in white stacked down the center. Her Converse were black, and he also didn't need to look further to know she'd written a literary quote on the white strip just below the inside of her ankle. She did it on all of her sneakers, the same way she used to drive her grandparents bananas by writing quotes on her jeans. She'd been wearing many of the same pairs of jeans and sneakers since she was a teenager. She gravitated toward the familiar. That and her utilitarian style were just a couple of the things Ben had always loved about her. She didn't care about money or material things. She cared about family and friends.

She stopped pacing and looked nervously at him. Their eyes connected with the heat of a thousand suns, and there was no mistaking just how deeply she cared about *him*, too.

"Is this how it's going to be from now on?" Piper asked. "The two of you lusting after each other so badly that neither one can speak? Because if you two need to hit the bedroom to get past that wickedness, I'll take this sweet little muffin for a walk and come back in an hour. But I prefer to know what the hell is going on first, Benjamin."

Ben huffed out a breath and said, "She might be mine."

"So I gathered when Aurelia said you guys were calling her Baby B, for *Baby Ben.*"

He paced, and Aurelia sank into an armchair as he gave Piper the lowdown on what had transpired over the last two days. As he spoke, he desperately wanted time alone with Aurelia to get everything out in the open between them, but that would have to wait. Piper might be the size of a pixie, but she was his most aggressive sister, and she asked a million questions, which he had to answer, because there was no deterring her. He told her about the two women he had yet to contact—the yoga instructor and the blonde in Los Angeles, though he hated the way it felt to say it *again* in front of Aurelia. Then he told her about the doctor and the paternity test, and when he was done, Piper blinked several times, as if she couldn't believe what she'd heard.

"Didn't Dad ever explain the birds and the bees to you?" Piper snapped.

"Not helping," he said stoically.

"A *baby*," Piper said. "A frigging *adorable* baby."

"I know," he said, feeling such a mix of emotions, he couldn't make heads or tails of them.

Piper gazed down at the baby and said, "There's a chance she's not yours, but who would leave a baby on someone's porch if she wasn't sure he was its father?"

"That's why my bet is on her being Ben's," Aurelia said, averting her eyes from Ben.

"It *is*?" He hadn't even gone there in *his* mind yet.

Aurelia nodded, finally meeting his gaze. "It makes sense, Ben."

"Maybe," he admitted. "I don't know what makes sense in this situation. For all I know she's trying to nail me as the father so I'll pay her off." He pushed to his feet, unable to sit still with that thought rattling around in his head again.

"You could be right, but I doubt it." Piper put the bottle down and lifted B to her shoulder, patting her back. "If someone wanted money they'd blackmail you about the baby, not *give* her to you."

All he knew was that he wanted two things at that moment—to have Aurelia beside him and Baby B in his arms. He'd wanted Aurelia for so long, wanting her closer made perfect sense. But the emotions he'd already developed toward the baby were harder to understand. They didn't fit into his view of himself or his future, and that threw him off balance.

"I'm on the verge of the biggest deal of my life, and I just made my feelings for Aurelia clear after *years* of wanting her." He turned to Aurelia and said, "*You*, wanting *you*. This timing sucks."

"Years . . . ?" Aurelia said softly.

He nodded. Needing something to do, he grabbed the towels from the duffel bag and layered them on the floor.

"What are you doing?" Piper asked.

"Getting ready to change her diaper. She'll poop in about a minute. I swear she's a shit machine."

"She goes a *lot*," Aurelia said as she dug through the duffel bag and withdrew wipes and diapers.

"Okay, first of all, this"—Piper waved her finger between the two of them—"this is the stuff *Dumb and Dumber* is made of. Why would you bring *towels* to Aurelia's apartment? She *lives* here. She has towels."

"I don't *know*," Ben snapped. "I didn't think about what I was bringing. I just shoved everything I could possibly need into the bags so we weren't stuck without something."

"Have you ever heard of a changing pad?" Piper asked with a hint of amusement. She kissed B's cheek and said, "It looks like Auntie Piper will have to go shopping because Bachelor Ben is a numbskull. I don't know what Aurelia's excuse is, but I'll get you all set up with proper baby stuff."

Ben glared at her.

"Just because we don't have experience with babies doesn't mean we're stupid," Aurelia said. "It just means we've come upon a situation in which we have no experience." She grabbed a bag from the counter and dumped a pile of books on the couch beside Piper. "Give us a day and we'll know everything there is to know about babies."

Ben couldn't hide his shock at the pile of baby and parenting books. "You said you couldn't do this . . . ?" *And then you went out and bought these books?*

"Yeah, well . . ." Aurelia sighed. "*That* wasn't about the baby. I had intended to tell you how I felt about you—not quite in the same way you showed me—but you were standing there wearing nothing but a towel, and my brain went blank."

Ben grinned, suppressing the urge to exclaim, *Hell yeah!*

Piper thrust the baby into his hands and said, "This is getting to be way too much information for me. What's your plan, Ben? When do you get the paternity results?"

"No idea. Soon, I hope." He kissed B's cheek, inhaling the sweet baby scent he was becoming overly fond of. "Tomorrow we're going to see the yoga instructor. I have to find out who the mother is."

Piper arched a brow. "'We're'? You know you're asking a lot from a woman whose tonsils you just inspected with your tongue."

"Can we *please* not talk about that?" Aurelia said. She looked at Ben, and her cheeks pinked up again.

Piper held her hands up and said, "Right. Well, Ben, I think you'd better get this shit under control before Sunday, when we're going to see Mom and Dad at Willow and Zane's for dinner." Willow and Zane were hosting a family dinner since their parents, and Bridgette and Bodhi, would be back in town. "I've got some free time tomorrow. Why don't I babysit so you can track down that yoga chick? I'll swing by the baby store tonight and get the things you don't realize you need, like a changing pad and a Diaper Genie." She eyed the bags and said, "Is it safe to assume you're staying here tonight? Or are you hiring a truck to take all your cargo back to your place?"

Ben looked at Aurelia and said, "I'll get back to you on that."

Piper left after the baby fell asleep on the blanket-bed Aurelia and Ben had made for her beside the couch. The second Piper was out the door, everything Aurelia had held in for the last two hours came tumbling out in fast, harsh whispers. "You kissed me! In front of Piper's crew! Our very first kiss *ever* and that's where you do it? How was I supposed to react to that? And in front of *Piper*?" She paced, unable to stop the accusations from flying. "You know everyone in Sweetwater will know about this by the end of the day. Piper will make a snarky remark, and then it'll be all over town. She probably won't even know she did it. She's like a *secret obliterator*. Not that we have to be a secret, but . . . our *first* kiss? And Piper and the *baby*? Did you see Piper's face? She loves B already! She's *shopping* for her. What if she's not yours? What if she is? Oh God, *Ben* . . ."

He pulled her into his arms and slanted his mouth over hers as he had downstairs, taking her in a passionate kiss that shattered her thoughts and left her light-headed.

He brushed his delicious lips over hers as light as a feather and said, "It wasn't planned. I had something much better planned, and I'll tell you about it, but first I need to say this. I agree my timing sucked. The last thing I wanted was an audience, but I can't hold back anymore, Rels. I can't hear about one more man asking you out or be there to hold your hand when he turns out to be an asshole. And I sure as hell can't kiss one more woman, hoping to fill a void where *you* belong."

She was overwhelmed with emotions, and "Ben . . ." slipped out. He'd been doing exactly what she had all this time?

He kissed her temple the way that always made her heart melt and said, "Let me finish. I know asking you to be with me when I'm in the middle of a paternity nightmare is a lot to hope for. I fucked up. I have no idea how, because I've never in my entire life had unprotected sex, but this is on me and I take full responsibility. And I'll understand if you want to walk away, even if it's only until I have this figured out. But I hope with every fiber of my being that you'll stick around, because baby or no baby, you're the only woman I want by my side."

Happiness bubbled up inside her, and she tried not to let it carry her away. "Do you have any idea how long I've wanted to hear that? But how can I know if this would ever have happened if we didn't find B on your doorstep? What if you want me because it's overwhelming to do this on your own?"

He took her hand and led her to the couch, pulling her down beside him. "I need to tell you how I had planned on confessing my feelings for you. How I'd planned on earning that first kiss."

"You better hope you're good at making things up on the fly." She knew Ben was a planner when it came to business, but not so much when it came to his personal life. The idea that he might have planned something so meaningful blew her away. *If* he really had.

He pulled out his wallet and handed her a folded piece of paper. She unfolded it and scanned the handwritten list. Her pulse quickened with every item she read.

1. *Glass slipper*
2. *Lights at night*
3. *Dancing beneath the stars*
4. *That look that Grandpa gives Grandma*
5. *Whispers and secret smiles*
6. *To be loved like Mr. Darcy loves Elizabeth Bennet*
7. *Moonlight walks*
8. P.S. I Love You *type of love that never ends*

The list went on, filling every line on the front and the back of the paper, and included so many of the comments she'd made over the years about things she wished for in a relationship, like waking up in a man's arms and finding him looking at her like he was so in love he could barely breathe and finishing each other's sentences. He'd even written, "That look Zane gives Willow," which she remembered saying she was jealous of when they were at the pub with them one night.

"Ben . . . ?" Her hands were trembling. She couldn't believe he'd remembered, much less written it all down. This was the most romantic thing ever, and it was better than movies, better than books, because it had come from *Ben.*

"It's all the things you've said you wanted."

"I know what it is, but why do you have it?"

"Because I wanted the night I finally told you how I felt to be everything you ever dreamed of. I planned to tell you at Bodhi and Bridgette's wedding reception, while we were dancing beneath the lights on the back patio."

Oh God. Her heart was beating so fast, she didn't think it could take much more. "But you didn't," she said, confused. Everyone knew he had two left feet and hated dancing. Was that why he hadn't followed through?

"Because you bought this place and said you were making a fresh start. I think, more specifically, you said you'd outgrown your life in Sweetwater, and I thought that included me."

She flopped back against the cushions and laughed. "Oh my God, Ben. We're so pathetic. I didn't think you'd ever want to settle down with one woman, and I didn't want to be the stupid girl hanging on for the eternal bachelor."

He leaned over her, boxing her in with his hands beside her shoulders, smiling down at her with those insanely kissable lips. She wanted to stay right there, with his chest brushing hers and his dark eyes looking at her like he never wanted to look away as he said, "There is no one I'd rather be pathetic with than you."

She didn't think, didn't hesitate or question herself, as she slid her arm around his neck and pulled his mouth to hers, kissing him as deeply and earnestly as she'd dreamed about for far too long. His chest was hot and hard against hers as he gathered her in his arms, never breaking their connection as he lifted and shifted their bodies, so they were lying on the couch. He wedged his thick thighs between her legs, his hard length rocking against her center. The weight of his body pressing down on her was so perfect, so exciting, she wanted to feel every hard inch. She clutched at his back, and his hand snuck up her side and over her breast. That first intimate, purposeful grope sent shivery thrills racing through her body. His hand was even stronger and bigger than she'd thought, covering her entire breast. His thumb played over her nipple in slow, mesmerizing circles, and she heard herself moan.

His lips left hers, and he kissed her jaw and her neck, and then he traced the shell of her ear with his tongue and nipped at her lobe. "Is this okay, Relsy? I'll back off if you want me to."

"Don't you dare," she panted out, pulling his mouth to hers again.

He reclaimed her mouth with renewed greed, and she pushed her hands beneath his shirt, feeling his back muscles bunch and flex. She didn't care that this was the first time they'd made out. She had wanted Ben for so long, she had no desire to resist. When he lifted her shirt over her breasts and teased her through her bra, her nipples tingled and burned. She arched up, whimpering into their kisses, wanting his mouth on her skin. He broke their kiss, searching her face, and he must have seen the invitation in her eyes, because he made a growling sound and dipped his head as he pulled the cup of her bra lower, freeing her breast. The first slick of his tongue made her moan and squirm. Her senses were already overloaded, but when he sealed his mouth over the taut peak and sucked it against the roof of his mouth, she buried her fingers in his hair, clenching her mouth shut to keep from crying out at the exquisite pleasure coursing through her. Every suck brought a pulse of heat between her legs, and when he grabbed her hands and thrust them above her head, recapturing her mouth in a penetrating kiss, she thought she might shatter into a million little pieces. His kisses were whole-body experiences, sensual and demanding at once. Possessive and captivating. Every seductive swipe of his tongue was magnified by an alluring rock of his hips. Feeling his hard heat against her in that magnificent rhythm made her wetter, *needier*, than she could ever remember being. Flashes of heat flared deep inside her, every thrust of his hips bringing them closer to the surface. If he could bring her this close to the edge fully dressed, she could only imagine what it would be like to finally make love with him.

He grabbed both wrists in one hand and drew back, his dark eyes sliding over her face, down her neck, to her breasts. Embarrassment washed through her as he visually devoured her, licking his lips, hunger brimming in his eyes.

"You're beautiful, Aurelia." He lowered his mouth and dragged his tongue around her nipple in slow circles. "I've waited so long for this, for *you*." He lowered his mouth over the sensitive peak again, sucking lighter this time, until she was a writhing, moaning mess of desire.

"Ben, Ben, *Ben*—" His name came out as a cross between a plea and a demand.

He shifted his body so he was lying beside her, and his mouth crashed feverishly over hers. Their teeth gnashed and their chests heaved as he worked her jeans open and pushed his hand into them. He gripped her hip, holding her against him. His long fingers pressed tantalizingly into her ass cheek.

He drew back, seeking approval again, and she loved him even more for it as she begged, "Touch me, Ben. God knows I can't wait to touch you."

He made a guttural, hungry noise as his hand slid beneath her panties and between her legs. Hearing that visceral sound made her go a little wild, thrusting her hips and grabbing his ass. His thumb found her magical spot like a heat-seeking missile, playing over her most sensitive nerves with deathly precision in a mind-numbingly slow rhythm. His thick fingers slid between her swollen, wet lips, teasing over her entrance as he ravaged her mouth, taking her right up to the edge of ecstasy. She was lost in his touch, his mouth, and the promise of more. She was standing on a cliff, unearthly pleasures teasing her closer to the edge. She rocked forward, urging him to take *more* with every stroke. But he continued his relentless taunts, making her body vibrate with need.

"Ben, please," she begged.

His fingers pushed inside her, sending shocks of heat sparking through her. She felt light-headed and grounded at once, pressure mounting inside her, prickling up her limbs, burning in her chest, and moving like a firestorm through her core. He did something with his thumb that sent her soaring, and she cried out. He captured her sounds with another fierce kiss, and she clung to him as her orgasm thundered through her. Her body bucked and quivered as he continued his masterful ministrations with his hands and mouth, until she went limp against the cushions.

"More," she whispered, and undid the button on his jeans.

He put his hand over hers, gazing into her eyes with a look that told her he didn't expect more. But she *wanted* it. "I've waited a long time, too," she reminded him.

He watched her lick her palm. Having his eyes on her made her want him even more, which she hadn't thought was possible. She pushed her hand into his briefs and wrapped her fingers around his thick length, moaning with the glory of *finally* feeling that part of him.

His forehead touched hers as he said, "Oh *fuck*, Rels . . ."

The way he said it, full of lust and appreciation, made her heart take notice.

"Kiss me," she said.

His mouth came hungrily down over hers as she worked him tighter, *faster*. His hips thrust harder with each stroke of her hand. Somewhere in the recesses of her mind she heard a faint whimper, but she was too lost in the thrill of making Ben feel good to stop. She felt his muscles tense, and his hips thrust faster, jerking strongly, fucking her hand harder as they ate at each other's mouths.

He tore his mouth away and said, "You're going to make me come."

For once in her life she didn't overthink or slow down. She was determined to bring him as much pleasure as he'd given her. She licked her hand again and took hold of his cock. "I sure hope so. You can make it up to me later."

He reclaimed her mouth with a guttural, appreciative noise, kissing her rougher. She felt him swell impossibly thicker in her hand, and she stroked faster. Somewhere in her frazzled mind she heard—*Oh my God! This is Ben!*—and other shocked exclamations, but that only amped up her desires. Her *greed* for the man she adored. She felt his body tense, and he shifted over her just as the first hot spurt hit her belly. His head fell beside hers as he rode out his release, chanting her name like a prayer—*"Rels. My Rels . . ."*

If she died right that second, she'd die a happy woman, feeling more complete than ever.

"Christ, woman. What have you done to me? I haven't come that fast in forever." He touched his lips to hers as those faint whimpers turned to a slow cry, and she realized it was the baby. Ben uttered a curse and panted out, "Sorry."

"It's okay. You take care of her. I'll get cleaned up." Her hand was sticky, and her belly stickier, but she didn't care. She was happier than she could ever remember being.

He peeled his body from hers and pressed a tender kiss to her lips. "Let me," he said, reaching for a package of baby wipes. As he gently cleaned her belly, he said, "I can take care of both my girls."

CHAPTER SEVEN

"NO WONDER THEY give parents nine months to prepare," Ben said as he read one of the parenting books Aurelia had bought. It was after midnight, and they'd finally gotten B back to sleep after her last feeding. "Listen to this. 'Babies as young as two days old recognize their mother's voice even if they hear only one syllable.'" He shot a worried look at B and whispered, "Do you think she misses her mother?"

He'd been reciting facts from the books all evening and worrying over each and every one. After he read that babies could only focus on objects within eight or nine inches of their faces, he began getting right in B's face when he spoke to her. It was heartwarming, but between feeding and changing B, eating the Chinese food they'd had delivered, and researching everything there was to know about babies, Aurelia felt like they'd talked about everything except the elephant in the room.

They'd made each other come!

Why was it that men were so confident and could just move on after something like that? Right after they did it he probably thought, *Man, that felt great, and we both came. We're good.* While her brain was racing in circles about how different things would be now and wondering if they'd made a mistake. Were they moving too fast? Would they last if B was his? His life—her life?—would change dramatically. This was what their lives would become, sneaking sex and learning how to parent.

One orgasm does not a relationship make.

Sure, he'd said he wanted more, but did he really mean it? They still weren't thinking straight. How could they? Tomorrow morning they were going to see Pretzel Girl, which brought a slew of new questions and emotions. What if she was B's mother? Aurelia might go off on her for leaving B on Ben's doorstep.

Her eyes fell to the sleeping baby. She smiled to herself as Ben's whispered promises sailed through her mind. *Shh, peanut. You're safe. It's okay to sleep now. Nobody is going to leave you alone ever again.* But what if she wasn't his?

"Rels," he said softly. He was sitting in the corner of the sofa with his legs on the coffee table, crossed at the ankle, and she was lying on the couch, leaning against his side. She tipped her face up, and he pressed a kiss to her forehead. "Did I wake you?"

"No. I was just thinking."

He set the book down and put his arms around her. "About?"

She shrugged. "Everything."

"Talk to me. *Everything* like how great it is that we can finally be together, or *everything* like *holy shit there's a baby relying on Ben and do I really want to be part of that?*"

He knew her so well it was scary. "Both, but not really the holy shit part so much. Only . . . yes, that part, too. My brain feels like it's whirling in a blender with worries about everything. I mean, Ben, this whole thing is scary, and fast, and what if we're together and you find out she's not yours? Then you might realize you don't want me in this way, that you reacted to the situation. And that's okay; it's just something to consider."

In one swift move he lifted her onto his lap and guided her arms around his neck. He brushed her hair from her shoulders and put his hand on her cheek, his face a mask of seriousness.

"Ben, you don't have to—"

He silenced her with a kiss. A simple, lingering press of his lips against hers that said more than words ever could. It was reassuring and loving, but more than that, it revealed his confidence in *them*, which she needed more than anything else right then.

"You've known me since we were kids," Ben said softly. "Have you ever once known me to make a commitment to anything without following through?"

She shook her head.

"Did you know that I wanted to ask you to your prom? But I was in college, and you were Willow's best friend, and I knew I couldn't be the boyfriend you deserved back then. But I wanted to be your date so badly, I stayed away for weeks before just so I wouldn't make that mistake."

She laughed. "You did not. You were just having too much fun with your college buddies."

"No. You're wrong, Rels. Ask Willow how many times I asked her if you were going to prom. At one point she got pissed and told me to ask you myself. But if I'd done that, I would have asked you to go with me, and that would have messed up any chance I would ever have had with you. Ask Talia if I talked about you while I was away at college. I'm pretty sure I covered up the truth about how I felt, but I talked about you a lot. I couldn't help it."

"You're telling me that you liked me back then, when I was just about the biggest tomboy around?"

"You still are the biggest tomboy around," he said playfully. "Well, other than Piper, who could probably whip Kase's ass."

They both laughed quietly.

"I have always liked that you're feminine but tough. You don't think I could fall for a pushover, do you?" He pressed a kiss to the hollow of her neck, sending rivers of heat down her chest. "Just like you could never fall for a guy who didn't know how to take control or shut someone down."

"You think you know me," she teased, but he was right.

"Should I make a list of all the things I know about you? Because that list I gave you earlier? That's about one one-hundredth of what I know about you. And just for the record, there are hundreds more facts about you that I don't know yet, but as your boyfriend—and make no bones about it, Rels, I'm officially your *boyfriend*—I will make it my priority to learn every single one of them."

He searched her eyes, and she wondered if he could see how much she trusted him and how hard this was for her. Or could he see that it was as easy as it was difficult? Both were true because he made the difficult parts easier. It was no wonder she was so confused.

Ben awoke in Aurelia's bed with a raging erection. Aurelia was fast asleep, draped over his chest, wearing nothing but a T-shirt and panties. Her bare leg lay over his, and her hand cradled his cock through his briefs. Beside the bed, B slept on a bed of blankets surrounded by pillows. It wasn't like she could roll away, but they both felt better knowing she was confined. Now he was in the worst quandary. Should he wake Aurelia with kisses and finally make love to her, taking the chance that the baby might wake up and interrupt? Or should he take a cold shower and work it out himself? That second idea sucked. *Hm . . . I'd like to see Aurelia sucking me into oblivion.* His cock twitched, and her hand curled around it.

She snuggled closer, pressing her hips against his thigh and making a sexy noise in her sleep. He felt heat through her panties. If that wasn't a sign from above, he didn't know what was. He kissed her forehead, and when she lifted her face, eyes closed, he gently shifted them both so he could kiss her lips. Last night had been incredible, though he was surprised she hadn't called him *Ten-Second Ben* because of how quickly he'd come. But he'd wanted her for so long, to finally be that close to her, physically and emotionally, had sent him reeling.

He'd make it up to her, though, *many* times over.

Starting now.

As he sank into the kiss, he realized she kissed the same way she looked at him now, with as much passion as challenge, and it was unlike anything he'd ever experienced. He cocooned her beneath him. He loved the way she *purred* into their kisses, snuggling into him. She was right that he hadn't wanted to take care of Baby B alone. Caring for a baby was as terrifying as it was rewarding. But she had been wrong to think that was *why* he'd wanted *her*. He had plenty of sisters who would be happy to care for such a sweet baby. The baby and Aurelia were as separate as they were intertwined, which was confusing, but it was life, and life wasn't always easy to understand. He'd always wanted Aurelia, probably since she was twelve or thirteen and had first refused to give him the time of day. The only way he could get her attention back then was by teasing her, earning that challenging snark he'd grown to love so much. The truth was, he'd want to be with Aurelia with or without the baby—and she was the *only* woman he'd ever want to care for a baby with.

A baby that was currently whimpering, causing Aurelia to laugh into their kiss.

"She has a new name," Ben said between kisses. "Baby Cock Blocker. We'll just call her CB from now on."

She swatted him. "You will *not!*"

He kissed her again and reluctantly climbed off her to pull on his jeans. He picked up the baby, cradled her tiny body in his hands, and kissed her forehead. "Good morning, CB."

Aurelia scowled. "Ben, no. Just *no*."

"Fine. We'll keep calling her Baby B. *Baby Blocker*."

Aurelia groaned and closed her eyes, although she was smiling.

He still couldn't believe they'd finally taken the leap of faith and were together. A couple. A damn good couple. The best fucking couple on earth, as far as he was concerned. He was one lucky bastard.

He sat on the bed and said, "I'll change and feed her if you'll whip up some breakfast."

"What's the alternative? Cold cereal, since that's all you know how to make?" Aurelia kissed B, lingering with her lips on the baby's cheek as she whispered, "I love how she smells." Then she pushed to her feet and said, "How about if you take a cooking class instead of taking over that hotel?"

He followed her out of the bedroom chuckling. "You're a demanding girlfriend."

"You haven't seen demanding." She glanced over her shoulder, her hair covering one eye, so sexy it was all he could do to stare. "Instead of complaining, why don't you get her changed and call Talia before Piper spills the beans? It'd break her heart to hear about B from someone other than you."

"I know. I think I'll stop by and see her this afternoon, tell her in person," he said as he changed the baby's diaper.

"That's an even better idea." She brought him a bottle of formula.

He kissed B's belly before snapping her onesie. Then he lifted each tiny foot to his lips and kissed them. "Have you ever seen anything as sweet as her?" He lifted her into his arms and kissed her cheek.

Aurelia gasped. "She's *smiling*, Ben. Do that again."

He kissed the baby's cheek again, earning the sweetest smile he'd ever seen. "The books are wrong. That was *definitely* a smile, not a reflex."

"Maybe Vic was wrong about her age."

"If she is mine, then she's just brilliant, and we can expect her to do everything earlier than expected," Ben said as he sat on the couch and began feeding her.

Aurelia laughed. "You're a nut, you know that? And you really need to start thinking about what you'll do if she *is* yours. I mean, you can't just work from home every day."

Tell me something I don't know.

There was a knock at the door, and they shared an inquisitive look.

"Would Piper come this early?" Aurelia asked as she took a carton of eggs from the refrigerator.

"She'd be the only one *coming* around here, thanks to CB," he said as he headed for the door.

"Ben!" Aurelia called out as he opened the door.

"Oh my God!" Willow squealed as she, Piper, and Talia barged in carrying enormous bags from the baby store in Sweetwater and a Pack 'n Play box.

Ben glared at Piper, who grinned like the smart-ass she was.

"What?" Piper said. "You didn't think I'd keep *this* a secret, did you? Besides, I needed help carrying all the baby stuff I bought yesterday. I'll go set up the changing pad and playpen." She carried the box and a bag past him.

Aurelia led her into the bedroom, giving Ben a *holy shit* look.

Willow dropped her bags and reached for the baby. "Wait until Mom and Dad hear about *this*. Come here, sweet thing."

"You can't tell them until I know if she's mine," Ben said, reluctantly giving her the baby.

"Give me the bottle. I can't believe you were *forever* on our case, protecting us from guys who you thought just wanted to get in our pants." Willow hurried to the couch and began feeding the baby. She smiled at the baby and said, "It looks like we weren't the ones who needed protecting."

"I didn't believe it when Piper told me," Talia said softly. "Why didn't *you* tell me?"

The hurt in her eyes slayed him. "I'm sorry, Tal. It all happened so fast, and I didn't want to get everyone riled up until I knew for sure if she was mine or not. I was going to come over later this afternoon and tell you about her."

"A *baby*, Ben?" Talia whispered. "Do you have any idea how much responsibility a baby requires?"

Talia was the most serious and careful of his sisters. She taught English lit at Beckwith University, a small private college in Harmony Pointe, and she was obviously teaching today, as evidenced by her black pencil skirt and peach blouse. Like Ben, she took after their father, with the same dark hair and eyes, while his other sisters shared their mother's fairer features. Also like Ben, Talia had a straightforward nature, which he'd always appreciated.

Until now, when he was exhausted and doing his best to keep up with the new demands on his time.

"No shit, Talia," he said more harshly than he meant to. "What do you think I've been doing since I found her? Feeding, changing, pacing the floor. My life is on hold right now."

He turned as Aurelia came out of the bedroom wearing a pair of yoga pants beneath her sleeping shirt, and Talia whispered, "From what I hear you're plowing ahead with *certain* parts of your life."

"Yeah, our timing has always sucked."

Talia put a hand on his shoulder and said, "Ben, you've been waiting for the right time with Aurelia forever. This *is* your right time. Otherwise you wouldn't have finally made your move."

"You have no idea how much I needed to hear that." He turned his back to Aurelia and Willow and confessed, "I feel so guilty for telling her how I feel in the midst of all this."

"If I've learned one thing from Derek and Jonah, it's that there is no perfect timing, and time not spent with someone you love is time wasted. Don't waste any more time." She glanced at Aurelia and said, "Besides, if that smile on her face is any indication, I'd say she's okay with your less-than-perfect timing."

He followed her gaze to Aurelia, who was looking lovingly at B. She lifted her eyes, catching Ben watching her, and the adoration in her eyes intensified. His fingers itched to hold her. It was alarming how empty his arms suddenly felt without Aurelia or B in them.

Piper came out of the bedroom, looked at the two of them, and said, "Again? What is it with you two? Can't you stop looking like you want to devour each other for five minutes?"

Aurelia's cheeks burned red, and she blurted out, "Breakfast! I was about to make breakfast. Who's hungry?"

"I would *love* one of Ben's famous frittatas." Willow looked pleadingly at Ben.

"You must have him mixed up with another Ben." Aurelia headed into the kitchen. "He can barely make cereal."

Oh shit. Ben tried to hide his smile as each of his sisters looked curiously in his direction.

Talia sat down beside Willow and the baby and said, "What are you talking about? He's a better cook than all of us."

Piper laughed at the shock and confusion on Aurelia's face. "*That* was better than a cold shower."

"Ben . . . ?" Aurelia crossed her arms, glaring at him. "What are they talking about?"

He went to her, and she stepped back, putting more space between them. "Come on, Rels. You can't blame me for wanting more time with you."

"More *time*? Seriously? You made me feel guilty when I didn't have time to make you breakfast."

He pulled her into his arms despite her struggles and said, "I'm sorry, but I just wanted you to *stay*. Is that so awful? I like being with you and watching your hot little bod moving around my house."

She rolled her eyes, but there was still fire in them. "What else have you lied about?"

"Uh-oh," Piper said.

"Nothing. I swear," Ben said. "And this wasn't really a lie; it was a hopeful coercion."

Aurelia lowered her voice and asked, "Does B have more than four potential mothers?"

He heard one of his sisters inhale sharply.

"*No*. Jesus, Aurelia. I'd never lie about something like that. I just wanted you to stay with me, that's all. Look, the cooking thing started as a joke. The first time I realized you had no idea I could cook, I was going to tell you after you made breakfast, but then I realized it bought me more time with you. And yeah, I took advantage, and I'm sorry. I'll cook breakfast for the next year to make up for it."

"Next *several* years," she said defeatedly. "And if you lie to me again, about *anything*, your ass is grass."

He drew her into his arms again, glad to see she was smiling, and said, "I change diapers. If I were really an asshole, wouldn't I have found a way out of doing that?"

She banged her forehead against his chest. Then she looked up at him and shook her head. "You're a pain."

"I know."

"And *you're* making breakfast today."

"I figured. Do you forgive me?"

She sighed and nodded.

"Damn, I'd have bargained for a lot more than that. Do my laundry, wash my car, do dishes *forever*," Piper said, making everyone laugh.

Ben pressed his lips to Aurelia's, and she pulled away quickly, her gaze darting to his sisters. Still holding her, he followed her gaze. As much as he'd wanted to keep Baby B a secret until he knew if she was his, seeing his sisters loving her up made him all kinds of happy, and he knew they were just as excited about him and Aurelia. He'd caught enough of their innuendos over the last couple years to know they'd assumed the two of them had hooked up or would eventually end up together. "Any of you have a problem with me and Rels being together?"

Talia was holding the baby now, and she said, "You've always been together."

"I think it's great," Willow added as she scrolled through her phone.

"I can't even imagine who else would put up with you." Piper waved to Aurelia's bedroom and said, "We set up the playpen, and I showed Aurelia how to convert it for the changing area and sleeper. You should be all set, and it's portable, so you can take it to Ben's. I've got a baby swing and a stroller in the truck. Want to get it now, or after breakfast?"

"What'd you do? Buy out the store?" Ben asked. Reality hit him with a dose of sadness. "She may not be mine, you know."

"Like I said yesterday, any woman who leaves a baby at a guy's house is probably pretty sure he's the father," Piper said. "But you keep living in the Land of Denial, Benny boy."

"She's right," Talia said. "I have to go to work, but I have a question. Why are you looking for the mother if you don't even know if you're her father?" She hugged the baby one more time and handed her to Piper.

"I can't just sit around not doing anything," Ben admitted. "And honestly, I'm *pissed* at the idea of someone leaving her alone. Forget the disruption to my life. What if something had happened to her? And Vic needs her immunization records. What if she hasn't had any shots? He said she needs *more* soon. It's just . . ."

"It's the right thing to do," Aurelia said. "He has a right to know who the mother is and why she gave her up. If the baby is Ben's, then he'll have to explain that to her one day, and if she's not"—she looked at Ben with sadness in her eyes, and he knew in that moment that she was becoming just as attached to B as he was—"then social services will need to know so when she gets adopted her history isn't a mystery."

Piper held B protectively against her chest and said, "She's not being adopted. She's Ben's. I know it."

Willow's phone rang, and as she answered it, she said, "Oh, yay! It's Bridgette on FaceTime."

Bridgette's voice rang out. "Let me see her!"

"Are you freaking kidding me?" Ben glared at Willow as he took the phone from her hand and met his youngest sister's wide, excited eyes. Behind her, Bodhi gazed over her shoulder, stone-faced as always.

"Ben!" Bridgette said. "You have a *baby*! I call dibs holding her Sunday night!"

She ran through the twenty-questions game, and afterward Ben handed the phone to Willow and cradled B in his arms, thankful to have her back.

As Bridgette oohed and ahhed, Bodhi said, "If this yoga girl isn't her mother, you should call my buddy Mason Swift. We worked together at Darkbird. He's done bounty hunting, and he's a PI. There's no one he can't track down." After several years in the Special Forces, Bodhi had worked for Darkbird, a civilian company hired to carry out danger-ous covert rescue missions. But after falling in love with Bridgette and Louie, he'd taken a job strategizing and training rescuers one week per month, with no chance of being sent away or risking his life. Bodhi's mother owned a flower shop in New York City, and he'd learned all there was to know about the business. When he wasn't training, he helped Bridgette run their flower shop.

Bodhi gave Mason's phone number to Ben and said, "He lives in New York City."

"Thanks, man. I appreciate this."

"Hey, Bridge, in other headline news," Piper announced, "Ben and Aurelia are sleeping together."

"What?" Bridgette squealed, and Bodhi treated them to a rare laugh.

"Piper! I hate you so much right now," Aurelia said, her cheeks turned crimson again. "We *haven't* slept together."

"Seriously?" Piper looked confused. "Baby-making Ben didn't try to—"

"Enough!" Ben snapped. He handed the baby to Aurelia and said, "Bridge, Bodhi, enjoy the rest of your honeymoon." He grabbed Piper's arm and hauled her toward the door. "Outside. *Now.*"

"What the hell?" Piper jerked her arm from his grasp.

"What's between me and Aurelia isn't up for commentary. And no jokes about B, either. This is a stressful time for all of us, and I don't need you making Aurelia self-conscious. She has enough to deal with right now. Got it?" She opened her mouth to speak, and he said, "Don't start. Every time your mouth opens, trouble comes out."

Piper smirked.

"Come on, let's get the baby stuff inside. What do I owe you?"

She narrowed her eyes and said, "A date with Fletch."

"Have you lost your mind?" he asked as they descended the stairs. "Not only is Fletch one of Talia's best friends, but I'm not in the match-making business. Besides, if I set you up with Fletch I'll have Harley breathing down my neck. No, thank you." Ryan "Fletch" Fletcher and Harley Dutch were both friends of Ben's, and he wasn't about to get between them. Harley owned a pub in Sweetwater where everyone, including Fletch, hung out, and he'd had his eyes on Piper for years, though she didn't seem interested.

"Harley, the *muff marauder*?"

Ben glared at her.

"We all remember the name Heaven Love gave him in high school. He might be hung like a horse, but I worry he's all kitten on the inside." She laughed. "Now *Fletch*, he seems like he'd be naughty in the bedroom. And those glasses? They give him a little extra something, don't you think?"

"Piper, *stop*. Why can't you get your own dates?"

"I can, mostly, but I'm told I'm too intimidating. God forbid a woman knows what she wants in the bedroom."

"I *don't* want to hear this."

She grabbed the stroller from the back of her truck and said, "If you're against Fletch, how about Aiden? That man's hiding something. He screams *Fifty Shades* Red Room to me. Don't you think?"

Ben shook his head as he grabbed the baby swing box. "*No,* and I wish I could erase the last two minutes with you from my memory."

After breakfast Ben spent almost an hour giving Piper instructions about how to care for B. Aurelia had to admit, seeing Ben so protective over a baby that might not even be his was a definite turn-on. He acted as if he'd been taking care of B his whole life. But on the way to the yoga instructor's house, Ben stared straight ahead, with a white-knuckled grip on the steering wheel, bringing reality back into focus. Aurelia had initially thought she could do this because Ben was her best friend. He'd been there for her so many times, so she was returning the favor. But now he was her *boyfriend,* and it was like a switch had flipped inside her head. She was about to see a woman with whom he'd not only had sex, but might have also created a baby.

She felt like she might throw up.

And Ben didn't look much calmer.

"Ben, are you sure about this?" she asked uneasily.

"No." His eyes never left the road. "I'm a little afraid if it is her, I'm going to give her hell, and I don't want to. I mean, I want to, but it probably won't help the situation." He glanced at Aurelia and said, "Are you sure you're okay coming with me?"

"No, but I'm here."

He reached across the seat, and as he took her hand, she noticed his was sweaty. "Thank you."

"This is messed up," she said. "I don't blame you or anything. Accidental pregnancies happen, but . . ."

"Listen, Aurelia. This is a lot for me, and it's *my* fault. I can't imagine how it makes you feel. I appreciate you coming with me and sticking by me, but if at any point this gets to be too much and you want out, just tell me. I won't hate you for it. I don't want to screw up your life."

"I don't want *out*. I just want answers. I know you do, too."

He nodded as he turned onto a dirt road just outside of town and pulled up in front of a quaint rambler. He looked a little green as he put the truck in park.

"Are *you* okay?"

"No," he confessed. "But I'm glad you're with me."

She looked at the house, trying not to think about Ben having sex with someone else inside it. "Did you drive all this way drunk the night you were with her?"

"I wasn't drunk. You know I don't get tanked."

That should make her feel better, because he wouldn't have risked lives on the road, but it just made the reality of his one-night stand hit harder. "This is where she lives? How can you remember that and not her name?"

"This is where we came that night. I had to focus so I knew how to get home. I know this makes me a dick, but her name wasn't important at the time. Jeannie or Jenny—whatever it was didn't make a difference. We were both only in it for the night." His chest rose as he inhaled a long, uneven breath.

"Can I ask you something that might be uncomfortable?"

A small, strained smile lifted his lips. "More uncomfortable than admitting to you all that I have about this situation? Or more uncomfortable than asking a woman if she dropped off a baby on my doorstep?"

"Both. How do you go from one woman's bed to the next like that? Doesn't it feel weird not having a stronger connection? How can you even . . . You know?"

His jaw tightened and he turned away, staring out the window.

"I'm not just being nosy," she said. "I really want to know."

"You've had one-night stands. You know what it's like. For a brief period of time you're not thinking about what you don't have. You're just thinking about *not* thinking for a little while. Disappearing into something that feels good so you don't have to feel bad."

The idea of Ben feeling bad tweaked her heart unexpectedly, especially given the circumstances, when jealousy should be her overriding emotion. "You have *everything*, Ben. An amazing family who loves you, friends, a career that most people only dream of, a house, a truck that cost more than the bookstore I just bought. What could you possibly feel bad about?"

He turned slowly toward her with a tense expression, as if it was all he could do to hold his emotions in check. "That I was filling a void where you should have been, and I knew it, but I never stopped to *fix* it." His eyes went glassy, and he said, "And now there's a little baby whose entire life will most likely be overshadowed by that weakness."

Tears burned in her eyes, not just because of what he'd said about her but because of how deeply he'd thought about B and the impact his actions might have on her life.

"I take full responsibility, Rels. But if you want to know what each of those times was about, I'll tell you. Those were the nights you had dates with other guys, and I'd have done *anything* to escape the gnawing in my gut caused by the thought of you being touched by someone else."

"Ben . . ." Her throat thickened, making it hard to speak.

"I'm sorry. As I said, this is all on me. I was an ass, always waiting for the right time. And in the end I chose the worst time of all."

Her thoughts were spinning so fast from his confession, the truth poured out. "Ben, I don't *do* one-night stands. There wasn't anyone touching me."

His brows slanted in confusion.

"I mean, *once*, in college," she admitted, "but not since."

"What about the football guy and the designer?"

She shook her head. "I didn't do anything but kiss them good night. Until last night I hadn't been with anyone since I broke up with Kent."

His eyes filled with disbelief. "Aurelia, I might have a kid. It's not like you have to hide indiscretions."

"I'm *not*. I didn't want you to know because you were going out and having fun, and there I was, hanging on to my unrequited emotions, which made me a loser."

He reached across the seat, and his arm circled her shoulder, pulling her closer to him. He pressed his lips to hers and said, "They weren't unrequited, and you could never be a loser. If anyone is a loser, it's me, for thinking a brief encounter could ever take my mind off you." He pressed a kiss to the back of her hand and said, "I'm sorry to put you through this, and I'm sorry to put B through this—and her mother, whoever she is. If I'd told you how I felt sooner, this might not have happened."

"I didn't exactly make it easy for you. I never thought you'd want a girlfriend, so every time you joked about getting together in that way, I blew you off."

"I still could have pushed."

"And I would have pushed back. Ben, you can't blame yourself for a relationship not happening when it was just as much my fault." She glanced at the house and said, "We should get this over with."

He swallowed hard, his brow furrowing. "What should I say to her?"

"I think you can lead with something like, 'Did you drop a baby off on my doorstep?'"

He laughed. "Smart-ass."

"Made you smile."

They climbed from the truck, and as she came around the front he said, "Are you sure you want to come up to the door?"

"Would you rather I didn't?"

"I'd rather you did, but I get it if it's too difficult."

She laced her fingers with his and said, "I already feel like I'm going to puke. What's a little more discomfort?"

Aurelia thought *she* was going to puke? Not only did he feel guilty as fuck for dragging Aurelia through this—and for the baby's sake—but now, as they approached the house, he was pretty sure he was going to pass out. "What if she thinks I'm here because I want to hook up again?"

Aurelia held up their joined hands and said, "Unless she's into threesomes, I think you're safe. You're *really* nervous, aren't you? I've never seen you like this. You're sweating."

He gave her a sideways glance. "What if it's *her*? I don't know that I'll be able to keep from giving her hell, and I'm really trying not to get attached to B, but—"

"You too?" She stopped walking halfway to the front door and stared up at him. "I've been trying so hard not to snuggle her too much, or think about how amazing she smells or how her cheeks are softer than anything I've ever felt. Or how I love it when she wraps her tiny fingers around mine. And when she's in my arms, sometimes I just want to cry for her, because she was abandoned by her mother. But I know she might not be yours, so I hold it all in because I'm afraid of how much it'll hurt if she's taken away."

Ben gathered her in his arms, resting his cheek against the top of her head. He felt her heart racing as fast as his.

"I've been doing the same thing," he admitted. "Last night, while you were sleeping, I just stared at her for the longest time, telling myself not to feel so much. But it's an impossible task because she's so little, and so frigging cute and innocent. I didn't even want to leave her with Piper to come here, and the thought of going to work . . . ? It feels like I'll be abandoning her, too."

Aurelia tipped her face up and said, "Maybe we shouldn't hold back. Maybe it's better for her if we let our love come out, so at least she'll know what it feels like to be loved. The books said babies feel everything their caretakers feel. And love is *good*, right? Even if we're sad if she eventually goes to someone else, isn't some love better than none?"

Relief swamped him. "God, Rels," he whispered. "You just made everything I've been struggling with feel okay. I agree. You and I held back from each other for too long. Let's not do that to B. Regardless of what happens here, let's show that sweet baby girl as much love as we can while we wait for the truth to come out."

"That sounds perfect to me." She smiled and said, "I'm a little less nervous. Are you still nervous?"

"Insanely . . ."

"Then take a deep breath, pretend you're negotiating a business deal. Imagine you've just taken over a big corporation, you're in the boardroom with other bigwigs, and you have to keep your cool. You've got this, Benny boy. I have faith in you."

And just like that, she centered him. He straightened his spine, holding tightly to Aurelia's hand as they climbed the front steps and knocked on the door.

A pretty blonde peeked her head outside, and after a few seconds recognition shone in her eyes. "Ben?"

"Yeah," he said uneasily, wishing he remembered her name. "Hi."

She stepped outside wearing a maternity shirt over a *very* pregnant belly and capris, pulling the door partially closed behind her.

Ben cleared his throat to hide his relieved smile, and he squeezed Aurelia's hand, reading the same relief in her eyes. Although he wasn't sure why he felt so relieved, considering that this nailed down the mother as the woman in Los Angeles, who would be about as easy to find as a needle in a haystack.

The blonde looked curiously at them and said, "What are you doing here?"

"I, um . . ." His mind went blank. "You're *pregnant*. Rels, she's *pregnant*," he said stupidly.

She rested one hand on her belly and smiled. "Married, too. It's been a long time since we've seen each other."

"*Married?* That's great," he said too enthusiastically. "Congratulations. I wasn't sure you'd remember me."

"Of course I remember you." She looked sheepishly at Aurelia and said, "We helped each other get over some stuff a while back."

The door opened behind her and an enormous man stepped onto the front porch. Ben was six one, and this guy had at least three or four inches on him and probably thirty pounds of muscle. He put an arm around the blonde and said, "Everything okay, Jenny?"

Jenny! That was it!

Jenny smiled warmly and said, "Yes, fine. Ben is . . . an old friend. He was just . . . ?"

"Uh, funny story." Ben fumbled for words. "We—"

"We were wondering if you taught couples yoga," Aurelia said quickly. "We heard it was really great for couples looking to connect on a higher level. But maybe you don't teach it anymore, since you're pregnant? So we'll just be going. Sorry to have bothered you." She tugged Ben down the steps and said, "Good luck with your baby!"

They hurried to the truck, both of them chuckling.

Aurelia flopped back against the passenger seat, exhaling loudly. "*Whew.* For a moment there I thought you had another baby coming, but then Paul Bunyan appeared."

They both laughed, but the thought wasn't really funny.

Ben started the truck and said, "*Couples yoga?* Connect on a *higher level?*"

"What did you want me to say? 'Sorry, Mr. Muscles, but Ben had sex with your wife . . .'?"

"They weren't married back then," he reminded her as he drove away. "I wouldn't sleep with a married woman. You know that, right?"

"I *know*. Now you can tell me how great I am for getting you out of that debacle." She flashed a cheesy smile, and her phone vibrated with a text. "Oh my gosh, Ben. My heart is melting."

He stopped at the corner, and she turned the phone toward him, showing him a picture of B in the baby swing with one of the pink blankets he'd bought her tucked around her. All the tension that had been simmering beneath his laughter disappeared, replaced with the most contented feeling.

"Isn't she the most beautiful baby you've ever seen?" Aurelia said softly.

His heart swelled with love, and when he shifted his gaze to Aurelia, it grew even bigger—because of the talk they'd had about showing their love for B and for the woman who was clearly going to give her more love while she was with them than she could ever hope for.

CHAPTER EIGHT

WEDNESDAY EVENING AURELIA'S apartment smelled better than an Italian restaurant. It had been an emotionally exhausting *and* uplifting day. Between their visit with Jenny, squeezing in work on their laptops, and caring for B, Aurelia had been in overdrive all day. She was glad Ben had offered to make dinner. He'd been adorable sneaking in gropes and kisses while he cooked, as if he had to *sneak* around the baby. But she had to admit, those furtive touches and sensual kisses had left her body humming all the way through dinner, which was delicious. Now, as she bathed B in the new baby bath Piper had bought and Ben did the dishes, even the *thought* of those stolen kisses made her hungry for him. But since she had no idea how long B would be awake, she tried to push away those naughty thoughts and focus on the baby.

"This is much easier than using a pillow, isn't it?" she said as she shielded the baby's eyes and rinsed her hair. She leaned in close, smiling into B's curious eyes. "You are such a good girl. You like your bath, don't you?"

As she gently bathed the baby, she felt overwhelmingly happy about finally allowing herself to open her heart completely to beautiful B. She marveled at her adorable little nose and Cupid's bow lips, her tiny fisted hands, and the way her downy-soft hair turned pitch-black when wet. She carefully wrapped her in a cute hooded towel, which made her look like a little bunny, and swaddled her the way Piper had taught her. There was so much to learn about caring for B, but Aurelia felt like she and Ben were doing pretty well for having been thrown into the situation. Ben always came out on top in sink-or-swim situations, but this was a *big* one, and she wondered if all new parents transitioned from freak-out mode to calm acceptance as quickly as Ben had.

She carried B into the bedroom and chose a snuggly white sleeper with little yellow ducks across the chest, which Piper had washed and left on the bed for them. She'd washed all of the new clothes and blankets. She'd also washed the baby things Ben had brought over. Of all Ben's sisters, Aurelia had always thought of Piper as the least maternal. Boy, had she been wrong. It had taken Piper as long to finally say goodbye to B as it had for Ben to give her instructions before they'd left that morning.

"Ready for some snuggly pajamas?" Aurelia said as she laid B on the bed and began putting on her diaper. "So now we know that your mama is the woman from Los Angeles." Her heart hurt a little at that, because part of her thought that the woman didn't deserve to be mentioned. She didn't deserve to have been given such a wonderful gift as this baby. But having grown up missing the mother she'd never known, Aurelia couldn't bring herself to take the possibility of knowing her mother away from B.

She dressed B and held her hands as she kissed her cheeks.

"Who your father is might be up in the air right now, but you should know that Benny and I love you, whether you're his or not." She kissed the baby's hands, and then she lifted her into her arms, breathing in her sweet smell. "You are safe, and you are loved, peanut, and no matter where you are in this world, nothing will ever take our love away from you." She moved her hand in soothing circles on the baby's back and closed her eyes, wishing there was some way for the baby to remember what she was about to say. "You need to know that just because your mom had to give you up doesn't mean she doesn't love you. It means she loved you *so* much she wanted the best for you. That's a lot of love, B, and I can only imagine how hard it was for her to leave you."

She sensed Ben's presence and opened her eyes.

He was standing behind her, and he leaned down to kiss the baby's head. "I love you, B," he whispered, and then he pressed a kiss to Aurelia's temple and said, "And I love you, too, Aurelia. I don't want to hold back anymore, not from either of you."

The now-familiar fireworks went off inside her, and she turned toward him. "Oh, *Ben.*"

He lowered his lips to hers, kissing her slow and sweet. But slow and sweet wasn't nearly enough. She'd waited years for this very moment. Her pulse was racing as he pulled back, and she trapped his lower lip between her teeth, earning a masculine, rumbly *growl.* Holding his predatory gaze, she dragged her tongue along his lip.

"Aurelia," he said in a long, heated breath. His eyes shot to the baby, and a sinful grin lifted his lips. "She's sleeping."

She turned toward the playpen, and Ben moved behind her as she bent over and laid the baby down. She felt Ben's hard length against her as she rose with her back to his chest. He brushed her hair to one side and began kissing her neck, sending scintillating sparks beneath her skin. His mouth was warm, and every touch of his lips made her insides swell and heat. When he sealed his mouth over her flesh, lavishing her neck and shoulder with openmouthed kisses, sucking and teasing until she was panting and even more needy, she pressed her bottom against him. His hands pushed beneath her top, palming her breasts. She ground against his erection, soaking in the feel of Ben Dalton not just *wanting* her, or *touching* her, but doing it *possessively*, whispering dark promises against her skin. "I want to love every inch of you, to taste your arousal, to feast on your body."

Desire pulsed inside her, growing and filling her until she felt it would seep out of her pores. He squeezed her nipples as he drove her wild with his mouth. Her body trembled and her knees weakened. Just when she didn't think she could take it anymore, he turned her in his arms, kissing her roughly and demandingly. His tongue plunged deep, devouring every dip and crevice of her mouth. He tore off her shirt between urgent kisses, separating only long enough to rip it over her head, and he made quick work of stripping them both bare. Good Lord, seeing Ben Dalton in briefs had been glorious—but seeing him in all his masculine beauty was beyond delectable.

His eyes locked on hers as he lifted her off her feet and onto the bed. Her mouth watered as she reached for him, but he grabbed her hands and pinned them to the mattress, kneeling between her legs.

"I have been dreaming of this for years. Tonight you're *mine*, Rels—all mine—and I'm going to love you until all those years we waited disappear."

He lowered his lips to hers in a scorching kiss that left her burning for more as his magnificent mouth traveled lower. He trailed tantalizing kisses and scintillating bites over each breast, slowing to love them until she was on the verge of release, writhing and moaning, arching and begging.

"*Ben*, please!" She rocked her hips in an effort to get what she needed.

"Shh, sweetheart," he whispered, and glanced at the playpen. "If you wake her, I'll have to stop."

She snapped her mouth closed, earning a wicked grin and *more* as his hands took over, fondling and caressing her breasts as he tasted his way down the center of her body. He nipped at her belly, dragged his tongue around her belly button, before plunging into it and then slowing to a mind-numbing rhythm. His tongue moved in and out of her belly button in ways she wanted to feel between her legs. She clenched her mouth shut, clinging to the sheets as he teased his way south, finally reaching the apex of her thighs. Thank God she'd shaved her legs and trimmed the promised land. She lifted her hips and spread her legs, giving him an open invitation.

He placed feathery kisses along her inner thighs, and she held her breath, willing him to take more. His hands slid down her belly and clutched her waist as his mouth covered her sex, and the first touch of his tongue sent her hips shooting off the mattress. He pushed them down and did something wicked with his tongue that sent pleasures tearing through her core and had her moaning uncontrollably. She closed her mouth, trying to quell the noises, but there was no way to silence the pleasure coursing through her as he licked and sucked and thrilled her beyond her wildest imagination. When he brought his hands into play, he sent her flying through the sky on ribbons of ecstasy. Every slick of his tongue, every touch of his fingers, took her higher, and when he pushed his fingers inside her and intensified his efforts with his mouth, light exploded behind her closed lids. Her hips tried to rise off the bed, but he held her there, deepening and quickening his efforts, sending her soaring again and again, until she could barely breathe. When she finally, blissfully, drifted back down to earth, he took his time loving his way up her body. Her nipples were overly sensitive, and he must have known, because he circled each one with his tongue before placing shivery kisses on the taut peaks. And then he lay over her, the head of his cock nestled at her entrance. He smelled like her, and when he kissed her, she didn't care that he tasted like her, too. She was so lost in him, so greedy *for* him, she heard herself whimpering.

"Are you on the pill?" he asked hastily.

"Yes, but maybe you should use three condoms just so your supersonic sperm don't get me." She giggled and felt him smiling against her lips.

"I'll do whatever you want, Rels. I want you to feel safe."

"I always feel safe with you. I trust you, Ben. I was only teasing."

"God, I love you."

He slanted his mouth over hers as he entered her inch by enticing inch, until he was buried to the hilt, filling her so completely she didn't want to move.

"Hold me just like this," she said against his cheek as she wrapped her arms and legs around him. "I want to remember every second of us."

He cradled her body beneath him, his strong arms reaching all the way around her as he said, "Do you feel that perfectness? Nothing could ever replace this, Rels, not in a million lifetimes."

She leaned back so she could see his face and was overwhelmed with love. "Kiss me."

Their mouths came together languidly, and she knew he was trying to savor every second, just like she was. But there was no slowing their passion, and their desires took over, thrusting and grinding to a frantic rhythm. She wanted to feel every slam of his hips, every press of his fingers onto her flesh, every nip and bite. Her insides pulsed and burned. She felt the pull of an orgasm just out of reach as he slowed his efforts, kissing her so deeply she lost sight of where she ended and he began. It was the most miraculous feeling of oneness she'd ever experienced. He pushed his hands beneath her ass, lifting and angling her hips so he could love her deeper. She bit down on his shoulder to keep from crying out from the immense pleasures he caused. Just when she thought she'd reached the peak, he withdrew all but the broad head of his cock, repeatedly stroking over the magical spot most guys couldn't find with a road map—sending her up, up, *up* again. And when she finally caught the brass ring, he thrust in deep and followed her over the edge. Her name sailed off his lips in a rough growl she knew she'd never forget.

CHAPTER NINE

BEN KISSED HIS way up Aurelia's ribs as the sun streamed in through her bedroom windows. He wondered how he'd ever found work—or anything else for that matter—so enthralling. Now he knew nothing could compare to the woman lying beside him. They'd done nothing but make love and care for B for the past thirty-six hours. Sure, they'd taken a few hours to catch up on work, but for the most part they'd either been loving up the baby or loving *on* each other, and he'd never been happier. Aurelia's apartment felt like more of a home than his big house ever had, which finally made sense to him. She'd always owned his heart, and how could a house feel like a home when she took part of it with her every time she left?

Aurelia made a sweet sound as she rolled onto her stomach and whispered, "Ben."

He crawled over her, pressing his erection against her ass, and kissed her shoulder. "Too tired for us, babe?"

"I want you," she said sleepily, eyes closed. "But you have to do all the work. I fed B at five."

She lifted her hips, and his arm circled her belly as he kissed her spine and said, "You can say *no*."

She looked over her shoulder, her hair covering one eye. "Have you *ever* known me to hold my tongue?"

"Actually, I love the things you do with your tongue." He nipped at her back, earning a sensual moan.

"Then we have something in common. Now stop talking, because . . ." She pointed to B sleeping in the playpen, and then she went up on her knees, aligning their bodies, and pushed back, her body swallowing his cock. Her head fell between her shoulders and she hissed, "I'm never going to be too tired for this."

Two incredible orgasms later, Aurelia lay in Ben's arms with her head on his chest. She ran her finger over his pec and said, "I think we've made each other into sluts."

He kissed her, laughing softly. "I'll be your slut, your slave, whatever you want, Rels. We waited so long, we deserve to be drunk on each other for an eternity, and I'm pretty sure we sent Ten-Second Ben packing."

She looked curiously at him. "Ten-Second Ben?"

"That first night on your couch . . ."

She laughed and slapped her hand over her mouth, eyeing the playpen. "Oh my gosh," she whispered. "That's *hilarious*. I would have called you Ten-*Inch* Ben."

Damn, that felt all kinds of good. "Now we're talking." He swept her beneath him, covering her face with kisses until she giggled and wiggled against him. "See why I love you?"

"It would have been embarrassing saying I was dating Ten-Second Ben, but Ten-Inch Ben? Now *that's* a boyfriend to be proud of." She pressed a kiss to his shoulder and said, "I have to meet Everly to go over inventory. Think you can handle B for a few hours this afternoon?"

"Of course." He kissed the tip of her nose.

His phone rang, waking B into a tearful wail. He cursed as he snagged the phone from the nightstand and said, "Sorry. I thought I had turned the ringer off."

They'd both turned their phones to silent because his sisters were calling and texting so often they couldn't rest. He'd finally had to ask them to stop and told them they'd see B Sunday evening and could dote on her and harass him then.

"You turned it on last night so you wouldn't miss that work call," she reminded him as she pulled on her panties. "It's okay. You owe me three orgasms and a scrumptious breakfast for waking her up." She grabbed his T-shirt from the chair by the bed and slipped it on.

"*Done.*" He answered the call as he pulled on his briefs. "Ben Dalton."

"Ben, it's Vic."

As if he'd had cold water splashed on his face, Ben pushed to his feet. "Vic, how are you?"

Aurelia stopped on her way out of the bedroom with B, worry hovering in her eyes.

"Good," Vic said.

"I assume you have news?"

"I do, Ben. The results are back, and they confirmed that you're the father."

Tears sprang to Ben's eyes as he sank down to the edge of the bed.

"Ben? Are you there?"

"Yeah. Thanks, Vic."

Vic went on to ask if he'd tracked down B's mother yet or had information about B's immunizations. But Ben's mind was spinning, and he answered absently, promising to call when they had more information.

Aurelia sat beside him, holding B tight, tears brimming in her eyes. "She's not yours?"

He shook his head, and tears slipped down Aurelia's cheeks. He slid his hand to the nape of her neck, drawing her forehead to his as his own tears fell, and he said, "She *is* mine."

The air rushed from her lungs, pushing out a surprised sound. "She *is*? And you're sad?"

"No, Rels. I'm so fucking relieved. I didn't know how much I loved her until I heard Vic on the line and realized I could lose her. She's mine, Rels. B's mine."

CHAPTER TEN

FRIDAY MORNING PASSED as if in a dream, with Ben and Aurelia both mesmerized by confirmation of his paternity. They'd cried, laughed, and hugged and spent hours just looking at and playing with B as if they could hardly believe she was his. And the truth was, no matter how many times Aurelia had told herself that B might not be Ben's, she'd never fully believed it. Or maybe she'd just wanted her to be his so badly, she'd refused to believe it.

Ben sat on the edge of the bed in a pair of worn jeans and a soft gray T-shirt, feeding B. They'd finally gotten around to showering a little after noon. His hair was still damp, he hadn't shaved, and his feet were bare, all of which made him look devastatingly handsome, but it was his contented smile as he fed B that made Aurelia's heart beat double time. The relief of knowing she was his had blown them both away and had also brought them even closer together.

"We need to get you a new shirt," Ben said with a lift of his brows.

She pulled on her jeans and looked down at her pink baseball shirt, which had white lettering across the chest that read, EAT, SLEEP, READ, REPEAT. She was meeting Everly in a few minutes, and this was one of her favorite comfy shirts. "You don't like it?"

"I think it would be more accurate if it said, EAT, SLEEP, MAKE WILD PASSIONATE LOVE, REPEAT."

"Hm. That should get Kase's attention," she said playfully.

Ben glowered.

She sat beside him on the bed to tie her pink Converse and said, "I think it should say FEED, CHANGE, MAKE LOVE, SLEEP, REPEAT. But then it would sound like I was dating a geriatric man."

He chuckled, and she leaned in and kissed him.

"You know I'm a one-man woman and only teasing about Kase, right? I have Ten-Inch Ben. Why would I want Granite-Faced Kase?"

He pressed his lips to hers and said, "I'm kidding. I totally trust you."

She tickled B's foot. "Are you sure you don't mind watching her while I work? When do you have to go back into the office?"

"She's my responsibility, Rels. Of course I don't mind. I'm going to schedule a meeting with Mason to get that ball rolling, and I'll call my attorney and Aiden, too. My whole life is about to change around her."

"It already has, Ben. There are so many things to think about. What about childcare?"

"I can't even begin to think about leaving her with someone else. Not even my mom, who you *know* will want to babysit. I'm going to continue working from home except when I have meetings."

"Oh gosh. *Roxie.* You need to tell your parents, Ben. They don't even know about her."

"Sunday, at dinner," he said emphatically. "I want a few days with just us before she and my sisters start directing our lives."

His family was wonderful, but they would definitely want time with the baby and to make sure Ben was doing all the right things. *She* wanted time alone with Ben and B, too, so they could adjust to their new reality. Getting up three times a night had nearly turned them both into zombies, even if taking care of B was as rewarding as it was challenging. The time they'd spent lounging around and sleeping when they could had been *necessary.* They were both exhausted.

Despite the fatigue, she didn't want to leave B with anyone else, either. Not that she didn't trust Roxie. She adored her and trusted her with her life. But if she and Ben were still adjusting, wasn't B, too? It didn't seem fair to thrust her care into someone else's hands so soon.

"I can take her with me to the bookstore when you have to go into the office," she suggested. "Then we wouldn't have to leave her with anyone else. But, Ben, how do you *really* feel about all of this? It's a lot for anyone to handle. I mean, I know you love B, but having a daughter will impact your business, travel, family. *Everything. Forever.*"

"I know. It's all I can think about. When Vic called, I was terrified of losing her. Almost as terrified as I was when you stormed out of my house saying you couldn't do this, and the other day when I offered you an out before we met Jenny. I would have understood if you had taken it, but I would have been heartbroken." He gazed down at the baby and said, "I may not have known that I wanted a baby in my life when we first found her, but now I can't imagine my life without her." He gazed into Aurelia's eyes with the most earnest, grateful expression and said, "I have to believe this was fate, because you'd just moved away and I was doing everything I could to keep you in my life. Then B came along and showed us how good we are together."

"I've always wanted to be in your life, Ben. We were just *stuck.* We were so young when we had our meet-cute, it made it difficult to figure out how to go from friends to lovers."

Ben's brow wrinkled. "What's a *meet-cute?*"

"It's a literary term. Never mind."

"You're not getting off that easy. Clue me in to your world a little."

Oh, how she loved that. "It's when two people who will later become romantically connected first meet, often in some quirky way."

"And to think you were going to hold that definition back from me," he said with an adorably serious expression. He leaned in for a kiss and said, "B might have finally brought us together, Rels. She was definitely our destiny. But the thing you need to know, deep down, when you close your eyes at night and wonder why on earth you're with a guy who has a baby, is that there has *never* been a time when I could imagine my world without *you* in it."

"Did you hear that?" she asked.

"What?"

"That *kerplunk*? That was me falling even harder for you." She pressed her lips to his, and then she kissed B's forehead. "Seeing you with B sends my heart into overdrive, but when you say things like that to me, it makes me feel like my heart might explode." She pushed to her feet and said, "I'm going downstairs before that happens."

He grabbed her hand, tugging her in for another kiss, but stopped a whisper away and said, "I love knowing you're right downstairs instead of a town away."

"Ben . . ." she said dreamily.

"Now get out of here before I put her in her playpen and"—he eyed the bed—"put you in *ours*."

Yes, please. "Somehow I think it's going to be hard to concentrate on inventory."

She was still thinking about his threat when she entered the bookstore. She spotted Everly coming out of the stockroom and tried to squelch those thoughts, but it was like trying not to let the world know she'd won the lottery.

Every one of Piper's crew watched Everly strutting toward her in a fringed suede miniskirt, black Harley-Davidson T-shirt, and leather booties. Aurelia didn't blame them. At five nine, with long, wavy brown hair and natural blond highlights, a perky nose, and mile-long legs, Everly could be a model. She could pass for eighteen as easily as her real age of twenty-six—until she opened her mouth and started spouting facts. The girl was as brilliant an artist as she was a genius on most topics, and she wasted no time on dolts.

Everly paid the men no mind as she approached Aurelia and said, "I was beginning to think you'd decided not to come down today. Do you have a secret hottie locked upstairs in your apartment?"

Aurelia grabbed her wrist and hauled her toward the stockroom. "There's been a major plot twist in my life. I'll fill you in."

Half an hour later, after Aurelia explained everything she and Ben had been through lately, Everly said, "A baby?" for the tenth time while they worked through the inventory in the stockroom. "Ben Dalton with a baby? I can't even picture it."

"He's amazing with her. Once he got past the initial shock of this tiny, pooping, hungry, needy creature, he stepped up to the plate. Of course, we're both still adjusting, but like he does with everything else in his life, he took control and figured it out."

"Sounds like Ben," she said with a sigh. "This is *big*, Aurelia. His family must be losing their minds."

"His parents don't know yet, but his sisters have been texting and calling ten times a day. Having a baby around is exhausting, but at least we have all the right stuff now, thanks to Piper."

"I would have paid anything to have seen the two of you the day you found her." She looked at Aurelia with a serious expression and said, "And you're sure about the whole you-and-Ben thing? I know how you feel about him. That's been obvious to everyone for a long time. But are you ready for instafamily?"

"It's crazy, I know, and I can't explain it, but there's no doubt in my mind or in my heart about either of them. Although I have to admit that at first I wondered if Ben wanted me because it was so hard to take care of her on his own." She thought about his confessions—how long he'd loved her and how he'd planned to tell her at Bridgette's wedding—and she said, "But now I know better."

Everly set a book into a box and reached for the tape. As she taped the box shut, she said, "So, are you moving in with Ben in Sweetwater?"

"No," she said. "We haven't talked about any of that, but I don't want to move back there. I can't go backward. I *love* my apartment." *Even more with Ben and B in it.* "I need to be here to receive deliveries, and we're opening in a few weeks."

"It wouldn't be the end of the world if you had to drive from Sweetwater."

"No, but this is my new beginning. This is where it's *supposed* to be. I feel it in my bones, the same way things with Ben and B feel right." But she knew Ben would never want to give up his house and his gorgeous property for a minuscule two-bedroom apartment. He probably wouldn't want to move away from his family, either, but did she want to give up her space?

Everly pushed the box to the side of the room and said, "Maybe this is where it was just supposed to *start*. New beginnings are called that for a reason, right? Changes happen. Love happens. *Babies* happen."

"I guess." Aurelia reached for another stack of books.

They worked on inventory for the next few hours, and then Everly showed her drawings of the mural she was going to paint in the children's area. Everly was going out of town for the weekend to attend a green-living conference. She made plans to return Monday so she could start the mural.

After Everly left, Aurelia headed upstairs, rehashing their conversation about moving. She knew she was overanalyzing and that it was too early in her relationship with Ben to even think about those types of logistics, and Everly was right. Driving from Sweetwater *wouldn't* be the end of the world.

But as she entered her apartment and found Ben and B fast asleep on the couch, his work spread out across her dining room table, his shoes by her door, and B's baby paraphernalia scattered around the room, she knew it wasn't the driving that bothered her.

She simply liked the world she and Ben were creating here in her cozy Harmony Pointe apartment, more than the one they'd been floundering in back in Sweetwater.

CHAPTER ELEVEN

BEN WAS TOO restless after B's 5:00 a.m. feeding to go back to sleep Saturday morning. He headed out to the dining room table, where he tackled emails and tried to prepare for Wednesday's meeting. But he had a hard time focusing on work. He'd spoken to Bodhi's friend Mason Swift and scheduled a meeting for Monday. He'd also spoken to Aiden, catching him up on the situation and explaining that his attorney was preparing paperwork to declare him as B's father. He reassured Aiden that he would be in the office Wednesday for their meeting. As Ben had expected, Aiden was understanding about his need to continue working from home while he wrapped his head around being a father.

A *father*.

That word had grown to monumental proportions, taking on new meaning over the past twenty-four hours. He'd never considered what it would feel like to be a father, what it would do to his psyche, his outlook, his *heart* . . .

Even when he'd known there was a chance he was B's father, what that actually *meant* hadn't hit home. But now it was all he could think about. When he held her, changed her, and fed her. When she was crying and he couldn't soothe her, or when she smiled and he wanted to memorize the preciousness of the moment. When he lay beside Aurelia, when he kissed her, when he tried to concentrate on his business, thoughts of fatherhood invaded his mind. There was no escaping the importance of those six little letters. It was *his* responsibility to protect that sweet little girl, to make sure she learned right from wrong, to help her feel loved and cherished. It was his responsibility to make sure she grew up confident and strong. A weaker man might wonder if he was qualified for such a task, but Ben didn't wonder. He knew it would take everything he had to be a good father, and he was ready to give her his all.

He prepared for fatherhood in the same way he had prepared for the night he'd wanted to profess his feelings for Aurelia, which in his eyes had been far more important than any business deal. He began with a list of goals, starting with financial ones, because those came easily.

Start a college fund.

Increase my life insurance.

Draw up a will.

With those out of the way, Ben thought about his father and the things he had done that had had the biggest impact on him as a child and as an adult. He didn't have to think long, because one thing stood out among all others. His father had always been there for him. Whether he was a phone call away or standing beside him didn't matter. Ben knew that if he needed his father's emotional or physical support, his dad would find a way to be there for him.

He added *Be present* to the list.

He remembered his father playing ball with him, reading to him, taking him to the library, and dragging his ass outside to help with one chore or another—raking leaves, washing cars, fixing the porch steps. There were dozens of odd jobs that Ben had found annoying at the time, when he would rather have been playing with his friends, but those were also the things that had taught him to be a responsible adult. His list came easily.

Show her unconditional love.

Build her self-esteem. Make sure she knows she's "enough."

Discipline with a strong lesson and never a harsh hand.
Include her in everything so she learns about the world.

As he made the list, he realized he didn't need to re-create the wheel. What he needed was to speak to his father.

If anything, he'd always imagined it would be one of his sisters having to break unplanned-pregnancy news to his parents. He sat back, breathing deeply, readying himself to hear disappointment in his father's voice. He grabbed his phone and pushed to his feet, heading to the bedroom to check on Aurelia and B. Aurelia was sprawled across the bed, her arms spread out to the sides, legs tangled in the sheets. She was wearing his shirt, which was bunched around her waist, and a pair of pink panties that made his body hot. Guilt tightened like a noose around his neck. Was it fair to drag her into all this? He knew how exhausted she was. He also knew she loved B as much as he did, even after only a few days.

But was it *fair*?

What constituted fair when he couldn't imagine a life without Aurelia by his side? When there was no other woman he'd ever want to raise his child with him?

He peeked at B, and his heart took another hit. She lay sleeping with her tiny mouth open, arms fisted beside her head. Maybe he should have sent Aurelia home the second she'd discovered B, because Aurelia had never stood a chance. It was impossible not to love his baby girl.

He pulled the bedroom door mostly closed and went outside, filling his lungs with the brisk morning air. The sun had barely breached the horizon, spreading ribbons of orange and red over the mountains and reminding Ben of the early hour. He debated waiting to call, but he wanted to speak to his father without having to juggle B or leave the room when Aurelia was awake.

"Ben?" his father answered groggily. "Is everything okay?"

"Yes. Sorry to call so early. I'm sorry to wake you guys. I just need to talk." *This is what being a father is, taking your son's call at the break of dawn and immediately worrying about him.*

"It's all right. Hold on." Ben heard his father tell his mother everything was fine and that he'd be right back. He pictured his father stepping from the bed wearing his standard nighttime attire—striped pajama pants and a white T-shirt—his salt-and-pepper hair standing on end.

He heard a door open and close, and then his father said, "Okay, Ben. What's going on?"

He'd spent a lifetime trying to be the honest, thoughtful man his father was. He'd screwed up many times, as people did, but he wanted to make his father proud. He felt the most astonishing mix of pride, for being that amazing baby girl's father, and disappointment in himself, for having to admit that the beautiful baby girl sleeping in the other room hadn't been planned. Those emotions slayed him.

"I . . . um . . ." He closed his eyes, debating not telling his father until he saw him Sunday, but he recalled something his father had told him when he was a teenager. *Even the ugliest truth is prettier than the most beautiful lie.* Hoping he wouldn't disappoint him too badly, he said, "I just found out that I have a daughter."

Silence stretched over the line.

"Dad?"

"Yeah, I'm here. Sorry. I thought you said you just found out you have a daughter."

"I did. I *do*." Ben explained how they'd found the baby and what had transpired since.

An incredulous laugh came through the phone. "I thought we dodged that bullet when our girls became adults."

"Thanks, Dad." Ben shook his head. "Just what I needed to hear. I know I fucked up."

"No, Ben. You *fucked*, obviously, but you didn't *fuck up*. It's a baby, not a disease, and in our family babies are always a good thing."

Tears stung Ben's eyes. He pinched the bridge of his nose and said, "Thanks, Dad. I needed to hear you say that." He looked up, blinking away the tears.

"Son, life is full of surprises. This one is unexpected, unsettling for you and Aurelia, I'm sure, but it sounds like you've already realized the beauty of the situation. And thank God Aurelia was there to help. She's a good friend, Ben, and I know you appreciate her. Life throws a lot of crap at us, and I hope you'll take a moment to soak in the goodness of this little miracle."

Great. More fucking tears.

"You said Bodhi's friend is going to track down the mother?" his father asked.

"That's the plan." He cleared his throat and wiped his eyes, regaining control of his emotions. "I'm going to see him Monday."

"And how are you holding up, son?"

"I'm okay. The first day or two was crazy, but then I got my head out of my ass."

His father chuckled. "And Aurelia? How's she doing?"

"She's exhausted, but we're closer than we've ever been. Really close, Dad. We're together, as a couple."

"About frigging time," his father said with a laugh. "Boy, if I'd have known all it would take was a kid, I'd have had someone drop one off on your doorstep two years ago. Watching you lust after Aurelia has been damn painful."

Ben laughed. "Thanks for the commentary, but I really need some advice."

"I gave you this talk when you were a teenager. *Condoms*, Ben. Don't leave home without them."

"*Dad,*" Ben said sternly, earning another chuckle from his father.

"Sorry, but come on, Ben. If we don't find humor in times like these, we'd all lose our minds. Wait until your mother finds out her love potions finally worked."

"*Christ,*" he said under his breath. "Dad, listen, I have two problems. The first is that I'm not sure if I'm doing the right thing with Aurelia. She doesn't need this type of responsibility in her life. She just bought the bookstore, and she's—"

"Stop right there," his father said. "For a guy who waited a long time to be with the woman he loves, you're giving yourself way too much credit. You can't make decisions like that for her. Aurelia's a bright girl. She'll do what she wants regardless of what you think is fair. You know she loves you. She has for a long time, son."

"I know that. And she loves B."

"Bea? That's my granddaughter's name? I love that."

"Dad, focus, please. I really need your help here." He had a fleeting thought about B needing a real name, but it was gone as quickly as it had come as more pressing worries hammered him. "What happens if this ends up being too much for her and she doesn't tell me because she's too attached to the baby? And not just that. I need advice on how to raise B. I'm making a list."

"A list?" His father chuckled again. "Ben, you can't raise a child by a *list*."

"I'm not. I'm just making sure I've got the main things down, so I don't screw her up."

"Oh, Ben. You've spent your entire life strategizing. You did it as a kid in every endeavor, from baseball to freaking Halloween. I remember you mapping out the streets, figuring out the quickest routes to cover the most houses and make sure you didn't miss the ones that gave out the best candy. You can't strategize fatherhood any better than you can strategize love. All you can do is be the best man you are capable of being—as a father and a significant other. Be *honest*, Ben, and love *unconditionally*. Never make promises you can't keep, and always give the other person space to make her own mistakes. That goes for kids *and* lovers. And maybe more important, give them a physical space of their own. Kids and adults both need a place to be alone with their own thoughts, to make their own decisions, and figure out how they feel about things."

"But B's just a baby. She doesn't need space."

"Trust me, Ben. Baby monitors are the best invention known to man. Get them. Use them. Your little girl needs to learn to sleep in her own room, or every time you and your *big girl* make a little noise, you'll wake her up."

"Right," he ground out. "You and I will *never* talk about me and my big girl in the bedroom again."

His father laughed. "It isn't exactly high on my list of priorities either, son."

"So you don't think I'm a selfish prick for asking Aurelia to be my girlfriend in the midst of my baby surprise?"

"Nah. The best unions are made under duress. Just ask your mother. I asked her to marry me in the middle of a fight."

"I've never heard that story."

"And you're not going to now. It's way too early for *that*. Listen, son. You're going to Willow and Zane's Sunday for dinner? Bringing our new grandbaby?"

"Yes. We'll come early so you can meet her before everyone else gets there."

"You know I have to tell your mom, right?"

"Yeah, I know. I'll send a picture, but everyone here is sleeping, so tell her not to call for a while. Babies are exhausting."

"Wait until she's a teenager."

"Oh God . . . don't remind me."

"I'd say you have years to prepare, but there is no preparing for teenage daughters. You always told it like it was. You were pissed off, happy, or somewhere in between, but you left no room for guessing.

The girls were all"—he raised his voice an octave and said—"'I'm not mad!'" He lowered his voice and said, "Then they'd slam their bedroom door, and if I didn't go make sure they were okay, I'd have a cryfest on my hands. Your sisters would go all"—he spoke in a higher pitch—"'You don't love me! If you loved me, you'd *want* to know what was wrong.'" He lowered his voice again and said, "And when I *did* try to find out what was wrong, I got the old"—his voice arced up again—"'Nothing! I'm fine! Leave me alone!'"

Ben laughed. "My daughter will not do that shit. We'll have an open, honest relationship."

"Said every new father on earth." His father sighed and said, "Good luck with that, son. I'll have a bottle of tequila on hand for those nights."

"My daughter isn't going to drive me to drink, Dad."

"Oh, the tequila's not for you. When your daughter is a teenager, your mother and I are going to camp out in your living room and watch the *show*." He snickered and said, "I love you, Benny. Give Aurelia a hug for me, and just in case you have any doubt, know that we love you, and we're here for you through anything. Okay?"

"Yeah, Dad. Thanks."

After he ended the call, he went quietly inside and finished making his list.

Be honest.

Only make promises I can keep.

Give her space to make mistakes.

Give her a space to call her own.

Aurelia padded out of the bedroom carrying B, both of them yawning. "Everything okay?"

He kissed them both and said, "Yeah. We should hit La Love Café for breakfast, then go nursery shopping. B needs a space of her own."

CHAPTER TWELVE

AURELIA PUSHED THE stroller down Main Street, tipping her face up toward the bright sun. They'd lucked out with a gloriously warm spring day. Harmony Pointe was nestled between Port Hudson, where Aurelia had attended college, and Sweetwater. It was just shy of an hour-and-a-half drive from New York City, and offered grand views of mountains as far as the eye could see. Cobblestone streets, brick-front eclectic shops, and old-fashioned streetlights added to the small town's charm. While Sweetwater was known for Sugar Lake, Harmony Pointe's Chiffon Park was the main attraction, with a large duck pond and a massive gazebo, which hosted lectures and musical events throughout the year. When Aurelia had heard about the events at the gazebo, it had felt like one more sign and clinched the deal for her purchasing the bookstore. She hoped to eventually do readings there, too.

"After my girls," Ben said as he pulled open the door to La Love Café & Gift Shop, which was owned by Everly's family and run by her sister Heaven and her brother, Echo.

His arm circled Aurelia's waist as he followed them in. She loved the *newness* of their intimacy, being a couple out in public. She'd thought about what it would be like, but nothing compared to the secret lustful looks he gave her or the feel of him pulling her closer, as he was now, like even a few inches between them was too much.

It might be her imagination, but since finding out he was B's father, he seemed to be carrying himself differently, more *proudly*. Earlier, she'd spotted a list on the dining room table with things like *Start a college fund* on it. Knowing he was taking fatherhood, and B's future, seriously made her fall even more in love with him. He'd spent twenty minutes organizing diapers, wipes, formula, and extra outfits into a backpack, which he now carried over one shoulder, and despite the warm weather, he'd stuffed extra blankets in the stroller. Aurelia shouldn't be surprised by his behavior, because she'd been just as bad, double-checking the backpack and gazing into the stroller every few seconds to make sure B was okay. It was strange not seeing her in the arms of one of them.

La Love was bustling with customers. Music played in the background as Heaven helped customers and Echo called out orders. Colorful lights hung over dark orange tables surrounded by brown chairs. As they made their way to the line, Aurelia admired Echo's abstract paintings hanging on the mustard-colored walls. Each piece of art was for sale. The jewelry Heaven made was also for sale, displayed in glass cabinets and hung from decorative trees at both ends of the counter.

"What are you hungry for?" Aurelia asked Ben, eyeing the bagels, pastries, and other delicious treats behind the glass.

A coy smile crept across his handsome face as he leaned closer and said, "You, Rels. Always *you*."

Heat flared inside her, and the air between them sizzled with desire. It was crazy how hot he could make her with just a look or a few simple words.

"Oh my goodness! Ben? Aurelia? And baby makes *three*?" Heaven exclaimed as she came around the counter despite the line of people Echo was dealing with.

Heaven was a pretty brunette with amber eyes. She wore a pair of purple batik pants, a lavender shirt that stopped two inches above her navel, and leather, beaded sandals. She was petite but curvy, like Aurelia.

"I thought Everly was *kidding*!" Heaven bent over the stroller, agog with instant adoration. "Isn't she just the sweetest thing?"

"Thank you," Ben said, holding Aurelia a little tighter and beaming like the proud papa he was.

Heaven's eyes moved between Aurelia and Ben. "And you two are an item now, huh?" She smiled and gave a happy little shrug-wiggle as she said, "It's about time!"

Ben laughed and pressed a kiss to Aurelia's temple. Oh, how she loved when he did that! As if he just couldn't hold back.

"I can't believe someone left this darling little baby on your doorstep," Heaven said. "That's like something out of a mystery novel. People are *nuts*! But she's a lucky girl, Ben. I know you'll take good care of her. What's her name?"

"B," he and Aurelia said at once.

"Baby Bea. Talk about adorable," Heaven exclaimed.

"Hey, sis," Echo called over the counter. "These orders aren't going to fill themselves."

Heaven did her signature shrug-wiggle again, smiling happily, and said, "If you get a chance, check out my new bookish jewelry. I know you'll love it! I made some really cool new charms." She lowered her voice and said, "Did you notice all the yoga-clad women?" She nodded toward the line at a group of women dressed in yoga pants, then whispered, "They're here every time Echo works. I swear he must put a flyer up in the yoga studio around the corner that says, *Tall, dark, and single right around the corner*!"

She returned to the other side of the counter, and they went back to waiting in line.

Half an hour later, after they'd finished eating, Aurelia went to check out Heaven's new pieces. Heaven's family owned an orchard in Sweetwater, and her father also made furniture and jewelry. He'd taught Heaven to make jewelry when she was in middle school. Heaven was a book lover, like Aurelia, and she also wrote poetry. They'd both attended

Boyer University in Port Hudson, New York, and joined the Ladies Who Write sorority, a group of women who'd bonded over their love of the written word. In college, Heaven had written a weekly poetry column in the school newspaper, and Aurelia had written a column called "Book Chat," talking up the hottest books.

As she looked over the charms of open books and quills, she thought about that column and considered trying to do something like that again. But she'd rather spend any extra time she had with Ben and B.

The baby started fussing, and Aurelia glanced at Ben, who waved her off as he put B on his shoulder and patted her back. She went to the other end of the counter to look at the necklaces, but when she got halfway there, B's cries escalated—and Ben looked a little panicked. She hurried over, noticing other customers looking at them.

Ben hiked the backpack over his shoulder and said, "I'm going to try changing her."

"Okay. I'll clean off the table." She began clearing their trash, trying to ignore the stares of the other customers, when she really wanted to say, *What? She's a baby. She cries!*

In the next second Ben barged out of the men's room and yelled across the café, "Aurelia!"

With her heart in her throat, she ran over. "What's wrong?"

He grabbed her arm, hauling her toward the ladies' room and speaking through gritted teeth as B's cries escalated to piercing wails. "There's no frigging changing table in the men's room. Please make sure there's no one in there. I'm commandeering the bathroom."

She hurried into the ladies' room, saw it was empty, and stuck her head out to say, "All clear."

"What kind of place doesn't have a changing table?" Ben seethed as they quickly changed B's diaper, her wails softening to a whimper. "Where are fathers supposed to change their kids?" He fixed B's clothes, picked up the backpack and the baby, and said, "Come on."

Aurelia followed him out of the bathroom as he blazed a path to the counter. He glowered at Echo, who was about six and a half feet tall, with shaggy brown hair, and said, "Why the hell isn't there a changing table in the men's room?"

Aurelia tried to hide her embarrassment, but she was also proud of him for speaking up.

Amusement rose in Echo's eyes. "Dude, this is a college town. We don't get many single dads in here."

"All it takes is *one*. *One*, Echo. One guy with a kid deserves a changing area." Ben took out his wallet and slapped down a debit card. "Ring up a cookie."

Looking bewildered, Echo said, "What kind?"

"Any damn cookie."

Echo rang it up, and Ben shoved his card in the processor. Aurelia nearly choked as Ben added a thousand-dollar tip and said, "Put a damn changing station in the men's room."

Later that afternoon, with bags full of nursery decorations, Ben was still feeling guilty about yelling at Echo and embarrassing Aurelia. As great as the week had been, it had been undeniably stressful. When he'd called his attorney, he'd realized how important it was to find B's mother. Their conversation had left him with a plethora of worries. What if she changed her mind once they found her? What if he *couldn't* find her? Not only did they have medical questions, but what would he tell B when she grew up and wanted to know why her mother had left her? That particular worry made his heart ache. Just like knowing he'd embarrassed Aurelia did.

"Hold up a sec." He guided Aurelia and the stroller out of the middle of the sidewalk, set down his bags, and gathered Aurelia in his arms. She gazed up at him with trusting eyes, looking at him like he was the best thing since peanut M&M's, but did he deserve that? "I'm sorry for flying off the handle at Echo and for embarrassing you."

"You've said that three times already. It's fine. I'm sure Echo knows you were frazzled because B was upset, and I was only embarrassed for a second."

"Still. I don't lose my cool often, and in the last week you've seen me totally out of my element more than once. I don't like that, and I don't want you to think I'm the kind of guy who will go off over little things."

She smiled up at him and said, "Afraid it's going to knock your cool quotient down a notch?"

"Rels, I'm serious. I shouldn't have gotten so mad."

"Okay, well, I've known you for years, and I'm pretty sure if you were the kind of guy who lost his mind over meaningless crap, I'd know it by now. Here's my honest-to-goodness thoughts on what happened. At first I *was* a little embarrassed, because you were so panicked. But then I realized two things. B needs a father who cares enough to make things right, and"—she flattened her hands against his chest and said—"that panicked, fatherly side of you? That was *serious* boyfriend porn. You were being protective of your baby girl, and you spoke up for all single dads in the area. That's awesome, Benny boy. I think I fell a little harder for you again today."

He touched his forehead to hers and said, "What did I do to deserve you?"

"Heck if I know." She smiled with the tease, and then she went up on her toes, meeting his delicious lips in a decadent kiss.

"If I'm hearing you right," he said as he picked up the shopping bags, "all I have to do to turn you on is stand up for my little girl?"

She began pushing the stroller as they walked toward the furniture store. "All you have to do is look at me, Ben. Get with the program."

He chuckled and stole another kiss.

They made their way to the furniture store and found the nursery section, which was stocked with cribs, dressers, changing tables, bookcases, and more in varying colors of paint and types of wood.

"Whoa," Ben said, looking over the sea of pastel-colored walls and furniture.

"Out of your element again?" Aurelia asked as she peeked at B.

"Slightly." He noticed a woman with short gray hair hurrying over. He smiled at the stout, friendly-faced woman, who looked to be in her fifties.

"Hello, there. I'm Peggy." She clasped her hands together, bending down to get a closer look at B, and said, "Oh, look at your darling girl. Are you shopping for this little princess?"

"Yes. We're looking for nursery furniture," Ben said.

"Well, you've come to the right place," Peggy said cheerily. "Did you have anything specific in mind?"

Ben looked at Aurelia, who shrugged, and then he said, "We want the best of everything."

Aurelia's eyes widened.

"Do you have a color scheme in mind?" Peggy asked.

Again he deferred to Aurelia, who said, "I kind of like white."

"A perfect choice. Follow me."

As they followed Peggy, Aurelia whispered, "Ben, she's seeing dollar signs. You don't need to spend a fortune."

"It's only money, and my girl deserves the best."

"Okay, Daddy Dalton. Bang that chest," she joked.

After Peggy explained the difference between convertible, mini, and standard cribs and gave them more information than they could possibly process about baby furniture, she left Aurelia and Ben alone to look around. Ben watched Aurelia checking price tags and running her hands over the furniture. It was easy to tell which pieces she liked and which she didn't by the look in her eyes. It was just as easy to tell which she thought were too expensive, as she peeked at the price tags, then dropped them like hot potatoes, moving away from them like she might get burned.

"Ben, this place is outrageously expensive," she whispered. "We can probably do better online."

"I know, but we're here, and I'd like to get her nursery set up. I want to get B nice things, babe. You know I can afford it."

"Just because you *can* doesn't mean you *should*," she said. "But you're a smart businessman. You know that."

He kissed her tenderly and said, "I love you, and I love how fiscally careful you are. But I also saw the way you were looking at that white nursery set with the inlaid roses, matching dresser, and bookshelf."

"No way, Ben. It's almost the same as that one over there." She pointed across the room at another nursery set. "But it's twice the price, and the only difference I saw was that the expensive one has curved sides. She's a *baby*, Ben. She's not going to notice curved sides."

"I get that, but we found her in a *basket*, Aurelia, and every time I think of her being left on my porch, *abandoned*, I just want to give her the world."

"I know you do," she said softly, taking his hands in hers. "But, Ben, you grew up with a big family who didn't always have money for shiny new things. You know that love matters most, not material things. I know you have more money than God himself, but you got that way by being smart, not by overcompensating for other people's faults. Overcompensate with your time, with your love and affection, and sock the money away in her college fund or something."

"Relsy, you never fail to make sense." He pressed his smiling lips to hers and said, "Maybe you're right, because if we have a big brood like my parents did, we'll need a *lot* of college money."

"Wait . . . What? *Big brood?* We're not even married."

"Yet . . ." He grabbed the bags and pushed the stroller toward the less expensive furniture, leaving her to pick her jaw up off the floor. *Oh yeah, baby. Get used to that idea.*

♥ ♥ ♥

After ordering furniture, which would be delivered to Ben's house Friday, they headed back toward Aurelia's apartment. When they reached Main Street, Aurelia spotted Fletch and his Bernese mountain dog, Molly, coming down the street. Fletch was a professor at Beckwith University and a good friend of Ben's.

Fletch grinned mischievously, eyeing the stroller with his vibrant baby blues. "I'd heard a rumor about the newest Dalton family member." He embraced Ben, giving him a manly slap on the back. "Congrats, man." Then he hugged Aurelia and said, "And I hear this big lug finally wrangled you onto his arm."

"That he did," Aurelia said as she crouched to love up Molly.

"So, all I have to do to get a beautiful woman is find a baby?" Fletch asked as he peered into the stroller. "She's a cutie, but I think I can do without the midnight feedings."

"No shit," Ben said as Molly came to his side, tail wagging, tongue hanging out, in search of attention. As he petted her, he said, "It's exhausting, but worth it. Speaking of women, are you seeing anyone?"

"Don't even go there, dude. Your mom keeps giving me bottles of body wash. I've been giving them away for faculty birthdays, and I scrub my hands with Brillo after touching them, just in case."

They all laughed.

"We're heading into the park. Want to join us?" Fletch waved across the street toward Chiffon Park, where people milled about on acres of lush lawns and winding trails.

There was a hill on the other side of the park, with an old farmhouse at the top that Aurelia had heard might be going on the market as commercial property. It was the perfect location for a quaint teahouse or café, as that was an iconic winter sledding hill.

Ben arched a brow at Aurelia, who nodded eagerly. "Sure," he said. "Let me just put these bags in Aurelia's apartment."

Aurelia gave him her keys, and he disappeared around the side of the building.

"How's he holding up with all this?" Fletch asked.

"He's good," Aurelia assured him. "Tired, but you know Ben. Once he realized the baby really needed him, he figured out the best way to handle things and went *all in*."

"And you? I know Ben's been into you for a long time, but this is a lot to take on all at once."

"Tell me about it. Single girl to single dad's girlfriend inside of a week's time. It's been a whirlwind, but just look at her." She gazed into the stroller and said, "You know, Fletch, a baby *is* a lot to take on, and I have no idea how this all happened so fast, but I'm all in, too." She thought about what Ben had said about a big brood, and she wasn't sure she was ready for all that yet, but the three of them? That she wanted. *Desperately.*

"I don't get it. I mean, she's cute, but I'm not feeling a paternal clock ticking or anything," Fletch said.

She met his assessing gaze and said, "How long did it take you to fall in love with Molly?"

"Ten minutes *maybe*. I got her from the Loves. One of their orchard dogs had pups. She was just a little bundle of fur when I got her." He waggled a finger at Aurelia. "I see what you're doing. I'd imagine a baby is hard to resist if you have some familial—or romantic—connection to it."

Aurelia laughed. "You should *hold* her. She's much harder to keep your distance from than a puppy."

He took a step backward. "No, thank you. Molly's enough responsibility for me."

"You know, B's only half the allure of the Ben-and-baby equation. You do know *Ben*, right? Big, handsome guy with a heart larger than this town? Trustworthy, great secret keeper? Not afraid to say when he's wrong? Well, that man had me *way* before B did," she said as Ben came around the corner of the building, his eyes locked on her, unleashing a flutter of heat in her chest. *Oh yeah, you had me all right.*

Ben draped an arm over her shoulder and said, "I put another bottle in the backpack just in case she needs it. Ready?"

"Am I *ever*," she said, and as they crossed the street she looked at Fletch and mouthed, *Thoughtful, too.*

Fletch smiled, nodding his agreement. "How are things coming along with the bookstore?"

"Great. They're almost done with the renovations, and Everly is starting a mural for the kids' section next week. I'm thinking about starting a monthly book club. You've lived here a long time. Do you think that would fly in this area?"

"Hell yes," Fletch said as they entered the park.

"That's a great idea, Rels." Ben winked at Fletch and said, "I bet Fletch knows lots of women at the college. He can probably pass out flyers."

Aurelia shook her head. "You're not using my book club as a dating pool for Fletch."

"Sorry, man," Ben said. "I tried to hook you up."

Fletch laughed and took a tennis ball from his jacket pocket. He unhooked Molly's leash, showed her the ball, and threw it.

They followed a path toward a gazebo. In the distance, kids fed ducks around the pond, a family sat on a blanket beneath a big oak tree, and an older couple walked hand in hand along a footpath. Molly skidded to a stop by the gazebo, retrieved the ball, and bounded toward them.

The baby fussed, and Aurelia stopped to take her out of the stroller. "Come here, little one." She kissed her cheek, and Ben pushed the stroller to the gazebo. "I love this gazebo. Fletch, do you ever attend the lectures they give here? Or the concerts?"

"Yeah, sure," he said as Molly dropped the ball at his feet. He picked it up and threw it again, sending Molly on another mad dash. "Do you think you guys will come to them now that you're living here?"

"Oh gosh, yes. I hope to, at least," she said, glancing at Ben.

"Sure. Whatever you want," Ben said.

"Once I hire staff and I've worked out all the kinks at the bookstore"—she sat on the gazebo steps—"I hope to be able to do readings here a few times a year." Talia had referred a couple of college students to work part-time at the bookstore, and Aurelia had scheduled interviews for the coming week.

"Will you dress up like you did for the readings at Pages?" Ben asked.

She looked curiously at him as he parked the stroller and sat beside her. "How do you know I dressed up for my readings?"

Fletch chuckled, and Ben scrubbed a hand down his face, grinning like a Cheshire cat.

"Ben . . . ?" She didn't remember ever telling him about dressing up. In fact, she didn't remember mentioning much about the readings other than that she did them.

"I might have . . . *um* . . ." He glanced at Fletch. Then he turned that panty-melting grin on Aurelia and said, "I caught a few of them."

"When? I don't remember seeing you. Wait a sec. You had meetings Thursday nights. Aida Strong *meetings*," she said with a wince of discomfort. "You couldn't have gone to my readings."

Ben looked like a kid caught with his hand in the candy jar. "You were my meetings, babe, not her. Second and fourth Thursdays of the month."

She couldn't believe he'd secretly gone to hear her readings. "I . . . *But . . . ?*"

"No *buts*. I was there, babe."

"But I never saw you at the bookstore."

"That was by design. I wanted to see *you*, but that didn't mean I thought you wanted to see *me*." He kissed B's head, and then he said, "You were the sexiest Scarlett O'Hara I've ever seen. And when you were Anna Karenina? *Whew*, Rels. I'm not gonna lie. You made for some pretty *interesting* fantasies."

A rumble of laughter burst from Fletch's lungs. "That's definitely TMI for this guy. I'll catch up with y'all another time." He threw the ball for Molly and walked off in the same direction.

"Ben, are you *serious*? Did you really come see me without me knowing?"

"Like clockwork, babe."

She filled with joy. "Do you have any idea how many nooky points that could have won you?"

He laughed and slid a hand to the nape of her neck, drawing her mouth closer to his. "I'm going to calculate how many times I went to see you, and you're going to have a lot of payback to do."

"Good thing I make good on all of my IOUs."

"If I have my way, you'll be paying me back for a *very* long time. But don't worry, I'll make it worth your while." He lowered his lips toward hers, and his warm breath coasted over her skin as he said, "When this little one goes down tonight, your man's *going down*, too."

CHAPTER THIRTEEN

AURELIA'S BACK HIT the cold, wet shower tile with a thud early Sunday morning as Ben thrust his rigid cock in deep, sending shocks of heat searing through her.

"Oh God, yes!" she panted out.

Ben's mouth crashed over hers, rough and demanding, as he pounded into her beneath the warm spray of the shower. She loved his strength and his ravenous desire for her. He'd made good on his promise last night. Having his greedy hands and his talented, insanely *wicked* mouth all over her had left her fantasizing about what she wanted to do to *him*. She'd woken up wet and needy, craving him like a drug, and decided to take their pleasure into her own hands. After B's 5:00 a.m. feeding, Aurelia had slithered beneath the covers and done just that. She'd loved him with her mouth and hands until he was nearly blinded with desire, but they were both afraid of waking the baby. Her brilliant boyfriend had swept her into his arms and carried her—and the baby monitor—into the bathroom. The steamy shower was the perfect buffer for their sounds as she clung to his slippery flesh.

He banded one arm around her back, and the other clutched her ass as he sent her up to the clouds, her body clenching hot and tight around him.

"Fuck, baby," he ground out. "I want you to come a hundred times, and then I want to make you come a hundred more."

"Later," she pleaded. "I want to feel you come with me *now*."

The darkness in his grin made her go ever wilder. She clawed at his slick skin, ate at his mouth, thrusting and grinding against him. He had to have the strongest legs and hips known to man, because his efforts never faltered. His grip was confident and unyielding, his kisses were all-consuming, and his love was inescapable. She felt his muscles tense, and then his body jerked with such force, his release sent lightning shooting through her core, and she surrendered to another mind-numbing climax.

He tore his mouth away, holding her trembling, bucking body beneath the warm shower spray, and spoke in a gravelly, lustful voice. "I love making love with you. But make no mistake, Rels," he panted out. "I'm truly, madly, *passionately* in love with *everything* about you, not just your incredible body."

A laugh slipped out before she could stop it. "I know, Ben. I see it in your eyes, and I feel it in your touch. But I should tell you, I'm totally into Ten-Inch Ben."

He smacked her ass, making her laugh again.

"Don't worry," she said through a wide grin. "I loved you when you were Ten-Second Ben, too."

"Hey," he growled. "We sent him packing days ago."

She held his face between her hands, so in love with him she couldn't tease him for a second longer. "You're the smartest, kindest, sexiest man I know, and there's no one I'd rather be naked with for ten seconds, ten hours, or ten million years than you."

Sunday evening they stocked up on baby supplies, folded up the Pack 'n Play, and headed into Sweetwater to have dinner with Ben's family. As Ben drove down the familiar cobblestone streets and Sugar Lake came into view, he was hit with a strange, detached sensation, like he was a visitor in his own town. He'd gone away to college and traveled often for work, and he'd never once felt the tightening in his chest or the sense of separation that came over him now as he turned onto Main Street. He passed Willow's bakery and Bridgette's flower shop, expecting the feelings to right themselves. When they didn't, he realized Aurelia's apartment, and her new town, had already started feeling like home.

He looked at his beautiful girlfriend, the woman who had always been by his side and in his heart, and then he glanced in the rearview mirror at his sleeping baby girl, and that discomfort dissipated, replaced with a sense of completeness.

"Are you nervous about seeing your parents?" Aurelia asked, reaching for his hand. "I know you talked to your father, but seeing them in person is different."

"Yeah, a little," he said as he turned down the street toward his childhood home, which Willow and Zane had purchased from his parents when they'd downsized. "I know they'll love B, but there's still guilt wrapped around getting a woman I barely knew pregnant. I wish I could have gotten B some other way—not just to ease the guilt I feel for my parents, but for you, Rels."

Aurelia glanced into the backseat as he parked in front of the five-bedroom white Victorian and said, "Want to know what I think?"

"Always," he said honestly.

"If it's true that babies feel everything we do"—she turned her loving eyes on him—"then I think you need to deal with that guilt and get it out of your system once and for all. It doesn't make a lick of difference to me how she came to be, and I'm sure it won't to your parents. What matters is that she's *yours*, and guilt will only taint the incredibleness of that."

"But when you look at her, you must feel *something*—Hurt? Disappointed?—because I had a baby with someone else?"

"I'm not going to lie. Sure, I was jealous, but I love you, so I think that's natural. And sometimes I feel pangs of that, but not nearly as much as I did the first two days. And I know that's on the way out, because I feel so much for her, and for you, and every day my love grows bigger. Soon there'll be no room for them. Besides, *yes*, you had sex with another woman, and that act resulted in a beautiful little girl. But you didn't have a baby *with her*, Ben. Maybe I'm just fooling myself, but I think there's a world of difference between having a baby *with* someone and welcoming that baby into a joint, loving home and what happened with Hotel Hookup that led to B."

He pulled her closer, taking her in a long, sensual kiss. He brushed his thumb over her cheek, marveling at her, and said, "Do you want to know why I only dated blondes who looked like Barbies?"

"You should really quit while you're ahead," she warned.

"I'm not a quitter." He smiled and said, "It was because they were the opposite of my type of woman. They were the opposite of *you*, Rels. They weren't real or naturally beautiful. They didn't have a genuineness that called out to me or a snort-laugh that made me happy every time I heard it. No woman could ever know me the way you do, and I'd never give them the chance to try."

"*Aaaaand* you've just jumped to the head of the race." She practically crawled over the center console to kiss him. He threaded his fingers into her hair, and she moaned into his mouth. He intensified the kiss, losing himself in her as she murmured with pleasure.

A knock on the window startled them apart, and Aurelia hit her head on the visor. "Ouch!"

Ben reached for her head, rubbing the sore spot as his mother's smiling face peered into the window. He unlocked the doors as Aurelia scrambled to the passenger seat.

His mother opened the back door and said, "You two go back to what you were doing. I'm just here to meet my granddaughter."

Aurelia blushed and mumbled, "*Ohmygosh.*"

His mother unbuckled the baby and gushed, "Hello, sweet little one. How's my precious girl?" She lifted her into her arms, closed the door, and headed up the driveway.

"Good to see you, too, Mom," Ben said with a shake of his head, earning a laugh from Aurelia. He waggled his brows and patted his lap.

"Hardly!" she said as she threw her door open.

They grabbed the bags and the Pack 'n Play, and Zane met them halfway up the driveway. He had gotten the short end of the stick when it came to supportive parents, but even when they were kids, years before he and Willow became an item, Ben's parents had made him feel like part of the family.

Zane laughed incredulously. "Congrats, dude. Look at you going full-on *Daddy Day Care*. Have I completely lost my running partner?" He gave Ben a slap on the back, then took the bags from Aurelia and embraced her. "I hear you two are finally an item. I guess that means congrats to you, too. Come inside. Willow and Roxie have been waiting with bated breath for that baby, so if you two want to take advantage and head to Ben's old bedroom for a no-baby-around make-out session, be my guest."

"We're good in that department, thanks," Ben said with a shake of his head.

They followed Zane inside, and Ben set the Pack 'n Play down in the living room, where his mother and Willow were loving on the baby.

"Oh, honey," his mother said. "You are not going to need that tonight. The girls and I are going to be fighting over this little darling all night long."

His father came out of the kitchen, smiling approvingly at Ben, as if stepping into fatherhood had given him a boon of some sort. Dan Dalton was tall and slim, and he looked more like the professor he'd been before retiring than the contractor he'd become after following his passion for custom-home building.

"Let me guess," his father said as he came down the hall. "Your mother confiscated the baby." He hugged Ben, then embraced Aurelia for a beat longer, whispering something that made her smile—and blush.

Bodhi, Bridgette, and Louie came through the front door.

"Uncle Benny!" Louie ran toward him, and Ben swept him into the air and hugged him. His eyes were as wide as saucers beneath his mop of brown hair. "Put me down! Mommy said you have a baby. I want to hold it!"

"*It's* a *she*, buddy," Ben said as he set Louie on his feet.

"I know! *B!*" Louie ran toward Roxie, who was cooing at the baby.

"Slow down, Louie," Bodhi called after him. At six three, Bodhi dwarfed Bridgette, and his love for her and Louie was just as immense. He clapped a hand on Ben's shoulder as Bridgette hugged Aurelia, and he said, "Congrats, man. On both counts."

"Maybe we need to start calling you *Potent* Ben," Bridgette said as she hugged him.

Bridgette was the youngest and had always been the wildest of Ben's siblings. She'd left college to marry a musician, only to lose him in a tragic accident shortly after Louie was born. She was an amazing mother to Louie, and though she'd missed her husband, she'd never complained about raising Louie alone. But Ben was glad she had Bodhi now, giving her and Louie the love they deserved.

Bridgette put her hand on her little baby bump, smiling up at Ben, her wavy several-shades-of-blond hair framing her face, and said, "Were you trying to steal our baby thunder?"

"Hardly, Bridge."

The front door opened, and Talia and Derek stepped inside. Their faces were flushed, and Derek's dark hair, which hung nearly to his shoulders, was messy and tangled. Talia averted her eyes.

Aurelia looked at Talia like she'd grown a second head and said, "I think your sweater is on backward."

Talia gasped and looked down as Piper appeared in the doorway behind her. Piper joined them, closing the door behind her. "Hey, Tal. I swear I thought I saw your car parked on that side road people used to . . . Is your sweater on *backward*?"

Talia blushed and hurried down the hall toward the bathroom, causing them all to chuckle.

Derek pushed a hand through his hair with a rakish grin and said, "We, uh . . ."

"Looks like someone took advantage of not having his father underfoot," Zane said with a waggle of his brows.

Everyone laughed and talked at once as they moved into the living room. Zane and Bodhi gave Derek grief about going *parking* like a teenager. Bridgette grabbed Aurelia's hand and said, "I want to hear *everything*," and dragged her toward the baby with Piper in tow.

Dan draped an arm around Ben, who said, "Welcome home, Dad." He noticed the way his father was looking at him differently. "What?"

"It's not every day my son becomes a father." He drew him into a manly hug and said, "Congratulations. Fatherhood looks good on you."

Ben hadn't expected the rush of emotions consuming him, but he didn't have long to swim in them. His father said, "Did you put the baby in her own room?"

"Not yet. I can't. I like having her close."

Dan shook his head, smiling as he said, "Just like your mother. That's okay. You'll know when it's the right time."

Talia entered the room wearing her sweater *properly* and made a beeline for the baby. "Okay, Nana Roxie. Give Auntie Talia a turn, you baby hog."

"Auntie Talia," Louie said as Roxie handed her the baby, "her name is *Grandma* Roxie." Having said his piece, he went to play with the toys Willow and Zane kept in a bucket by the fireplace.

"Hear that, baby?" Talia said sweetly, nuzzling the baby. "It's *Grandma* Roxie. Did you have fun with Uncle Fletch and Molly yesterday at the park? I heard all about how cute you were. You are the most precious little muffin, aren't you? Found on the front porch like the best gift *ever*, huh?"

Ben listened to his usually too-proper sister spewing baby talk in a high-pitched voice, and he could do little more than stare. Boy, had his studious sister changed. By the surprised looks in the room, everyone else was also confounded by her baby talk.

"Derek, what have you done to her?" Bridgette asked. "She wasn't this way even when Louie was born."

"I was too," Talia said.

A murmur of disagreement made its way around the room.

Derek put his arm around Talia and said, "I don't know what you guys are talking about. Tallie *loves* babies."

"I think someone's maternal clock is ticking," Roxie said.

"I love this baby, but better her than me," Willow said.

Roxie looked at Ben and said, "Ben, she's a beautiful girl, but I have a few questions, some of which are about her mother." She turned a softer look to Aurelia and said, "Aurelia, honey, you know I think of you as a daughter. I always have, and now that you and Ben are together, if my questions are going to make you uncomfortable, please tell me."

"Roxie, she's your granddaughter," Aurelia said. "Your *first* granddaughter. This is a huge moment for all of you, and I would expect, given the circumstances, that you have *lots* of questions, and I *want* you to ask them."

Ben's heart took a hit at both his mother's thoughtfulness and Aurelia's response. "We don't have any secrets, Mom." He went to Aurelia, standing beside the couch where she sat, and laced their fingers together.

"Okay, honey," Roxie said. "Your father told me that you're meeting with Bodhi's friend Mason tomorrow. Do you need a babysitter?"

"I'm watching her," Aurelia said.

"We're going to try to work around each other's schedules so that we don't have to leave her with anyone else for now," Ben explained. "I think she needs the stability."

Roxie's lips curved up in an approving smile. "That's wonderful, and I'm here if you need me. Babies can be exhausting."

"We know," Ben and Aurelia said in unison.

"What can you tell me about her mother, Ben?" Roxie asked. "Was she outgoing or shy? What color hair did she have? What's she like as a person? It must have been so hard for her to leave the baby. What a selfless act, putting her child's well-being above her own. Whatever the circumstances, I'm glad she was smart enough to bring her to you."

He knew his family would always be there for them, but hearing his mother's unconditional acceptance felt monumental.

"This is a little embarrassing," Ben admitted. "I don't really know much about her. Her name is Caroline, and I met her in a hotel bar where I was staying. I think she worked as a waitress there, because she said her shift had just ended. She's blond, nice, outgoing." He cringed inside, hating himself *again* for using sex as a salve for his pain. "She was trying to get over a breakup, and I was . . ." He could say anything and his family wouldn't question it. But when he looked at Aurelia, brushing his thumb over the back of the hand that had cradled his heart forever and guided him through this whole ordeal, the truth spilled out. "I was trying not to think about Aurelia being out on a date."

A sea of emotions rose in Aurelia's eyes as she said, "See? B's here because of me, so it kind of makes sense that I'm the one who found her," with a humorous lilt in her voice.

Ben pulled her up to her feet and wrapped his arms around her. "She's our destiny, babe."

"I know," she whispered.

Ben was so lost in her, he caught only pieces of the conversations going on around them. His mother said something about her potions finally kicking in, and someone else—Bodhi, maybe—said Mason would get the answers they needed. Then everything turned to white noise, and there was only him and Aurelia and the pulse of love between them.

"Ben!" Piper snapped, like she'd said it more than once. "What are you going to call her?"

Still lost in Aurelia, Ben vaguely registered Piper's question and said, *"Mine."*

"Oh boy, someone's lovestruck," his mother said, and everyone laughed.

"The *baby*, Ben," Piper said. "You can't call her *Baby Ben* forever."

Aurelia went up on her toes and whispered, "She has a name."

"She sure does," Ben said. "Her name is *Bea*. B-E-A. Bea Dalton."

Despite knowing Bea would be the center of attention tonight, Aurelia had been nervous that her and Ben's new relationship would become a topic of conversation. But they'd made it through a delicious steak dinner, talking about Bea, catching up on Louie's exciting week with Willow and Zane, and, of course, hearing all about Bridgette and Bodhi's honeymoon in Hawaii. It seemed everyone had accepted her and Ben's coupledom as if it had been a given.

As they finished the chocolate pecan pie Willow had made for dessert, Bridgette said, "I think my favorite thing about Maui was that everything was totally relaxed. There was no hustle and bustle. We never felt rushed."

"Hard to get that feeling when you never leave your hotel room," Zane said with a smirk.

Willow elbowed him. "That sounds amazing."

"I'll show you amazing," Zane said as he kissed her cheek.

Dan and Roxie shared a knowing smile, their eyes holding for a beat longer, and *darker*, than usual. Aurelia looked away, both embarrassed to have caught the desire between them and happy for two of the people who had always shown her what love and family should be like. She used to daydream about what it would be like to be Ben's girlfriend. Now she knew. He'd held her hand throughout dinner, whispered private jokes, and kissed her openly—and also just below her ear, teasing her with a tantalizing slick of his tongue after each whispered secret. She had never felt so close to him. She should have known it would be this beautiful between them. Ben had forever been draping an arm over her shoulder or taking her by the hand, leading her places, or letting her use his chest as a pillow. They may not have shared kisses or tongue action when they were just friends, but they'd always been right there by each other's side.

"It was incredible," Bridgette said, bringing Aurelia's mind back to the conversation about their honeymoon. "The pool at the resort had a waterfall *and* a view of the ocean."

"We want to take Louie there one day," Bodhi said, reaching for Bridgette's hand.

"I don't want to never leave a hotel room," Louie said with a mouthful of pie, making everyone laugh. "I could stay with Zane and Willow again. Or with Uncle Benny and Auntie Aurelia! They have a baby now, and I love Bea!"

Aurelia held her breath, wondering who was going to explain to him that she and Ben didn't live together, even if it looked that way.

"So, Mom," Talia said, apparently oblivious to Aurelia's worries. "How was the Monroe House?"

"Hm?" Roxie looked up, sharing another secretive smile with Dan.

"The *inn*," Talia said. "Was it as great as it looked online?"

"Oh yes," Roxie said with a blush. "The lobby was nice, and room service was really good."

Ben and his siblings exchanged uncomfortable glances.

"Efficient," their father added, staring down at his empty plate. His gaze darted to Roxie, and they both tried to stifle laughs.

"Ugh!" Ben threw down his napkin and said, "I can't unhear that."

"Or unsee it." Piper set down her fork and said, "Time to clear the table."

"It's just *S-E-X*," Roxie said with a roll of her eyes.

"Ew," Ben and his siblings said in unison as they all pushed to their feet and began clearing the table.

Roxie sat back, laughing softly, and said, "Where do you think y'all came from?"

"I for one do not want to think about *that* at all," Willow said as she carried her plate to the kitchen.

"They came from you and Grandpa," Louie announced. "When two people love each other they make babies, like Mom and Bodhi and Ben and Aurelia."

Aurelia looked at Ben, who shrugged as if he was at a loss about correcting Louie's assumption, too. Luckily, Bea whimpered, waking up from her nap in the playpen and giving Aurelia the perfect excuse to escape the other surprised looks.

"I'll get her!" Louie pushed from his seat and ran toward the playpen.

Bodhi followed him over and said, "I'll get her, Aurelia. I haven't had any baby time yet. Louie and I can hold her together."

Ben headed for Aurelia just as Bridgette sidled up to her and said, "Do you and Ben want us to clear that up for Louie?"

Ben put his arms around Aurelia, looking at her like she held the answer. "Should we let him think she's ours?"

Oh boy . . . This was *big*. Her pulse raced at the prospect of what his question implied, but she forced herself to slow down and think rationally. "As good as that feels to my heart," Aurelia said, "my head tells me it's not right. One day Bea needs to know the truth, and you don't want Louie to feel like we lied to him."

A smile curved Bridgette's lips. "Oh, big brother, you have no idea how lucky you are."

As Bridgette walked away, Ben brushed his lips over Aurelia's and said, "I know exactly how lucky I am."

"How lucky we both are," she corrected him.

He kissed her tenderly, and then he went back to helping with the table. Aurelia glanced at Bodhi, crouched beside Louie and holding Bea. She looked even tinier in his massive arms.

Bridgette sidled up to Aurelia again and said, "It's a nice view, isn't it?"

"It's like the Incredible Hulk holding a Cabbage Patch doll."

Bridgette rubbed her belly and said, "Soon I'll be able to see that wife porn every day." She sighed dreamily. "Gosh, Aurelia. I'm so in love with that man."

Aurelia's gaze fell on Ben as he picked up a pile of plates, his eyes hitching to hers as he blew her a kiss, and she said, "Me too."

"You love *my* husband?" Bridgette looked at her like she was nuts.

"What?" She felt her cheeks burn and said, "Oh gosh. *No.*"

"I think she was talking about Supersperm over there," Piper said as she picked up a platter from the table.

Ben glared at Piper, who laughed and headed into the kitchen.

Later, after everyone had loved up the baby and they were saying their goodbyes, Willow hugged Aurelia and said, "You three make a perfect little family."

"Shh. Don't jinx it," Aurelia whispered as Ben came to her side with the backpack over his shoulder, the Pack 'n Play in one hand, his other hand loaded up with the bags they'd brought. They really needed to learn how to pack for short visits. They'd been so worried about forgetting something, they'd brought practically Bea's entire wardrobe, as well as bottles, blankets, and other paraphernalia.

"Ready, babe?" Ben's chest brushed the back of her shoulder, like he wanted any contact he could get since his hands were full.

"You mean I have to give up my granddaughter?" Roxie asked, snuggling Bea one last time. As she put the baby in Aurelia's arms, she gave her one last kiss and said, "Will we be hearing wedding bells soon?"

Aurelia's eyes shot to Ben.

"Good night, Mom," Ben said sternly. "Love you."

"I love you, too. All three of you," Roxie said. "Don't hesitate to call if you need anything."

Relief swept through Aurelia. She and Ben had enough on their plates without his family pushing them to get married.

"Thanks, Mom," Ben said. "I think we've got it."

"We'll see," Roxie said, looking at Bridgette like she was in on a secret they weren't privy to.

"Thank you," Aurelia said as they headed out to the truck. "I thought for sure your sisters were going to jump on that wedding-bells train."

He flashed an arrogant grin and said, "I know how to shut down a conversation that would have gone on forever with my sisters around." He opened the back door for her to put Bea in her car seat and said, "Besides, the faster we got out of there, the quicker I can get you in my bed."

She snort-laughed, and he gave her a chaste kiss.

"By the way, we're staying at my place tonight, and if you want to know why?" he said with a sinful look in his eyes. "It's because it's *closer*."

Ben's house felt colder than normal, too quiet, *and* too big, like it had been empty for too long. But Aurelia kept that to herself, because they had enough to deal with resituating Bea's things. They carried everything into the living room, and as Ben began emptying the contents of the bags, Aurelia fed Bea. *Bea*. She couldn't imagine calling her anything else.

"I love her name," she said as he carried the formula into the kitchen.

"Me too," Ben called out.

She smiled down at the precious girl in her arms, who was making the sweetest sounds as she ate. *Sweet baby Bea.*

When Ben returned to the living room he said, "She probably needs a middle name."

"Maybe when Mason finds her mother, you'll want to use whatever name she'd given her," she suggested.

"What if she never gave her one? She didn't put a name in the note." He huffed out a breath. "Do you think he'll find her?"

She shrugged. "I hope so. Vic said he needs to know about what shots Bea's had, and I'd hate to think that we'd never know the reasons her mother left her."

"Yeah." He picked up the Pack 'n Play. "I'll get this set up in the bedroom. Come with me?"

She followed him up to his bedroom and sat on the bed to burp Bea while he set it up. She loved watching him do things for the baby. *Who am I kidding? I like to watch him do everything.*

He checked each hinge to make sure it was locked in place, and then he shook the whole playpen. "Okay. She's good to go."

"I forgot to grab a diaper. Would you mind?"

"Sure." He headed back downstairs, returning a minute later with a diaper. "Got it."

She motioned for him to come closer and kissed him. "Wipes?"

"Damn."

She heard him hurrying down the steps as she laid Bea on the bed. Bea opened her mouth and wiggled her arms, like she recognized Aurelia. Aurelia thought she might burst, she loved her so much. "Hi, baby girl," she said, offering her finger, which Bea immediately grabbed hold of. "Even though I was right in the same room with you tonight, I missed you. But I'm glad you got to spend time with your grandma and grandpa, all your aunts and uncles, and your little cousin, Louie." She thought of Flossie and knew she'd love to see Bea.

"Got the wipes," Ben said, and he set them on the bed. He ran his hand up Aurelia's back and said, "I hate it here."

"What are you talking about?" she asked as she changed Bea. "You love your house."

"I thought I did. But I think I loved knowing it was mine. It's never felt like a home except when you were in it."

She lifted Bea to her shoulder, patting her so she'd fall asleep, and thought about what he'd said. A few minutes later she felt Bea's body go limp and whispered, "Well, now me and Bea are in it, so it should feel good."

"It just feels *wrong*." He dipped his head to kiss Bea's cheek. Then he took her from Aurelia and placed her gently in the playpen.

Aurelia slid her fingers into the waist of Ben's jeans, pulling him closer as she said, "Then let me make it feel *right* . . ."

As she unzipped his pants, he said, "It's just too big. Everything is too far apart."

She sat on the edge of the bed and yanked down his jeans and briefs, and the wickedness that rose in his eyes nearly made her lose her mind.

"*So* big," she said as she wrapped her hand around his cock, loving the way he watched her. She dragged her tongue from base to tip, and he groaned appreciatively. "So *close*," she whispered, and slicked her tongue around the broad head.

His chin fell to his chest with a hiss, and he buried his hands in her hair. She lowered her mouth over him, taking him to the back of her throat. His hips rocked as she loved him. His hands fisted tighter, causing scintillating stings along her scalp. She'd never enjoyed giving oral sex, but with Ben everything was different. Seeing the heat in his eyes, feeling the restraint in his body as desire mounted inside him, and hearing the sinful noises he futilely tried to silence made her want to make him lose control.

She sucked harder, worked him faster. He ground out a curse and withdrew from her mouth, pulled her up to her feet, and took her in an urgent kiss.

"Love kissing you," he said hungrily as he made quick work of stripping them both naked and tossed her on the bed, following her down.

He entered her in one hard thrust, and they both moaned—immediately silencing themselves. Their eyes shot to the playpen, where Bea was fast asleep.

Ben's gaze hit Aurelia's with the ferocity of a lion who had just captured his prey, and that look drew a needy whimper from deep within her. His mouth covered hers hungrily, taking, loving, *devouring* her as they fell into a feverish rhythm. He pinned her hands to the mattress, and then his magical mouth claimed her neck.

"Oh God, *Ben*," she whisper-pleaded as he drove her to the brink—and held her there.

He drove deeper, sucked harder, catapulting her into delirium as she shattered into a million little pieces.

"I love you, baby," he ground out against her cheek as he surrendered to his own powerful release.

CHAPTER FOURTEEN

"TWO-STORY HOUSES ARE for the birds," Ben said as they walked into Aurelia's apartment the next morning. Bea had woken up twice last night, and he'd had to run downstairs to retrieve a bottle, and by the time he'd made it back upstairs, she'd been doing the wailing-stop-breathing thing that gave him a heart attack every damn time she did it.

Aurelia yawned and flopped onto the couch with Bea in her arms. "At least you got a good leg workout. I know you hate missing your morning runs."

"I do, but what I hate more is leaving you guys to go see Mason today." Ben dropped the playpen and bags, feeling guilty for having to leave her with Bea when she had her own work to do. But Mason liked to meet with his clients in person, to assess them, Ben guessed, though Mason had mentioned a contract and other paperwork. "Are you sure you're okay with Bea?"

"We're fine. Everly's starting the mural, and we have a delivery of books coming, so I'll be doing a lot of inventory. I'll bring Bea with me and work while she sleeps. I have two interviews lined up, but I can hold her while I do them if she's awake." She kicked her feet up on the coffee table and bent her knees, repositioning Bea on her legs. "Right, sweet pea? Daddy needs to go to his meeting and stop worrying."

"I have that meeting with Aiden Wednesday."

"I know. We're *fine*, Ben, today and Wednesday. You'll have her when you don't have meetings, and that'll give me time to give my undivided attention to the bookstore."

He sat down beside her, and she dragged her eyes appreciatively down his chest and said, "I love you in Armani." Turning her attention back to the baby, she said, "But we love Daddy in anything, don't we? Mostly *naked*, though." She'd whispered *naked*. "One day I won't be able to say that in front of her."

"But I hope you'll never stop thinking it." He turned her face and kissed her deeply. "Rels, I've been thinking. Let's stay here during the week. You need to be able to go up and down to your shop, and I can work from your apartment just as easily as I can work from my office."

"Fine with me."

Bea took hold of Aurelia's finger, and Aurelia made kissing noises. Bea's eyes widened, and her mouth opened in a smile. An honest-to-goodness smile!

"Did you see that, Rels? She *smiled!*"

Aurelia laughed. "That's because she's the smartest, cutest baby girl on earth."

"Make her do it again," Ben urged.

They spent the next fifteen minutes making kissy faces and soaking in all of Bea's adorable smiles.

"Remember what the books said? She might be too young to smile," Aurelia said between kissy faces. "These are probably reflex smiles, but you know what that means?"

Ben hugged her against his side, overflowing with love. "That she has the best reflexes on earth?"

"Exactly!"

"There's no way her smiles are caused by reflexes. Not when her little arms flap like an excited bird. I can't leave you guys," he said, feeling too torn to walk out the door. "How can I go all the way into the city, focus on my meeting with Mason, and then drive all the way back? I'll be gone all day. I'll miss so much with Bea, and I'll miss *both* of you like crazy."

"You *have* to find her mother, Ben. Bea will be doing all of this when you get back."

He groaned. "If you're wrong, there'll be hell to pay." He gave her a chaste kiss, and then he kissed Bea and said, "Be good for Relsy." He pushed to his feet. "She'll probably be *crawling* around by the time I get back."

Aurelia laughed. "Don't forget to take the letter that we found with her. I put it by your keys this morning. Did you grab it?"

"Yeah, I did. Thank you again for being with me in this."

"I think you should thank me for the years I was with you *before* this. Bea's an adorable incentive, and you know I love her, but never forget it was always *you* first, Benny boy."

Ben carried her words with him on the long drive into the city. He'd expected to experience at least a modicum of relief at having an ounce of freedom from his new, ever-present responsibilities, but as he drove, he longed to be with Aurelia and Bea. He cranked the music, driving faster than he should, reaching for the feelings of invincibility and adventure that had propelled him through thirty-plus years of life. But as he flew down the highway, what went through his mind wasn't excitement at having breathing room. Nope. He couldn't shake the knowledge that he was being foolish and irresponsible. What if he got into an accident? His attorney was still drawing up the papers to have him declared as Bea's father. What would happen to her if something happened to him? Would she be taken away from Aurelia? Would Aurelia *want* her without Ben?

His chest knotted at the thought.

He knew she would want Bea, but the idea of Aurelia shouldering that responsibility alone was too much to bear. He eased his foot from the gas pedal and felt the knots in his chest loosen. Pushing away the notion that he should grab the stars of freedom, which he no longer wanted, he focused on the road and his upcoming meeting with Mason.

By the time he arrived, he was more determined than ever to find Bea's mother.

He sat across from Mason Swift after giving him the details he could remember about Caroline, studying the man who was as stone-faced as Bodhi. He had military-short dark hair, manicured scruff, and a steady gaze that rode the fine line between intimidating and regal. He wore a crisp black dress shirt and expensive slacks. His stare told Ben he was not into bullshit, and his Movado watch revealed a penchant for quality. Ben just hoped that *quality* carried over to his job. He didn't give a rat's ass if the guy wore sweatpants and told time by the sun—which this guy could probably do—as long as he could find the woman who had abandoned Bea.

"What are the chances of finding her?" Ben asked.

"That depends on how solid your information is. *If* Caroline is her real name and *if* she works for the hotel, then we'll find her. That'll take a little time. Assuming we find a match, then we'll see if she's *still* working there, and—"

"And if she's not still working there? At least you'll have her home address, right?"

His brows lifted. "*If* she's still living at the same address." He sat back, the muscles in his jaw bunching. "Clearly this pregnancy came at a bad time. Maybe she'd lost her job or her home. Maybe she was sleeping with the boss and he fired her when she got pregnant. We won't know until we get our first lead. If we find out her full name or an address—present or past—we can then track her down with credit card records, assuming she has one. We'll also check with hospitals in the area to see if we can track her down that way, but that's a stretch.

A baby that's abandoned has a higher chance of having been born at home." He paused, and then he said, "Ben, you're a businessman. You understand the complexities of human nature. This woman could be anywhere. We're looking for the veritable needle in a haystack."

Ben leaned forward, worrying with his hands. "What can I do to help find her?"

"Sounds to me like you and your girlfriend have already done all the right things. You've come to the best. If she can be found, I'll find her. You're sure there's no one else it could be?"

Ben shook his head. "Not that I remember."

Mason cocked his head curiously.

"I know how that sounds, but seriously, I can't remember anyone else."

"No judgment here, Ben. I work for you."

"Thanks. I appreciate that," he said, but he still felt like a dick. It didn't matter that everyone had hookups. *Everyone except Aurelia, apparently.* "Do you get this kind of thing a lot?"

"Babies left on a doorstep?" Mason almost cracked a smile, but it did nothing to soften his rigid exterior. "Not specifically, no. But tracking down someone a client has slept with? Sure, and a whole lot worse. I used to be a bodyguard. Let's just say there are reasons certain people *need* bodyguards. I spend a lot of time tracking down those *reasons.*"

Aurelia had always believed there was nothing she couldn't handle, but by midday Bea was beginning to make her question that. The day had started out calmly enough. She'd put the bouncy seat that Piper had given them to good use. Bea loved it, which gave Aurelia time to tackle emails, confirm the book signings for her grand opening, and get Everly set up to start painting. But as the day progressed, Bea got fussier, and nothing seemed to soothe her. Aurelia had practically worn a path in the hardwood floors trying to mollify her. She'd even gone up to the apartment, thinking the familiar sights and smells might help. But it seemed to make things even worse, and every time she'd put Bea down, she'd cried.

It had started raining midday, so taking her for a walk in the stroller wasn't an option. Eventually Bea had taken a short nap, and Aurelia had started working on inventory. When Bea woke up, she was still fussy even after being fed and changed. Aurelia tried to do inventory while holding her. It had taken twice as long to get through a box of books, but at least she'd gotten through a few. Now she was trying to interview Lazarus Parsons, a nice college kid with cocoa skin, short dreadlocks, and just about the friendliest smile Aurelia had ever seen. Aurelia had been pacing with Bea throughout the interview in a futile effort to keep Bea from fussing, and Lazarus paced alongside her, kindly answering her questions.

"I worked in the library in high school. For the last few months I've been working at the pizza place because the hours are flexible, but books are my *jam*," Lazarus said. "I want to be a writer one day, and I read just about everything—nonfiction, fiction, graphic novels. Professor Dalton said your hours were flexible."

"Yes," she said, trying not to show how frazzled she felt as she bounced the crying baby on her shoulder. "I was hoping to get ten to fifteen hours a week. Is that doable?"

"Yeah. No problem."

Bea let out a loud wail, causing Kase and the other workers to look over. Aurelia cringed. "Sorry!" she called out to them. "I'm so sorry about this, Lazarus. I know how unprofessional this looks, and I assure you, working here won't be like this all the time."

"That's okay. I have a three-month-old niece and three younger siblings. Have you tried laying her on her belly across your legs and . . . I can show you, actually." He looked around and pulled over a chair, then sat down and held out his arms. "I babysit a lot. My mom got remarried and had two more kids. They're four and five now. I learned this trick for when they had bellyaches."

"Oh. Um, sure, thank you." She handed Bea to him.

"Hello, baby girl," he said with the confidence of a boy who's had loads of experience with babies. He laid her on her belly across his legs and began bouncing his legs as he patted her back.

Aurelia dropped to her knees beside him. "Are you sure about this? Will that hurt her brain? You're not supposed to shake babies. What if she pukes?"

He chuckled as Bea's whimpers became softer.

"It does something good to their stomachs." He patted Bea's back, and soon she quieted. "It would make me puke, but I'm not a baby."

"Holy cow. You're hired."

He grinned. "For real? 'Cause I would love to work here."

"Yes, for real, but you've got to tell me all your baby secrets."

They finished the rest of the interview in blissful quiet, and when she took Bea back, she was fast asleep. She walked Lazarus out and went to check on Everly's progress. She didn't dare put Bea down for fear she'd wake up.

Everly stood on a ladder painting the background, which was mostly done. The right side of the wall was varying shades of light blue with fluffy white clouds, which blended into darker blues as the mural progressed toward the left, ending in midnight blue with sparkling white stars forming the words, OH, THE THINGS YOU'LL SEE . . . She'd painted bubbles to give the lighter blue skies a sealike appearance. The final picture would include colorful fish, a smiling crescent moon, green plants with bright pink and white flowers, and in the center an ark filled with characters from children's books: *Clifford the Big Red Dog*, *The Cat in the Hat*, one of the monsters from *Where the Wild Things Are*, and several others.

"That's beautiful," Aurelia said softly.

Everly continued painting, and Aurelia realized she had earbuds in. She moved toward the wall and waved to get her attention.

Everly pulled out her earbuds and said, "Sorry. I plugged in when Bea started crying."

"It's okay. Sorry about that. The mural is amazing. Kids are going to love it."

"Thanks." She smiled at Bea and said, "She finally tuckered herself out?"

"Lazarus, the guy I just interviewed, showed me a trick that worked like a charm."

"I hope you hired him."

"Damn right I did. I'm glad my other interview rescheduled. It was embarrassing trying to interview while she was screaming." Bea whimpered again. Aurelia patted her back, bouncing a little in hopes of soothing her, but her cries escalated.

"Wanna run after Lazarus?"

"*Ugh.* I'm going to try the thing he showed me. I feel so helpless not knowing how to help her."

"Good luck." Everly climbed down the ladder and headed for the bathroom.

Aurelia sat down, laid Bea across her lap, and bounced her legs while patting her back exactly as Lazarus had shown her—but Bea continued wailing. She tried bouncing slower, faster, rubbing her back in circles, up and down, and straight across, but nothing helped. Finally she gave up and put the baby on her shoulder, patting her as she paced. Her phone vibrated, and she pulled it from her pocket and saw a voicemail from Ben, only now remembering that it had vibrated when she was interviewing. She put it on speakerphone and set the phone on the counter, needing both hands to try to soothe Bea.

"Hey, Rels," Ben's deep voice boomed from the phone. "I'm on my way back from Mason's. He was great." Bea's whimpers quieted. "How are things going there? I miss you guys. I hope everything's okay." Bea stopped fussing. "Love you both."

The message ended, and Bea let out another bloodcurdling wail. Aurelia fumbled with her phone, replaying the message, and Bea quieted again. *Holy shit.* Every time the message ended, Bea cried, but the sound of Ben's voice silenced her.

Aurelia spotted Everly coming out of the bathroom and called out, "Ev! Come here!" She played the message again. "Do you see this? She misses Ben. I need to find an audiobook that sounds like him. Can you help me?"

Bea cried again, and Aurelia restarted the message as they headed for the boxes of audiobooks.

"Find anything by Zachary Webber. I think he narrated *Anything for Love* by Charlotte Sterling."

"Wait until Ben hears you have a thing for Zach Webber."

"Hey, it's not that easy to conjure a sexy voice, but you can bet your butt it was Ben in my fantasies, not Zachary. I pray this works before we all lose our minds." She restarted the voicemail while simultaneously scanning titles. "Here it is! Wait! I can listen to the audio on my phone. That's easier. Can you hold Bea for one sec? She'll cry, but hopefully Zach's voice will remedy that."

Everly took the baby as Bea let out another shrill cry. "Holy crap. *Hurry!*"

"I'm trying!" She navigated to the audiobook and hit *play*, turning it up as loud as it would go.

She took Bea from Everly as Zachary's soothing and commanding voice filled the air, sending chills down Aurelia's spine at how similar it was to Ben's. Bea's crying hitched and, after a few short gasps, dialed down to sporadic whimpers. Aurelia rocked from side to side.

"We need rocking chairs," she said.

"The heck with rocking chairs. You need Zachary Webber's voice box." Everly hiked a thumb over her shoulder in the direction of the mural, and then she turned and headed back toward her paints.

Zachary's voice did wonders, but the book had a male and a female narrator, as it was told from both the hero's and heroine's points of view. Every time the woman's voice came on, Bea cried. Aurelia fast-forwarded through those sections, making a mental note to find a book narrated by only Zachary.

After twenty minutes she got brave and set Bea in the bouncy seat with the phone beside her. She listened contentedly as long as Aurelia skipped the woman's narrations. After the first few times, Bea only whimpered briefly at the sound of the woman's voice, as if she knew Aurelia would quickly make the transition. She might have lungs like a hyena, but she was definitely the smartest baby on the planet.

When Ben walked in more than an hour later, Bea had finally fallen asleep. Aurelia sat in the middle of several stacks of books, holding a slice of pizza, and shushed him with a finger over her lips. "She *just* fell asleep."

His brows slanted. He cocked his head to the side, his eyes serious. "You let her listen to *porn?*"

"What?" She realized Zachary was narrating a sexy scene. "It's not *porn*. It's contemporary romance, and for your information, Bea cried almost all day." She told him about her chaotic afternoon. "When I listened to your message on speakerphone, she quieted right down. Zachary sounds a lot like you, so—"

"You listen to this stuff? Wait. Don't answer that." Ben pulled her into his arms and said, "I'm sorry you had a bad day."

"It wasn't bad, but it could have been better." She kissed him, and then she held up the slice of pizza for him to take a bite.

"I'll have her all day tomorrow, so you can make up for lost time today." He took a bite of the pizza and said, "It's cold."

"Welcome to our new normal."

CHAPTER FIFTEEN

BEN CRADLED THE phone against his shoulder Wednesday morning, talking to Bridgette as he fed Bea. She had gotten up three times last night, and he felt like a walking zombie. "Four to six *months* of sleepless nights? I was hoping you'd have a few tips that might help her sleep through the night."

"Don't you remember how exhausted I was when Louie was a baby?" Bridgette asked. "Oh, wait. My memory of those crazy days is starting to come back to me. As I recall, you scoffed at me and said that you were used to staying up half the night and you couldn't understand *why* I was so tired. So even if I had tips, why should I share them with you?"

He knew she was only joking, but she was right. He had been an arrogant twentysomething when Louie was born, and though he didn't remember saying that to her, he probably had.

"You're right. I deserve to be light-headed with exhaustion in my meeting this morning."

"Believe it or not, that's going to be easier than watching Bea. How's Aurelia this morning? Do *not* leave without giving her time to shower first, or she'll never get one in. Are you letting her get any sleep? I know you're a new couple, and there's the whole insatiable-appetite-for-each-other thing going on, but the girl needs her sleep if she's going to help you with the baby."

"Bridgette," he warned.

Bridgette laughed. "Oh my God, Ben. Don't even pretend you're not all over each other. Everyone noticed the other night at dinner. It was like you were two just-uncorked champagne bottles. Lust bubbled out of both of you."

He closed his eyes, remembering how Talia had walked in on them making out in the pantry when they'd offered to do the dishes. "Stop," he said. "She slept as late as she could, and she's taking a shower." He knew Aurelia had a full day's work ahead of her, including an interview and book deliveries, and she was also hoping to get a jump on filling the bookshelves. He worried about how much she had on her plate, but Aurelia assured him that she could handle it.

"Why don't you just ask Mom to watch Bea for a few hours?"

"No. I'll be working from home the rest of the week. We've got this, Bridge."

"Uh-huh," she said lightly. "You know, both of you are used to doing everything on your own, but it's okay to ask for help."

He heard Aurelia in the bedroom and said, "That's why I called, asking for tips. Remember?"

"Okay, you're right. Here they are. Hire a night nanny, which you can *easily* afford, or sleep in separate rooms so *one* of you can get some sleep. You do have a house you can go to, Ben. Give the girl a break. She's gone from being a single woman opening her first business to basically being the stepmom to a baby inside of two weeks. That's a *lot* to deal with."

He gritted his teeth as Aurelia came out of the bedroom looking a little more bright-eyed than she had earlier—and sexy as sin in a tan miniskirt and a thin white sweater. He dragged his eyes down her body to the black high-tops on her feet and spotted the red ink of the quote she'd written on them. A quote he knew by heart, because she'd written it there when she'd first moved back to Sweetwater. *It's the possibility of having a dream come true that makes life interesting.*

She pointed to Bea and mouthed, *Want me to take her?*

He shook his head and smiled. "Bridge, I've got to get to my meeting. Thanks for the help, and tell Bodhi that Mason was awesome."

After ending the call, he kissed Aurelia. "Good morning, beautiful."

"What did Bridgette say?"

"That it'll be four to six *months* before she sleeps through the night."

"That's okay." She put her hand on his waist, kissed Bea, and said, "We'll just start going to bed earlier. What's four to six months in the grand scheme of things?"

"I couldn't love you more, you know that?" He kissed her again. "I could take her with me today," he suggested, imagining himself as Superdad, cradling the baby while negotiating schedules with Aiden and the staff.

"Ben, *no*. We're a team. Yesterday you were in the game. Today it's my turn. Tomorrow you'll be in it again." She rubbed Bea's back and said, "We've got this, right, sweet pea?"

He set down Bea's bottle and lifted her to his shoulder. Then he put his arm around Aurelia, pulling her in closer. "Isn't it supposed to get easier to leave you two with time?"

"You're just in daddy mode right now. Once you get into the office, the fiercely aggressive businessman inside you will come roaring out, and you won't even remember why you didn't want to leave this morning." She pulled out her phone and snapped a picture of him and the baby. "I'll text this picture to you so you can stare at her during the meeting." Her eyes flicked playfully up to his and she said, "I'm sure Aiden will appreciate you being sidetracked and getting all googly-eyed in the boardroom."

"I'd like to get you all googly-eyed in the *bedroom*." He slapped her ass. "Swap with me." He handed her the baby and took her phone, snapping a picture of the two of them. "*That's* the picture I want to stare at."

Aurelia hammed it up as Ben took more pictures. She puckered against Bea's cheek with smiling eyes; then she held Bea above her head, which Bea loved.

"Let's both kiss her cheeks at the same time and take a selfie," she said, moving next to Ben. "*That's* the picture *I* want to stare at."

It took five tries to fit them all in the picture, and they both ended up laughing. He might be exhausted, but everything he had never known he'd wanted was right there in that room, and he wouldn't trade either of them for the world.

"Can you text me *all* of those pictures?" he asked as he set her phone on the table. "I have a surprise for you."

"A surprise? I was hoping for another one of your fabulous foot rubs tonight."

He leaned in for a kiss. Monday night Bea had fallen asleep on his chest while he was reviewing documents for his meeting on the couch and Aurelia was reading another baby book. They'd had their feet in each other's laps, giving foot massages. Aurelia had fallen asleep with a small smile on her face, and given the chaotic day she'd had at work, that smile meant the world to him. They'd slept there, with both his girls safe and happy, until Bea had woken up to eat.

"Nothing will preclude another foot rub, babe. Promise." He went to the bookshelf and retrieved a small handheld recorder from the top of a row of books.

"You hide things up there?" Cradling Bea in her arms, she said, "I'm making a mental note to have a library ladder installed."

"Oh, so you don't want me to give you surprises?"

She pretended to zip her mouth closed.

"You said that Bea was calm when she heard my voice, so while you were in the bookstore yesterday, I taped myself reading to her."

"Are you *kidding*? You did that?" She cradled Bea in one arm and pulled him closer. "You're the best daddy in the world, you know that?" She pressed her lips to his and said, "Thank you!"

"I've got a lot to learn, but I'm hoping that might make things easier for you today. Now you can stop listening to Zachary Whatshisname."

"You mean *Bea* can stop listening to him," she said.

"I meant *you*. At the end of the tape there's a reading meant for your ears only." He kissed her again, and she smiled so big, it illuminated the room.

"Benjamin Dalton, did you read something *naughty* for me?" she asked with a lift of her brows.

"You'll have to listen and see." He grabbed his keys. "Text me if you need anything. I'll keep my phone on vibrate during the meeting. I love you, babe." He kissed her. Then he kissed Bea's head and said, "See you soon, peanut. Be good for"—holy shit, he almost said *Mommy*—"Relsy, okay?"

Ben downed coffee throughout the day as he met with their finance and legal teams about the offer they were preparing for Barrister Hotels. His mind whirled as they went over figures and discussed travel plans and schedules. Ben had worked his ass off to make this deal come to fruition. His head should be in the game so deep, nothing else registered. This was the American dream, finally seeing all his hard work come together, and yet his mind wasn't even in the outfield. It was miles away with his daughter and Aurelia, and rehashing his earlier conversation with Bridgette.

"Ben?" Nadia Clayton, the head of their financial team, was a cut-throat redhead. She sat ramrod straight, wore her hair in a tight bun, kept their finance department on an even tighter rein, and she was staring at Ben over the rims of her black-framed reading glasses.

Shit. He'd zoned out and hadn't heard the question. He glanced around the table at the rest of their financial and legal teams, who were watching him expectantly. He looked at Aiden, hoping to catch a sign of what he'd missed. But Aiden was staring down at his phone, thumbing out a message, his brows slanted angrily.

"Sorry, Nadia," Ben said. "I missed the question."

She smiled inquisitively and said, "It wasn't a question. I wanted to be sure you heard the figures. By conservative projections, if we follow the outlined strategies, we should see a thirteen percent profit within the first twelve to eighteen months, with a four- to five-year projection netting one point eight billion dollars."

"Thank you, and the wholesale partnerships?" he asked.

"We went over the partnership agreements again from the two lower-earning locations," she said, "and we concur that bringing in new wholesale partnerships should create an immediate increase in revenue."

"Ben, we'll need teams ready to deploy as soon as the deal is done," director Garth Anziano added. "As you know, two of the locations have had declining reviews for the past several months. We'll need to focus on restaffing immediately in the European and island locations."

"Got it," Ben said. "All of that was to be expected—"

"Sorry," Aiden interrupted, pushing to his feet with an anguished look on his face. "I need to take this call privately."

Ben wondered what was going on to have caused that look and said, "We'll hold discussions until you return." He was thankful for the break. As the others talked quietly over documents, Ben sent Aurelia a quick text. *Hey, babe. How's it going?* Her response came in the form of a picture of Bea's tiny hand with the caption, *Can you see me wrapped around her tiny fingers?* She'd added a kissing emoticon and a heart.

Aiden returned to the room red-faced, his jaw clenched. He was usually the epitome of a poised professional, but as his hands curled into fists, Ben knew something bad had happened, and with Remi's stalker situation, he feared the worst.

"Clear the room," Ben commanded. "We'll reconvene shortly."

As everyone gathered their laptops and documents, Ben pulled Aiden to the side, speaking quietly. "What's going on? Did something happen to Remi?"

Speaking through gritted teeth, he said, "Something is *going to* happen to her when I get back to LA." He shook his head and said, "Her bodyguards lost her. How the fuck do you lose a twenty-five-year-old woman who can't go outside without being hounded by the press?"

"Jesus. Do you think it's her stalker? Did you call the police?"

"I wouldn't be standing here if I thought she was in immediate danger." Aiden paced the floor. "She ditched them again, and you know how I know that? She sent me a text threatening not to return to her house unless I fired her bodyguards."

Ben chuckled, then quickly schooled his expression. Remi hated having bodyguards. She also despised the press and everything about being an actress, although she loved acting. "Can't you track her phone to find out where she is?"

"You know my sister. She nixed that ages ago."

"Sounds like Remi. Where could she go and not be seen?" Ben asked. "Does she have a friend she'd stay with who wouldn't out her?"

Aiden shook his head. He had the classic good looks of David Beckham, turning heads everywhere he went. But Ben knew that between business, watching out for Remi, and managing her career, Aiden didn't have time for much else.

Aiden turned a seriously strained face to Ben and said, "I know you worked your ass off for this deal, and this morning I had every intent of offering to take over your end of the travel, but I can't do it. Not knowing Remi might be putting herself in danger."

"I'd never expect you to do that," Ben reassured him. "Let's figure out where Remi is and get her to safety. Then we can figure out the business. Family first. *Always.*"

Aiden scoffed. "I have lived my entire life putting her first. Why does she do this time and time again?"

"Dude, she's not a kid anymore. She feels hamstrung by the press, by the frigging stalker, and even though it's wrong, she probably feels that way by her bodyguards. I get why she took off, even though I don't agree with it. But you've got to get through to her. If you think this stalker is trouble, she can't do this shit."

Aiden ground his back teeth and said, "He's trouble. He broke into her house last week. I've got to track her down, and I know the timing sucks, but I can't concentrate on this project, and I have a feeling you can't, either. You've looked like a caged tiger since you walked in here."

Ben stared out the window and crossed his arms. When he'd earned his first million, he'd thought he'd made it. When he was on the cover of *Forbes* magazine, he couldn't imagine anything feeling more incredible. But nothing compared to seeing Bea smile or waking up with Aurelia in his arms. More money, more hotels, none of it would mean shit if his life with them fell apart. It didn't take much for him to realize what he had to do.

"But Garth and Miller can," Ben relented. Miller Crenshaw was another lead director at their firm, with skills equivalent to Garth's.

Aiden's eyes narrowed. "What are you saying?"

"That maybe it's time to stop being a control freak and let others lead. We've groomed them to step up to the plate. Let's give them a shot at the big game. We can oversee it from a broader perspective, let them do the travel, work with the teams to analyze what needs to be done. Hell, we can still make the final decisions, but have them do the intricacies that we usually handle."

Aiden slid his hands into the pockets of his slacks. "This is a trick, right? Because you won't even let anyone make you coffee."

Ben grinned. "I've changed."

"I hear diaper duty and a good woman will do that to a man. You sure, Ben? This isn't the type of thing you can take back once it's done."

"Sure we can. We own the company. We can do anything we want. But we won't have to. Garth and Miller have been loyal employees. They've earned this, and so have we." He patted Aiden on the back and said, "I met with that investigator I told you about, Mason Swift, and hired him to find Bea's mother. You want to call him about Remi?"

"No. I've got a guy. I already sent him a message. I'm thinking about getting her chipped, like you would a pet."

"Dude . . ." Ben laughed, and then he said more seriously, "Think I can do that to Bea? For when she's a teenager?"

It was after five o'clock when Ben finally left the office. He stopped on the way out of Sweetwater and picked up peanut M&M's, bubble bath, and a bottle of wine, excited to share his decision with Aurelia. He drove to Harmony Pointe thinking about all the trials and tribulations Aiden had experienced while raising Remi and what his own parents had gone through with him and his sisters, and he had no doubt that he'd come to the right decision. Handing management of this new takeover to trusted employees was absolutely the right thing to do. There was too much on his plate for him to give his full attention to business development, especially when he'd rather give it to his girls.

As he drove down Main Street, passing the park, it was easy to picture Aurelia standing before a crowd in the gazebo, dressed in one of her period costumes as she read a passage from a classic novel. He used to love watching her when she was unaware of his presence. It had been easy to slip between the rows of books and watch her from afar, openly admiring her confidence as well as her beauty. She didn't need a stage to command the attention of customers. When she read, her inflection alone had stopped people in their tracks. When she'd told Ben she was doing readings, he'd thought she was nuts to put herself out there like that. People could be harsh critics, and New Yorkers weren't known for their gentle ways. The first time he'd gone to see her read, he'd done so wanting to protect her from those critics. But within the first few minutes, he'd known she was meant for that very spotlight. Aurelia didn't merely *read* the passages. She *became* the characters, as if the words had awakened another person lying dormant inside her. She was captivating from start to finish. He'd never wondered if he'd return for a second reading. He'd *known* he wouldn't miss a single one.

He passed Chapter One, smiling to himself. Aurelia had found her new beginning all right, and he was so fucking thankful it included him and Bea. He parked around back, grabbed the goodies he'd bought, and took the steps two at a time up to her apartment door.

"Rels?" he said as he threw open the door.

"Shh!" Piper shushed him from the couch, where she was feeding Bea—and sitting next to Remi Divine.

"What the . . . ? *Remi?* Aiden is out of his mind with worry. What are you doing here?"

"Long story," Remi said with a sigh. She had a dark baseball cap pulled low over her forehead, and she wore a pair of torn jeans and a flannel shirt tied at the waist, the sleeves rolled up to her elbows.

"Nice disguise," he said sarcastically, as if a flannel shirt and hat could hide her identity. "Where's Aurelia?"

Piper pointed to the bedroom. "She's sleeping. Willow and I got SOS texts from her. Willow was in the middle of making a wedding cake, so I came over."

"SOS?" Ben closed the distance between them, looking at Bea. "What happened?"

"Let's just say it was a *long* day," Piper said.

"No one's hurt?" Ben asked.

"No," Piper said. "Just exhausted."

Ben set a serious stare on Remi and said, "I'll deal with you in a minute."

He went into the bedroom and found Aurelia curled up on the bed, hugging a pillow, tears streaming down her cheeks—and his voice playing from the recorder. He set the things he'd brought for her on the dresser and crawled onto the bed, gathering her in his arms. Her eyes were puffy from lack of sleep and from her tears, and her nose was pink from crying. How could he have been so selfish?

"Babe, what happened? What's wrong?"

"I *tried*, Ben. I thought I could do it all, and I didn't want to let you down, but this is *so* freaking hard. Bea must hate me. She cried so much today. Everything I did was wrong."

"Bea doesn't hate you, Rels. She loves you. I'm so sorry. Why didn't you call me?"

She swiped at her tears. "Because you have enough on your plate, and I kept thinking I could figure it out. I *wanted* to figure it out, but nothing worked. Now I'm behind on inventory, and I'm supposed to see my grandma for lunch tomorrow, and I'll probably have to put that off." She snuggled into him and said, "I'm so sorry, Ben. I don't mean to be such a loser. She's *one* baby. Women care for babies all the time. I just *suck*. I think we need help, and I hate saying that, because I want to be with her all the time. But apparently I'm not good enough at it."

"No, sweetheart. *I* suck. This is my fault. Bea is my responsibility, not yours." He held her tighter, kissing her temple. "You're great at taking care of Bea. That's not the trouble. You're exhausted, and you're just starting your business, and we came in and took over your life in the blink of an eye. *I'm* sorry, Aurelia. I'll take Bea to my house for a few days—"

"No." Her face crumpled, rivers of tears sliding down her cheeks. "I don't want you to leave. I just need a minute to catch up on my sleep or something."

His father's advice sailed through his mind. *Give them a physical space of their own . . . a place to be alone with their own thoughts, to make their own decisions, and figure out how they feel about things.*

"You need more than a minute, babe. You need your life back, at least parts of it."

"I want *you and Bea* in my life," she insisted.

"I know. That's not what I meant. You can't be expected to put your business on hold for my baby. I love that you're part of our lives, but I want you healthy and happy, not overwhelmed and sad. We need help with Bea, and I'm going to line some up. But we can figure that out later. Right now I want you to rest." He brushed a lock of hair, damp with tears, from her cheek and kissed her there. "Did you know Remi is here?"

She nodded. "She's hiding from her bodyguards. I told her she could stay with us for a few days."

He made a mental note to let Aiden know she was okay. "Good. You could use the girl time."

"Ben . . ."

"It's fine, babe. I *love* you, and I hate that I did this to you. I'll take Bea, and you do your own thing."

"But I don't want to do my own thing," she pleaded. "I want to be with you and Bea."

"You may not realize it, but you need a breather, Rels, and that's okay. When you're feeling better, we'll figure this out." He held her until she stopped crying, and then he held her longer, because for the second time that day, he had to leave the person he always wanted by his side.

When Aurelia fell asleep, he thanked Piper for being there for her, and after Piper left, he said to Remi, "You need to call your brother."

"I just need a night, Ben," Remi said pleadingly. "*One* night without having people breathing down my back. If you think about my timing, it's like fate stepped in. I think Aurelia and I can both use a good dose of Flossie tomorrow."

He gritted his teeth to keep from arguing with her. Then he picked up the playpen and Bea's carrier, in which she was sleeping, and headed out of Harmony Pointe with his baby girl and all her supplies, feeling as though he were leaving a piece of them both behind.

CHAPTER SIXTEEN

AURELIA STUMBLED OUT of the bedroom at ten o'clock Thursday morning feeling like she'd slept for a month, despite having gotten up twice during the night. She'd woken both times with a start, having thought she'd heard Bea crying. But she'd been met with an empty bedroom. Her sheets smelled like Ben, and she'd lain awake wondering if Bea had woken up right then and if Ben was doing okay with her. She missed them even more than she'd thought she would, and when she'd seen the M&M's and wine Ben had left on her dresser, it had driven that longing even deeper.

"I was beginning to wonder if I should put a mirror under your nose and make sure you were still breathing," Remi said from her perch on a barstool by the counter.

"Sorry. I guess I was more exhausted than I realized." She poured herself a cup of coffee and climbed onto a stool beside Remi, who was bright-eyed and fully awake. "Isn't it only seven your time? How long have you been up?"

Remi shrugged. "I haven't been sleeping much lately." She sipped her coffee and said, "A stalker will do that to a girl."

"Remi, that's not funny."

"I know." She looked down at her coffee. "They broke in last week. It was creepy. They smashed the glass cabinet where I keep my awards, but they didn't take anything. Although I didn't check my underwear drawer." She laughed half-heartedly. "I didn't want to know."

"That's so scary. Why on earth are you dodging your bodyguards? I'd stick to them like glue."

"Because I'm sick of living my life under a microscope. I feel like I'm in jail." She rested her head on Aurelia's shoulder and said, "Thank you for letting me stay with you. Are you okay?"

"No," Aurelia admitted. "I feel like such a loser."

Remi sat up and said, "You mean because you're *human*?"

"It's just, I *love* Bea and I *love* Ben, and I want to be with them. He trusted me with his daughter, and I had to have his *sister* come to my rescue."

"You are *way* too hard on yourself. I went online to this parenting site this morning to see what other parents do when they feel like this, and, *girlfriend*, you are not alone. Women are hiding in their pantries, bawling their eyes out, and then sucking it up the rest of the day to care for screaming kids. Most of the moms with babies Bea's age take naps when the baby does, and you're going full speed all day and probably all night."

"Well, they've gone through childbirth. It's different."

"Ohmygod. Really? You can't believe that. I mean, sure, they hurt all over, and I'm sure giving birth is hard work, but you can't think that caring for an infant isn't just as exhausting, whether or not you gave birth to her. Plus, you're trying to set up a business *while* caring for her. Give yourself a break. I couldn't do it, and I'd bet Ben's sisters couldn't either."

Aurelia sat up and said, "All I know is that I love her and Ben, I missed them last night, and I miss them now. And I don't want to cry in a pantry, but thank you. It feels good knowing I'm not that far from normal. You know all those commercials where you see the new mom loving up her baby? The ones where everything is sunshine and smiles? Someone should make commercials with new moms who have their clothes on backward, their hair askew, and dark circles under their eyes, shuffling around like zombies."

Remi laughed. "I'll bring that up to my agent."

"I'm not kidding. I mean, when it's me and Ben, we do okay. How do single moms do it all without tons of help? The media is *so* misleading."

"Want to hear something funny?" Remi asked, looking a little uneasy.

"Yes. Please make me laugh."

Remi climbed off the stool, looking cute in a pair of black leggings and a white shirt that probably cost more than Aurelia's car, and said, "When I heard you bought this place, I was jealous."

"Why? You have *everything*. You're an A-list actress, everyone loves you—"

"Even my creepy stalker," Remi said in a singsong voice.

"Stop smiling. *That's* creepy."

"Sorry. But you're right. The media is misleading. You think I have it all." Remi sauntered over to the refrigerator and said, "But I wasn't kidding. I'm sick of living under a microscope. I want a simpler life with friends like you and the Daltons who love me for me and not because I'm an actress. I want Aiden to stop feeling like he has to protect me all the time." She grabbed an apple from the fridge and said, "But I want to keep acting, so we both know my life will continue to be what it is until *I* make a change."

"Oh, Remi. I wish I had the answers for you. I wish I had the answers for *me*."

"Your answers seem simple," Remi said. "Ben has obviously loved you for a long time. I remember when I first met him, he gave off this vibe like he was comparing everyone to someone else. I even asked Aiden about it."

"Really? What did Aiden say?"

"That Ben could have any woman he wanted and to stay away from him." She laughed and bit into her apple. "Are you going to shower before we see Flossie, or what?"

"Yeah. Let me just send Ben a quick text and make sure he and Bea are okay." She grabbed her phone from the coffee table, where she'd left it last night, and when she turned it on, three text messages appeared. The first was from Willow. *Are you okay? Sorry I was busy yesterday. Call me. Love you.* The next two were from Ben. One was the picture of her and Ben kissing Bea on the cheeks that he'd taken yesterday, but it was one of the ones where she was cut off. The next message read, *We left our hearts in Harmony Pointe. Love and miss you. B&B.*

Tears filled her eyes.

"Uh-oh." Remi peered over her shoulder at the messages. "Aw, Aurelia! *That's* what I want. That's *everything* right there . . ."

"That's my Ben," she whispered as she thumbed out a response. *Thank you for knowing what I needed when I was too exhausted to think straight. I miss you guys so much. We're going to my grandma's. I'll call you when I get back. Love you both. Xox.*

Flossie McBride was a sprite of a woman at four ten, with long silver hair and a penchant for fashion that Aurelia had always admired but definitely had not inherited. The few times she'd tried to find a style she felt comfortable in other than jeans, comfy tees, and sneakers, she'd felt like an impostor. It was her grandmother who had helped her accept and embrace her own style with three simple words—*You are perfect.* She'd spoken those words just about every time Aurelia complained about not being enough in any aspect of her life. Her grandmother's loving compliment sank bone deep over the years, giving Aurelia more confidence than any style ever could have. Although Flossie had always been a leader in the confidence department. She'd kept her maiden name as a way to honor her father at a time when it hadn't been typical to do so.

As Aurelia knocked on her grandmother's door, she realized that in her love for Bea and Ben, she finally knew the unconditional love it took to say words and truly mean them.

The door opened, and her grandmother's crimson lips stretched wide into the closed-mouth smile Aurelia loved. She was dressed in black slacks and a long-sleeve black shirt, with a double strand of faux pearls hanging to her navel and a lemon-yellow shawl that draped to her knees. Her long silver hair was swept up in a braided updo that always looked to Aurelia like her grandmother had spent hours in a salon. But Flossie rarely spent hours doing anything, except maybe cooking. She was energy in motion most of the time, though these days, during visits with Aurelia, she liked to stay in and talk, rather than race around to see gardens, museums, or a show, as they used to.

"My sweet bubbelah," her grandmother said. "And Remi, my faraway girl. What a lovely surprise to see you again. Come here, my sweethearts." She waved her open arms and hugged them both at the same time.

Aurelia filled her lungs to capacity during their long embrace. She hadn't realized she'd been living on partial breaths, rushing from one thing to the next, for *weeks*, probably for the better part of a year. But her grandmother's warmth had always centered her. Even in the craziest of times, during finals week in college or when she was making the decision to move from the city to Sweetwater, a simple hug, a phone conversation, or one of her grandmother's beloved handwritten letters would make everything clearer.

"Come inside, my lovelies," Flossie said. "I've just made a feast!"

As they followed her in, Aurelia's heart filled up as she took in the aromas coming from the kitchen. She'd know the scent of her grandmother's bourekas and meatballs anywhere.

"Grandma, you didn't have to go to all this trouble," Aurelia said.

Flossie waved dismissively. "Thank goodness I did. Remi needs a good meal before she blows away with the wind." She wrapped her hand around Remi's arm and said, "You are going to eat today, aren't you?"

"Absolutely," Remi said. "After the last few weeks, I deserve a home-cooked meal."

"Good girl," Flossie said.

Aurelia looked over the living room. When her grandfather had passed away, she'd wondered if she'd feel his absence in a smaller way over time, but he was *everywhere*. His smiling face was proudly displayed in elegant frames on the surface of nearly every piece of furniture, which they'd moved from their home in Sweetwater where Aurelia had grown up. Even the furniture held warm memories. She'd broken the iron-and-glass curio cabinet when, at nine years old, she'd tried to do a cartwheel in the living room. After cleaning up the mess, her grandfather had coaxed her into trying again until she got it right. The intricately carved end tables that had always been piled high with books now held books and photographs. Even the windowsill overlooking the gardens below displayed pictures of her grandfather, of Aurelia's mother, Abigail, and of Aurelia and a number of her friends. The same blue-tufted sofa where Aurelia had lain when she had the flu as a little girl boasted multicolored pillows, anchoring the cozy room beneath an enormous colorful abstract painting of a wild horse running through water. Its mane and tail flowed behind it, and its powerful body was angled as if leaning into a sharp turn. Her grandmother had always likened the wild horse to Aurelia's mother. *Abby was my free-spirited girl.*

"It smells wonderful," Remi said as they followed Flossie into the kitchen. She towered over Flossie.

Flossie took Remi's hand and said, "I've made bourekas, meatballs with tahini and tomatoes, and chicken soup."

"What's a boureka?" Remi asked.

"Only the world's best comfort food. They're buttery, crisp dough stuffed with any number of delicious fillings," Aurelia said. "Grandma, did you make strawberry-and-cheese bourekas?"

"Bubbelah, what do you think? I made spinach and cheese and strawberry and cheese. And yes, I made enough for you to take some home." She began ladling soup into bowls. "Why don't you girls carry the rest of the food to the table, and then we'll catch up. I want to hear all about Chapter One. And, Remi, what brings you to the East Coast? A *man*, perhaps?"

"I'm trying to escape the men in my life," Remi said as she carried a dish of meatballs in a creamy sauce to the table. Each meatball had half of a cherry tomato and a sprig of parsley on top. She set the dish beside the platter of bourekas Aurelia had just set down.

"She's got an unwanted admirer, Grandma," Aurelia explained as she set out silverware and drinks and Remi carried the soup bowls to the table.

"A stalker?" Flossie's silver brows shot up in surprise above her gray-green eyes. "Goodness, Remi. What does Aiden have to say about all this?"

As they took their places at the table, Remi said, "If he had his way, he'd keep me under lock and key every second of the day."

Flossie's shoulders sank, and her lips pursed. "Remi, bubbelah, did you run away *again*?"

"It's not like I do it *all* the time." She dished meatballs onto her plate. "Just when I feel like I want to scratch my eyes out."

"Aiden loves you, sweetheart. He's been your protector since you were twelve. That's a long time for a brother to watch over his sister. And he's helped you grow a magnificent career," Flossie reminded her.

"I know. And I love him for *all* of that," Remi said. "But is it wrong that sometimes I just want to be a twentysomething girl who nobody knows? Whose brother goes out on dates instead of interrogating every-one who asks *me* on one?"

Flossie giggled. She'd always had a high-pitched giggle, not a laugh. Aurelia's grandfather used to say it was what made him first fall in love with her. "No, baby. That makes you *human*."

"That sounds familiar, doesn't it?" Aurelia pointed out, reminding Remi of their earlier conversation.

"This is why I love coming home to see everyone." Remi sat up straighter and said, "You understand me. You don't treat me like a celebrity."

"You said *home*," Flossie pointed out. Remi had a house in Cape Cod and one in Los Angeles, both of which she'd called home before meeting Willow and the rest of the Daltons. "That means you're right where you're supposed to be. But don't make Aiden worry. He's a good man, like Benjamin."

Aurelia exchanged a glance with Remi as she ate her soup. She hadn't told Flossie about Bea or her relationship with Ben yet. She'd wanted to tell her in person.

Flossie kept her eyes trained on her spoon as she dipped it into her soup. A knowing smile stretched her lips as she said, "Well, if that's not the look of a secret, then I don't know what is."

"It's not a secret, Grandma. I just wanted to tell you something in person. A lot has happened recently."

Flossie dabbed at her mouth with her napkin and said, "You're young, you're starting a business, and you've just moved to a new area. You're due to have *many* blessings coming your way."

Remi sighed and said, "Can I call you Grandma? I love everything you say."

"Bubbelah, you can call me anything you want." She reached across the table and took Remi's hand. "But you need to look deep inside yourself and figure out what you're really running from. Not even a loving grandmother can figure that out for you."

Remi's finely manicured brows knitted. "Okay. I promise." She took a bite of a spinach-and-cheese boureka and closed her eyes. "Mm. This is *scrumptious*."

"Thank you. And no promises, Remi," Flossie said. "Life's too fluid for them. Just do the best you can and know that you're perfect just as you are. But if you want to make yourself different in some way—less of a worry for your brother, for example—you have the power to do that."

"That's her subtle nag," Aurelia said with a smile. "Grandma, you know how close Ben and I are."

"Two lovebirds standing on separate branches," Flossie said.

Aurelia couldn't mask her surprise. "What? I never knew you thought that about us."

"Honey, I might be old, but I'm not blind or deaf. You and Benjamin have been dancing around each other for a long time. And if I hadn't suspected before, seeing the way he hovered over you at Grandpa's funeral put it out there for all to see." Flossie held up her index finger as she rose to her feet. "I'll be right back."

She hurried through the living room and disappeared into the bedroom, returning with two framed photographs. She handed one picture to Aurelia, placing her hand on her shoulder as she asked, "What do you see?"

Aurelia looked at the picture of Ben standing between Willow and Talia, with his arms around them. They were all smiling, *laughing*. The picture had been taken during Thanksgiving the fall before her grandfather had suffered his stroke. Their families had celebrated together.

"Ben and his sisters," Aurelia said.

"Mm-hm." Flossie handed her the other picture, this one of her and Ben, taken the same evening. "And what do you see in this one?"

Ben had his arm around Aurelia, and they were both smiling for the camera, but there was no mistaking the difference in Ben. He resonated happiness, his fingers curled over her shoulder, holding her flush against his side. Even his smile was different, bigger, more natural, more meaningful.

"Wow," Remi whispered. "They always say a picture is worth a thousand words, and that's proof of it."

"Without you, Benjamin is a lovely man with a heart of gold," Flossie said.

Aurelia looked at her grandmother and asked, "What do you suppose he is with me?"

"*Fulfilled,*" Flossie said.

That one word stole her breath. "If you saw this between us then, why didn't you ever say anything?"

Flossie sat down and placed her napkin on her lap. "Sweetheart, you can't hurry love any more than you can hurry a soufflé. You know he checks on me, and we talk."

Aurelia's mouth fell open. "He *checks* on you?"

"Just since Grandpa died. He calls to see if I need anything. He's such a sweetheart. I suspect the man we're seeing now is the *real* Benjamin. I think he's been holding back, secretly fearing he'd let you down."

Aurelia swallowed hard as her grandmother's words reiterated Ben's confession. *I was in college, and you were Willow's best friend, and I knew I couldn't be the boyfriend you deserved.*

"That's the sweetest thing I've ever heard," Remi said.

"Ben could never let me down," Aurelia said honestly.

"He is a real mensch." Flossie patted Remi's hand and said, "Just like Aiden. Two of a kind, those boys. Real gentlemen."

"Grandma, did he tell you that we're together now, as a couple?" Aurelia asked.

"He didn't have to. I heard something different in his voice, and you just confirmed it." Flossie placed her hand over her heart and said, "This makes me so very happy, Aurelia."

"Thank you. It makes me happy, too, but there's more." She told her about Bea and everything she and Ben had been through with her.

"*Bea . . .*" Flossie's eyes dampened. She blinked several times and whispered, "Just perfect."

"She is perfect, but I wish I had babysat, or been around more babies, when I was younger. I love her, Grandma, and I feel like I'm failing her."

Flossie giggled again. "You're contradicting yourself. If you truly love her unconditionally, you cannot fail her."

"I'm not so sure that's true," Aurelia said. "While I had her yesterday, I was so tired, and I tried everything to calm her down, but she cried her little eyes out all afternoon. I had to ask Piper to come and take over."

"That's what love is, honey," Flossie said. "Failing her would be *not* asking for help, getting so frustrated you yell at her, or worse. She's a tiny baby—whom I can't wait to meet, by the way—all she needs are the essentials: warmth, love, sustenance."

"But I don't understand what she wants sometimes," Aurelia said.

"That's okay, because neither does she. Babies cry, honey. It's not easy getting up every few hours to eat and learning about this big new world. You said yourself she missed Benjamin. That's a big thing to a little baby. And babies are intuitive, which means you probably missed him, too. She might have been crying because she wanted both of you together." She sipped her drink, watching Aurelia, and Aurelia knew she was letting her words sink in before asking, "What do you want now?"

"*Them,*" Aurelia said without hesitation.

"Then you can't fail either of them, or yourself." Her eyes moved between Aurelia and Remi, and she said, "Girls, one thing you should learn to do in every aspect of your life is to follow your heart. If you do, you can't go wrong. Things won't always be easy or run smoothly. You'll have mountains to climb, battles to fight, but if you lead with your heart, you'll both survive and come out as better people on the other side."

"You make it sound so easy," Remi said. "I can't imagine anything with a baby is easy, considering life is never easy."

"Baby, teenager, adult. None of it is *easy*." Flossie smiled and said, "Let me tell you both a little story. When Aurelia's mother was fifteen, she was a sass-mouthed little thing. She never knew when to stop arguing, and she'd push me to my limit every chance she got. One day we were driving home from the shopping center, and she was yelling at me for one thing or another. I can't remember what, but it was important to her as a teenager. I asked her to speak rather than yell, but she was blinded with anger. So I pulled over six blocks from home, and I let her out of the car and told her to walk the rest of the way."

Aurelia and Remi exchanged surprised glances.

"Some people might think that's a parental failure," Flossie said. "But I couldn't lead with my heart with her yelling at me. If she kept it up, I'd have said things I could not take back. Now, even though Sweetwater was a safe place back then, I still drove to the end of the next block and pulled over. I could *barely* see her in my rearview mirror, and when I thought she could make out my car, then I drove to the end of the *next* block. I did that all the way home."

Aurelia laughed. "And what happened?"

"Oh, she was *livid* when she got home, but *I* felt better. It enabled me to take the breather I needed, and then I was able to talk while she yelled. Eventually she ran up to her room and slammed the door. But when she got hungry she came downstairs, sullen and pouty. And you know what? That was okay. Because life can be rocky."

"What did you do?" Remi asked.

"I hugged her, and she stood rigid as a wall. But," Flossie said with a spark of joy in her eyes, "she knew I loved her even though she was being a sass-mouthed brat at that moment." She looked at Aurelia and said, "If that little one knows you love her, everything else will fall into place. It's okay to be exhausted and to feel lost. Calling Piper was the right thing to do. You're learning, baby, and where children are concerned, that learning never ends."

"Thanks, Grandma. You're so good at making me feel better."

Flossie reached across the table and patted Aurelia's and Remi's hands. "The world is filled with unhappy people trying to bring others down. Family should always try to lift your spirits."

"Maybe you can help me," Remi said.

"I can try, Remi. Are you doing what you love most?" Flossie asked.

Remi nodded. "Yes."

"And you're *sure* of that? Because my first love was music—"

"Music?" Aurelia asked. "I thought books were your greatest love."

"Your grandfather was my *greatest* love. But my first love was singing. I wanted to be in the opera, but for love, one adapts and changes. When your mother was born, I set aside my affinity for music and nurtured my love of literature, which fit better into my life as a mother."

They talked for a long while about love and life, and Aurelia told her all about the bookstore and the two employees she'd hired: Lazarus, the baby whisperer, and Hollis Marks, an English major with freckles, hair the color of pennies, and a knack for all things literary. She was excited for Flossie to meet her staff and see the bookstore when the renovations were finally complete. She and Remi would both be at the grand opening—if Aiden didn't lock Remi up after he found out she was in town.

With a container full of her grandmother's food, she hugged Flossie goodbye. "I love you, Grandma."

"I love you too, bubbelah. This is for you." She put a key in Aurelia's hand and covered it with her own.

"A key? What is this to?"

"To our storage unit in Sweetwater. You know where it is. The crib you and your mother used is in it. It's yours, darling, along with anything else you'd like for Bea."

193

Aurelia hugged her. "Thank you. This means the world to me."

"And you mean the world to me," Flossie said sweetly. "You never knew this, but your grandfather and I called your mother Bea."

Aurelia blinked several times, trying to understand. "You called her Abby."

"To everyone else we referred to her as Abby, because that's what she preferred when she first went off to kindergarten. But when we spoke of her privately, she was always our little *Bea*, which means *bringer of joy*, or *she who brings happiness*."

"Oh, Grandma." Aurelia tried to speak past the lump in her throat.

"It's definitely fate," Remi said.

"Yes, you're right, Remi. Bea is the perfect name for the baby who opened Aurelia's and Benjamin's hearts to each other. And I'd like to think this is your mother's way of showing us that she's smiling down on us."

Aurelia was still wiping away tears as she climbed into the car. "We need to go shopping."

"Shopping? You hate shopping," Remi reminded her.

"I hate shopping for *me*."

"I need a better disguise than a baseball cap and dark sunglasses if we're going shopping."

"Suck it up, buttercup. I'm your bodyguard today, and I'm on a mission to show Ben just how much I want him and Bea in my life. Stalkers beware, because nobody's going to get in our way."

"Come on, peanut." Ben lifted Bea's carrier from his truck Thursday evening, relieved to see Aurelia's car parked behind her apartment, since he'd been trying unsuccessfully to reach her for hours. But now he hesitated at the bottom of the steps, second-guessing himself. What if she was sleeping? Wasn't the break supposed to allow her time and space to think her own thoughts? To do her own thing?

"I know," he said to Bea. "But I want to *be* her *thing*. Let's go get our girl."

As he headed up the steps, the apartment door flew open and Aurelia and Remi bounded out, both of them laughing hysterically. He stopped halfway up, realizing they hadn't spotted him yet, so he said, "Hey."

They both looked at him, and Aurelia's face brightened. "Ben! I was just coming to see *you!*" She ran down the steps as Ben ascended them.

Remi held up her hands, moving out of their way. "Don't say it, Ben. I'm going to see Aiden right now."

"Good. But I already narced on you. I told him to give you a day."

"Ohmygod. You and Aiden really are two of a kind." Remi glanced at Aurelia, who was bouncing up and down excitedly, and said, "I'm outta here before I get an eyeful of lusty kisses and gropes."

As Remi descended the steps, Ben gazed into Aurelia's beautiful eyes and said, "I know I promised to give you space, but we missed you."

"Life is too fluid for promises," she said quickly. "I was coming to see you! I didn't want to be apart for a second longer. I love you, and I missed you both *so* much. I woke up *twice* last night, and I hated not having you guys there."

She crashed her mouth to his, and he swept one arm around her, pulling her against him as he took the kiss deeper. Bea made a happy little sound, and they both laughed as their lips parted.

Ben stepped onto the landing, still holding Bea's carrier. Aurelia crouched beside her and said, "Hi, sweet pea. I missed you so much, too." She took her out of the carrier, closing her eyes as she snuggled her and said, "I love you, perfect girl. I'm sorry for yesterday, but we'll figure this out together."

Aurelia's eyes popped open and she said, "I have so much to tell you, and to show you." She fumbled with her keys, and Ben took them to unlock the door. As they stepped inside, she said, "First, I'm sorry for being human."

Ben laughed. "Ah, Flossie made you realize it's okay not to be superhuman?"

"No, *you* did, Ben. She just made me see it more clearly. Our lives and careers are too busy to think we can do everything on our own."

"I know." He set down the baby carrier and closed the door behind them. "My mom is going to help out for a few hours each day, so we can work, or rest, or . . ." He leaned in for a kiss, earning a blush. "And I didn't get to tell you last night, but Aiden and I are letting Garth and Miller take over the new investment. I'm not going to travel and leave my girls."

"That's great about Roxie, but, Ben, you worked for more than a year on that deal. You can't give it up."

"I'm not giving it up, Rels. I own the company. I'm just lightening my load so I can pay attention to the things—the *people*—that really matter. I'll do what needs to be done, and I'll have to do a little traveling here and there, but hopefully you and Bea can come with me on those brief trips. I want you both to know you can count on me." He wrapped his arms around her and said, "The furniture is being delivered to my place tomorrow, and then my mother is going to babysit Saturday *overnight*, so I can take you on a real date."

"She doesn't have to take her overni—" Her words were silenced by the press of his lips.

"You're my girlfriend, and there's no way you're missing out on romantic, fun dates with your man or the incredible all-night lovemaking I've got planned for us."

Her eyes sparked with heat. "That sounds promising. I listened to your tape." She pressed closer, angling her body to allow room for Bea as she lowered her voice seductively and said, "You sound way hotter than Zach." She whispered, "And the striptease scene? How did you know that was my *favorite* scene in *Claimed by Love*? I've got Brett Eldredge's 'Lose My Mind' all queued up on my phone . . ."

Just thinking about stripping for her made him hard. He eyed the baby, feeling like a dick because he wished she were sleeping so they could act out that wickedly hot, romantic scene.

Before he could get his brain to function enough to respond, she said, "But that'll have to wait, because I have something to show you."

She took his hand and led him to the guest bedroom. "I know you're making a room for Bea at your place, but since we stay here so much—and I hope we'll continue to—I thought she should have her own room here, too."

Ben's heart thundered against his ribs as he took in the nursery. A mobile of Winnie-the-Pooh characters hung above an oak crib with yellow sheets and pink padding around the bars. There was a rocking chair by the windows and a matching changing table against the far wall, beneath which were stacks of diapers, baby wipes, pink and yellow blankets, and more baby supplies. On the wall above the changing table was a quote in blue letters with two bees flying around it, trailing a swirly line of tiny hearts, followed by a famous Winnie-the-Pooh quote: "As soon as I saw you, I knew an adventure was about to happen." An antique white-and-oak bookshelf stood between the windows across the room, filled with stuffed animals and children's books. He turned and saw one of the pictures of him and Aurelia kissing Bea's cheeks that they'd taken in the kitchen, blown up and framed, hanging on the wall beside pastel letters she'd stacked in rows of three that read,

BEA
UTI
FUL

"I hope it's not too presumptuous," she said nervously. "My grandmother gave me the key to her storage unit. This is the crib me and my mom used. My great-grandfather built those shelves and the changing table for my mom. I know they're not new or fancy, but—"

He silenced her with another kiss and said, "It's perfect, Rels. *You're* perfect. Even when you're overwhelmed, you're perfect. I *want* you to presume, baby. We want *you*. Period."

"I want you, too." Tears brimmed in her eyes. "I made you a key to my apartment."

"Aw, babe. You *do* love me," he said teasingly, because he'd given her a key to his place two years ago, and while he'd had a key to her old apartment, she had yet to give him a key to this one.

"It's not like my life hasn't been crazy since I bought this place."

He kissed her again and said, "You know I'm kidding. Thank you, and I'm glad things went well with Flossie today."

"She told me you've been checking on her. Thank you for doing that. I didn't know this, but my grandparents called my mom Bea." She looked at the baby and said, "Grandma thinks that finding her on your doorstep, and naming her Bea, was a sign that my mom was smiling down on us." Tears slid down her cheeks.

He took the baby from her, gathering them both in his arms, and said, "She is, Rels."

She rested her cheek against his chest, rubbing her hand over Bea's back, and said, "Did you know Bea means 'one who brings joy'?"

"No, but that's perfect for our girl—which reminds me . . . Bridgette bought us a present." He pulled a pacifier out of his pocket and said, "Meet the pacifier, bringer of no more tears."

CHAPTER SEVENTEEN

"YOU NEED TO calm the heck down," Remi said over FaceTime Saturday evening.

"Calm down? I'm going on my first real date with the man I'm practically living with." Even though they were spending weekends at Ben's and Aurelia had plenty of clothes at his house, she'd come home to get ready for their date so she could find the perfect outfit. Ben was picking her up after dropping Bea off with his parents. "He's going to be here in less than ten minutes, and I'm totally freaking out. I've been with Bea so much, I keep thinking, I should *not* dress like this!"

She might not be Bea's mother, but she felt such a strong maternal pull, it was a little hard to separate having baby puke on her shoulder and enticing Ben to nibble on that shoulder. Her dark purple boatneck dress fit her like a second skin, with tight three-quarter-length sleeves, the bodice dipping in at the waist and hugging her hips. The skirt was slit on the left side and cut at an angle, exposing her left leg from midthigh down and crossing over her right leg just above the knee.

"On the mannequin the dress looked sexy but refined, like a classic novel," she said. "But on me it looks like I stole it from the pages of an erotic romance novel. And the spike heels are too much, right? I wanted to be closer to Ben's height, but they make me feel like a . . ."

"Vixen?" Remi suggested.

"Yes! And it's as unexpectedly empowering as it is shocking to see myself like this, and a little frightening that I love that empowered feeling."

Remi busted out laughing. "Girl, you look scorching hot, and Ben deserves five flames. He *adores* you, and you *should* feel empowered. You're a gorgeous, smart woman who is caring for his baby! Now it's your turn to be pampered in all the very best ways. And that dress? That's going to seal the deal."

"I'm not used to dressing like this for anyone, especially Ben. He sees me in jeans and sweats all the time."

"Which is *exactly* why it's *perfect*," Remi coaxed. "If you sent a picture of yourself to his sisters, they'd lose their minds. Willow would be like, 'Go, girl!' Piper would probably have to sterilize her *eyes*, Talia would blush a red streak, and Bridgette would say something like, 'Ben will not know what hit him.' I, on the other hand, think Benny boy will know *exactly* what hit him, and you'll never make it out the front door."

"So, no part of you is cringing inside? Thinking I look like I'm trying too hard?"

"You are *supposed* to try hard when you're in love," Remi said. "Not that I would know. I'm pretty sure Aiden's going to put a location collar on me."

Aurelia laughed. "You said he wasn't that angry, just worried about you."

"He was. *Is.* But I have to be in LA Tuesday, and Aiden's coming with me, of course. We'll be back for the grand opening, but I'm sure going to miss you."

"Me too, Rem." A knock sounded at the door, and Aurelia's heart skipped a beat. "He's here, and he knocked. He doesn't ever knock. I gave him a key."

"It's a date, doofus. Like Flossie said, he's a mensch. *Go.*" She blew Aurelia a kiss and ended the video call.

Aurelia tried to calm her nerves as she went to answer the door, but when she peered out the peephole and saw Ben's handsome face, his scruff manicured to perfection, his dark eyes glimmering back at her, her pulse skyrocketed. She squeezed her thighs together in anticipation of what those sexy whiskers promised for later.

She opened the door, and her stomach tumbled. She was used to seeing Ben dressed nicely, but his dark dress shirt hugged his biceps, his slacks accentuated his thick thighs, and the way he was looking at her, like he wanted to tear her dress off with his teeth, brought a whole new level of hotness.

"Damn, babe, you look incredible." He swept his arm around her, hauling her against him in a heart-stopping kiss. "Maybe we should stay in tonight."

His reaction made her body flame. *Yes* was on the tip of her tongue, but she loved his reaction so much, she wanted to see *more* of it. There was power in dressing like this after all. If tonight were a chapter in a book, she would title it "Enticing Ben."

"*Big Ben* is going to have to wait until later. This girl needs to eat before we play," she said, because who knew when she'd get the courage to dress like this again.

"How about I *eat* while we *play*?"

His devilish grin *almost* had her relenting, but instead she used it to fuel her desire to drive him even crazier. She grabbed her purse, hooked her finger into the waist of his slacks, and stepped outside, closing the door behind her. "Come on, Benny boy. Let's go light the town on fire."

Ben wasn't the only thing that took Aurelia's breath away tonight. He'd gotten a private booth at Temptations, the hottest new nightclub and restaurant in Harmony Pointe. She'd never seen any place like it. The restaurant was on the second floor, with hundreds of inset white lights in the domed ceiling. Private booths and tables were set up along the perimeter of the restaurant. Glass walls around the center created the appearance of a loft, overlooking the nightclub below. Music from the band serenaded them. Buffered by the extra-high first-floor ceiling and glass walls, it added ambience without overpowering their conversation. They shared appetizers of crab and shrimp fondue and dinners of steak and chicken in a savory wine sauce and roasted vegetables. They talked and laughed, as they always had, but it was so much better as a couple. They fed each other tastes between steamy kisses, and Ben couldn't seem to keep his hands off her. By the time their server brought dessert, Aurelia couldn't remember why she'd been nervous in the first place. She loved turning him on!

Ben was sexier than ever, and at the moment he was trying to feed her *another* strawberry dipped in chocolate. "No, please, Ben," she said with a laugh. "I can't eat another bite. I'm stuffed, but dinner was incredible. This whole place is amazing. How did you get a reservation so fast? I heard they were booked until Christmas."

"The owner's a buddy of mine." He lifted the strawberry to her lips, and his eyes darkened. "Come on, Relsy, one more bite, for me."

"*One*, and then that's it, or I'll burst the seams of this dress."

"That'll save me from having to tear it off you. Open up, sexy girl."

She opened her mouth, and he put the tip of the strawberry between her lips. As she bit into it, he said, "*Mm-mm*. There is nothing sexier than seeing your lips wrapped around something of mine."

"Then maybe we need to get out of here," she said seductively.

A low laugh rumbled out of him. He set down the strawberry with a predatory look in his eyes, and then he leaned in and slicked his tongue over her lips. She closed her eyes, barely breathing as his hand traveled up her leg, and he tucked his fingers between her legs, firmly against the thin material of her thong, and whispered, "Soon, baby, but first I have something else planned."

The sounds of a man clearing his throat startled them apart. Ben didn't move at first, looking out of the corners of his eyes, but then he shifted his hand lower on her leg and put a little space between them, glowering at the gorgeous man standing beside their table. His shirtsleeves were rolled up to his elbows, revealing muscular, tattooed forearms.

"Excuse me, sir," the man said. "We don't allow that sort of behavior here. Ma'am, would you like me to escort this wretched beast away from you?"

Aurelia gasped, instantly turning the heat Ben had sparked into rage. "*Excuse* me?"

"Rels, this—"

"No, Ben," she interrupted. "This guy is being rude. Listen, Adam Levine wannabe, we're having a lovely dinner and this gentleman is my boyfriend."

"Rels—"

"Ben, I've got this," she snapped, her eyes never leaving the tatted-up bigmouth. "So why don't you keep walking before I call the manager?"

She turned toward Ben and caught him stifling a laugh. She shot a look at the other guy, who was also grinning, and realized she'd been played.

"Will the *owner* do?" the guy asked.

She groaned. "You both suck, you know that?"

"I'm sorry, babe," Ben said. "This is Jared Stone, and as he said, he owns the place. He's got a warped sense of humor, but he's a good guy. Jared, this is my girlfriend, Aurelia Stark."

"I'm sorry, sweetheart," Jared said. "It was all meant in fun."

"That's okay," she said, relieved that he wasn't really an asshole. "Paybacks are hell, by the way."

Jared chuckled. "I bet, but I have to say, that was impressive. Which begs the question, what's Ben got to hook a woman as beautiful and feisty as you?"

"They don't call him Ten-Inch Ben for nothing," she said sassily.

Ben flashed an arrogant grin and pulled her closer, kissing her temple.

"Yeah?" Jared lifted his chin and said, "Well, they don't call me—"

"Dude!" Ben cut him off.

Aurelia laughed. She liked Ben's possessive side, and she liked his funny friend, too.

Smiling, Jared said, "I just wanted to stop by and say hi. I hope you enjoyed dinner."

"It was incredible," Aurelia said. "Sorry for going off on you."

"No worries. I'm glad I finally got to meet the infamous Aurelia. Have a great night. Ben, we'll be in touch."

As he walked away, Aurelia said, "'Infamous Aurelia'?"

"I might have told him about you a few dozen times." He touched his forehead to Aurelia's and said, "Do you know how much I loved seeing you fight for my honor?"

"Probably as much as I loved the kiss we were enjoying before he interrupted us."

"Ah yes. . ." He took her in another tantalizing kiss.

Thank goodness she wasn't wearing lipstick, because Ben wasn't just kissing her; he was *devouring*, *claiming*, his thumb moving in slow, intoxicating circles on her inner thigh. As he drew back, he graced her with a series of lighter kisses that left her dizzy.

He took out his wallet, threw a few hundred-dollar bills on the table, then took her hand and said, "Come on, Relsy. We're going dancing."

She was sure she'd misheard him. "You don't dance."

"I slow danced with you at Bridgette's wedding."

"Ben, this isn't a *slow dance* kind of place, and we both know you have two left feet," she said as he led her down the steps toward the nightclub below, where neon blue, purple, and red lights rained over the dance floor.

Ben couldn't wait to get Aurelia on the dance floor. His girl had *serious* moves, the kind of moves that could make a dead man hard—and he'd spent way too many years watching her dirty-dance without him. He kept her close as they wove through a mass of bumping and grinding bodies. The scent of sex and foreplay hung in the air, amping up his anticipation of finally showing Aurelia what he'd learned for her.

"Ben," she shouted over the pounding music. "You don't have to do this. I know you hate dancing."

"You *think* you know me," he said with a wink.

Adrenaline coursed through his veins as he found a spot in the crowd, and as he'd known she would, Aurelia started dancing. Her shoulders and hips swayed seductively, as if the beat lived inside her. At first he barely moved, letting her think he was the same old Ben. The guy who had been born with two left feet. But she was a sight to be reckoned with, all her sexy curves gyrating and bumping to the seductive beat.

She thought he couldn't dance. Didn't she know that Ben had never come up against anything he couldn't overcome with the right incentive? And Aurelia was a damn good incentive. His love for her had driven him to secretly take *months* of dance lessons in hopes of impressing her the night of Bridgette's wedding. *Better late than never.*

He let the beat sink in, and then he fell into sync, matching her every move with one of his own. The surprise and appreciation in her eyes gave him the approval he needed to let the dirty dancer he'd discovered in himself come out to play. Her arms rose above her head, and he pressed closer, bringing her thigh between his legs. His hips thrust and gyrated, his hands danced down her arms and up her torso, his thumbs brushing over the sides of her breasts. Her breathing hitched, and even in the dim lights he saw flames in her eyes. He leaned in, their bodies snaking against each other, making him rock hard. He lowered his lips to hers, probing possessively as their hips ground to their own private beat. Ben was so lost in her, clutching her ass, devouring her mouth, the music and people around them blurred together. He didn't know when one song ended and the next began, and he didn't care. Time passed in a sweltering, libidinous rush of grinding and groping. He kissed her slick, salty skin, ate at her luscious mouth, and pawed her gorgeous ass, earning the most sinful look he'd ever seen. *Oh yeah, baby. You like that?* She'd been casting those wicked looks his way all night.

Now it was his turn.

He slipped one hand beneath the slit of her dress, clutching the back of her thigh as she ground against his erection. Under the cover of the dimly lit dance floor, his fingers moved higher, and his cock throbbed at the feel of flesh instead of panties. He grabbed her bare ass, and his fingertips brushed over the thin strip of her thong. She moaned, and though he didn't hear it, he felt her chest vibrate against him, and he thought he might lose his fucking mind. He lowered his mouth to her neck, sucking and biting, earning a grind and thrust of her hips with his every effort.

"When'd you learn to dance?" she panted out next to his ear.

"When I realized I never wanted to see you dance with any other man."

Her arms circled his neck, and he claimed her mouth. She crushed her softness against him. He buried his hands in her hair, angling her mouth beneath his, sinking deeper into their kisses, swallowing her sounds of pleasure. The beat of the music, the feel of her fingers digging into him, begging for more, and her hungry kisses heightened the sexual tension that had been sizzling between them all night. Other than during his lessons, Ben had never danced with another woman like this. He'd been saving it for Aurelia. He'd wondered if he'd be nervous, but he was so focused on enjoying every second of bringing her pleasure in this new and different way, anxiety had no way into their private, sensual bubble.

When their lips parted, she turned in his arms, grinding his arousal against her ass. She shimmied lower, brushing her back against his erection before dancing upright again. Lust thrummed inside him as the erotic beat of the music climbed to an explosive crescendo. He turned her toward him, keeping hold of her arms as they danced. He wanted to strip her dress off and pound into her to the same fervent beat, and he finally understood that *this* was what she'd craved all those times she'd begged him to dance with her. This was why she'd danced with his sisters, turning away the men who'd tried to cut in when they were out at clubs. This was why she'd gotten forlorn when he'd turned her down because he hadn't wanted to embarrass himself on the dance floor. She'd wanted this chemistry, this intense sexual connection with *him* and only him. Wasn't he a lucky bastard. He'd been an idiot to wait so long, but he had forever to make it up to her.

Heat pulsed through his core as the music slowed, and he held her body against him, leading her in a slower, even more erotic dance. With one hand pressed to her lower back, the other splayed between her shoulder blades, bringing her chest against him, he moved painfully slowly and purposefully hard, sure she would *feel* and *sense* his darkest thoughts. The lustful look in her eyes told him she was right there with him.

He pressed his cheek to hers, inhaling her familiar scent, and said, "I want to go down on you right now, to feel you come on my mouth." Her fingers dug into the backs of his arms, and she whimpered, spurring him on. "Then I want to make love to you rough and wild, until you come so hard you can barely breathe, and just when you think you've had enough, I'm going to take you punishingly slowly, until you're begging for more."

"Take me home, Ben. Take me all those ways and more."

They stumbled up the stairs to Aurelia's apartment, making out like horny teenagers who might never get another chance. Ben fumbled with the keys. When they pushed through the door, he kicked it shut behind them and swept her up into his arms.

"Ben!" she squealed as he carried her into the bedroom.

As he set her on her feet beside the bed, his heart climbed into his throat. She was dangerously beautiful, and looking at him with such trust and love, he was momentarily rendered mute. He took her hands in his and kissed each finger as he found his voice.

"When you look at me like that," he whispered as he moved behind her and unzipped her dress. "Wearing this dress." He brushed her hair over one shoulder and kissed her there. "Dancing with you." The dress slipped off her shoulders and puddled at her feet, leaving her in her black thong and matching bra. He ran his hands slowly down her sides, from her breasts to her hips. "It's almost too much to bear."

He toed off his shoes and stripped off his clothes. The room was silent, save for their breathing. He brushed his hard length lightly over her bottom as he removed her bra. As he dragged her thong down her legs, he trailed kisses down her bottom, her hamstring, and all the way down her calf. She stepped free from her thong, still wearing her heels, and as he stood, he slowed to enjoy her warm flesh again, running his hands up her outer thighs as he kissed the curve of her ass. She made a whimpering sound, and he gripped her hips, nipping and licking each rounded cheek. He dipped lower and slicked his tongue between her legs, tasting her arousal, lingering there, licking and loving her until she was shaking and moaning. Only then did he move higher, pressing kisses on his way up, along her spine, to the base of her neck.

His arms circled her from behind, and he whispered between shoulder kisses, "You're my strength." *Kiss, kiss.* "My weakness." *Kiss, nip.* "My world."

He kissed lower again, moving around her as he trailed open-mouthed kisses along her hip, giving rise to goose bumps. He lingered around her navel, and she clutched his shoulders, trembling with desire. He took his time, savoring every inch of her warm flesh as he kissed up her belly, between her breasts, up her neck, to her sweet lips. Her nipples brushed against his chest, and he drew back so he could see her beautiful face. His breath left his lungs with a sense of awe and adoration. He guided her hand to his shoulder and laced their other hands together. A smile curved her lips as he began slow dancing.

There was no stopping his heart from pouring out. "You're my oxygen, Relsy."

"Ben," she whispered.

His eyes met hers and drew him deeper into her. Their mouths came together in a luxurious kiss that wound through his veins, spreading heat through his chest and lulling him into a different state of mind. Gone was the urgency, the need to *take* or dominate, replaced with the sheer, soul-deep desire to love and cherish. He guided her to the bed, kissing her as he lowered them to the mattress. He loved his way south, slowing to tease her nipples the way he knew drove her crazy. Every slick of his tongue, every suck, nip, and tease, brought a needy sound, a rock of her hips, a breathless whisper—*"Ben—"*

He heard that dizzying plea in his dreams, and he wanted to hear it every single day for the rest of his life. He moved down her body, cherishing every inch, and then he made his way back up to see the blissful look on her gorgeous face. He was overcome with love. He'd promised her wild sex, but as he held her beneath him, as he kissed her with all the love and devotion he possessed, all he wanted was to be inside her so she could feel the strength and power of his love as her own.

He drew back, gazing down at the woman who owned him so completely, he wasn't sure how to survive without her. Her green eyes moved slowly over his face, and then, as if she'd read his mind, she said, "Make love to me, Benny. We can be wild later."

"Oh, sweetheart, I'm going to do just that." He kissed her deeply, cradling her beneath him, feeling her heart beating in time to his as their bodies became one, and he whispered, "I always knew we'd be good together, but I never imagined it would be like this . . ."

A long while later, after they'd made love slowly and sensually, and then wildly and without inhibition, Aurelia lay with her back against Ben's chest in a warm bubble bath. It was wonderful making love without worrying about waking Bea. No, it was better than wonderful. It was *magnificent* seeing Ben so unrestrained. He was a sexual animal, and oh, how she loved it! They'd christened the bed, the couch, and when they went to the kitchen to get a snack, he'd swept the dishes off the counter, sending them crashing to the floor, and then they'd christened the counter. Her love for him was endless, and their passion grew with every kiss. She had never felt so in love, or so at peace, as she was right then, so why, as she lay in a romantic bath with the man of her dreams, was her mind tiptoeing to Bea? Was it weird that as much as she'd love to have the rest of the night to cuddle with Ben and not have to worry about feedings or changing diapers, she *wanted* those responsibilities?

Ben kissed her temple and ran his fingers down her arm. "What are you thinking about, Relsy?"

"Us." She tilted her head so she could see his handsome face, and he lowered his lips to hers in a temptingly warm kiss.

He traced her jaw with his fingers and said, "And?"

"Bea," she confessed. "I can't help it. I miss her."

"Oh, baby," he said with a rough voice. "Me too. I was trying not to say anything because I didn't want to ruin the moment."

"Thoughts of Bea could never ruin any of our moments. Do you think your mom would mind if we picked her up now? Even though it's late?"

A dazzling smile, alive with affection and delight, brightened his face, and he said, "There's only one way to find out."

She squealed and popped to her feet, dripping with bubbles. He snagged a towel and wrapped it around her. He kissed the tip of her nose and said, "Let's go get our girl."

CHAPTER EIGHTEEN

THURSDAY MORNING AURELIA sat in the rocking chair they'd bought for her bedroom, feeding Bea as the first spray of sunlight peeked through the curtains. Bea made contented sounds as she ate, as if every drop was exactly what she needed. Aurelia kissed her forehead and glanced at Ben, lying in his briefs on top of the covers, one arm stretched over his head, the other on his stomach. Their lives hadn't woven together seamlessly, but how could they with a new baby and so much of her life still up in the air? They'd stitched and patched their busy lives together, but wasn't that what happiness was made from? Helping each other when things got to be too much? Reading each other's minds and stealing away for a quickie when Bea finally fell asleep? Easing each other's fears about finding—or *not* finding—Bea's real mother?

Ben stretched and rolled onto his side, a sleepy smile curving his lips. "Want me to finish?"

She shook her head and blew him a kiss. They'd fallen into a schedule of sorts, though it was fluid and changed often. With Roxie watching Bea for a few hours each day, they were both able to catch up on work. The mural was finished, and the bookstore was almost ready for the grand opening. Aurelia was having a hard time deciding what to read at the grand opening, but she had it narrowed down to either *Pride and Prejudice* or *Alice's Adventures in Wonderland*. Ben's latest deal was transitioning smoothly and moving right along, but there were late nights and stressful days, so they alternated nighttime feedings, sharing the burden of exhaustion. They'd both put certain parts of their lives on hold, and now that things were falling into place and they had a schedule of sorts, she hoped to give Ben a little room to reclaim the parts of his life she knew he missed. And the truth was, she missed seeing her friends, too. Not that she regretted giving up those visits or resented Ben or Bea for it. Life was give-and-take, and with Ben and Bea she'd been given the best gifts of all.

"I've got her," she said. "I was thinking about taking Bea to the bakery this morning. I miss seeing the girls, and I thought you might want to go running with Zane and Bodhi. Willow was at Roxie's the other day when I picked up Bea, and she said Zane missed running with you."

"You sure you don't mind?" He stretched his long legs over the side of the bed and sat up.

"Not at all. To be honest, I'm impressed that you haven't lost your mind from not running. I know how much you love it."

He reached for her hand, giving it a squeeze, and said, "I miss jogging with you, too. Maybe we should start scheduling an extra hour of Roxie's time once or twice a week, so we can go running together."

"Actually, since we stay here in Harmony Pointe during the week, why don't we ask Lazarus? He's so good with Bea, and he lives in town and could probably use the money."

"Sounds good to me."

He dropped to his knees and knee-walked to her with a playful smile. He kissed her thigh, and then he kissed Bea's cheek. Aurelia couldn't resist caressing his face. He shaved less often these days, and she loved his scruff.

"Mother's Day is next Sunday," he said. Every year he went to his parents' house for a big Mother's Day brunch, and she had breakfast with Flossie. "I know you usually have breakfast with your grandmother, but I was wondering how you'd feel about bringing her to lunch with my family instead. We can pick her up the day before, and since we'll be at my house for the weekend, we have room for her."

They'd taken Bea to meet Flossie last Sunday. When she'd opened the door and seen Ben cradling the baby, with one arm around Aurelia, she'd gotten tears in her eyes and said, *All my bubbelahs in one place. What a blessing today is!* She'd promptly confiscated the baby and spent the next couple of hours gushing over her.

"I think she'd love that."

"I hope you're taking notes, because I'm going to need them," Bodhi said later that morning as they ran around Sugar Lake.

"You're great with Louie, and Dahlia survived puppyhood," Zane said with a chuckle. "I'm sure you can handle a baby."

"You are the definition of clueless, Zane." Ben glanced at Bodhi and said, "Dude, this is all you need to know. Life as you know it is going to end when your baby is born, and not just because when you're changing diapers and walking around like a zombie you'll no longer feel like *Bodhi the ex-military stud*, but because your worldview will change dramatically." Not only did Ben drive more carefully, take fewer risks, and notice things like which restrooms had changing tables since Bea had come into his life, but he also looked at Aurelia differently. The way she loved and nurtured Bea, her willingness to set aside her own needs for his daughter, and a million other things she did drove his love to a deeper, truer love than he'd ever known.

"My world view changed when I met Bridgette and Louie," Bodhi reminded him. "I can't imagine it changing even more, but Bridge says everything is different with a baby. She's worried about Louie being jealous and getting enough attention, so I'm already making plans to babysit so she gets one-on-one time with him after the baby comes."

"Dude, nix that word—*babysit*—from your vocabulary. I was talking to Bridgette the other day on the phone and I said I was going to babysit while Aurelia ran an errand. Bridge bit my head off. Apparently it's not called *babysitting* when it's your own kid."

Bodhi's brows knitted. "Damn. I'd better not forget that."

"At least you have time to prepare. Bridgette's not due until October," Zane said. "Ben's been thrown into it."

"You can say that again," Ben said as they sped up. "But from the way Willow fawns over Bea, I'd say you're not far off from fatherhood yourself, Zane."

Zane glared at him. "Bite your tongue, dude. The only thing I want to be woken up for in the middle of the night is hot sex."

Bodhi laughed.

"Dude, she's my sister. There are certain things I do *not* want to hear," Ben reminded him. "One more thing, Bodhi. I wouldn't trade Bea for the world, but definitely line up babysitting so you and Bridgette get some time together. Having a few unencumbered hours makes a world of difference."

"Bridge has all that worked out," Bodhi said proudly. "This is my first rodeo, but it's not hers. She's already made arrangements for my mother to help out at the flower shop for the first few months, and Roxie's going to take the baby whenever Bridgette needs a break." Bodhi's mother, Alisha, had recently sold her flower shop and moved next door to Bodhi and Bridgette. "Our kids are cousins. How cool is that? And our babies are going to be close enough in age to go to school together."

"Our babies will grow up raising hell together," Ben said. "See, Zane? Another reason to have a baby sooner rather than later, so yours is close in age to ours."

Bodhi smirked and said, "I think Roxie's been working on that."

The color drained from Zane's face. "Shit. What's she laced her potions with this time?"

"I'll never tell." Bodhi sped up to a full-on sprint.

"Damn it!" Zane ground out as he and Ben took off after him.

Ben's phone rang, and as he pulled it from his running belt he said, "Go on. I'll catch up." His chest constricted at the sight of Mason's name on the screen. He slowed to a walk as he answered the call. "Mason, how's it going?"

"Pretty well. Have you got a minute?"

He wiped the sweat from his brow with his forearm and said, "Sure. Of course."

"I'm sorry this has taken some time, but we tracked down the mother, Bernadette Caroline Thatcher. She goes by Caroline, as you know. She was a waitress at the hotel where you met her, but she no longer works there. She took maternity leave a few weeks before the baby was born, and two weeks after she was born, she resigned. No one there has seen her since. We linked her to a flight to New York City, where she rented a car a few days before she left the baby at your place, but she never used her return ticket. Although the rental car was returned. We've tracked a few expenditures in New York City, but it's been more than two weeks, and her trail has gone cold."

"What do you think that means?"

"It could mean anything. She could have gone to stay with friends or family. My guess is that she wanted a fresh start, doesn't want to be found. But we've checked local hospitals and clinics, just in case something happened to her. She hasn't shown up anywhere. Her parents are deceased, and I haven't been able to locate any other relatives. The good news is, we tracked down the hospital where your daughter was born."

Mason relayed Bea's birth and hospital information, and then he said, "I sent you an email with all of the data so your attorney can fast-track the paperwork. I know you were worried about the baby's immunizations, and at least you can breathe a little easier knowing she's had them."

"Thanks, man. Did she have a name on the birth certificate?"

"She did. Jane Thatcher. She was six pounds, two ounces."

"Jane." Tears burned in Ben's eyes. Jane was such a plain name. Could she have put less thought into naming her little girl? "Thanks, Mason. What happens now?"

"Your attorney should have enough to get you legal guardianship. The rest is up to you, Ben. Do you want me to continue searching for her?"

He wanted to find her, to see her face-to-face and ask why she'd never contacted him before the day she'd dropped off Bea. But at the same time, he wished she'd stay away for good. He remembered what Aurelia had said about knowing what had happened so Bea wouldn't go through life wondering why her mother had left her.

"No," Ben said. "I don't want you to, but I think you should. I need closure, for Bea's sake."

After the call, Ben didn't catch up to Zane and Bodhi. He called Aurelia.

"Hi, handsome. How was your run?"

"Cut short. I just heard from Mason." He relayed the information he'd learned, and with tears in his eyes he said, "Soon she'll be legally mine, Rels. We're one step closer to never losing Bea."

CHAPTER NINETEEN

MOTHER'S DAY ARRIVED with sunshine and the promise of a gloriously warm day. Aurelia heard Ben talking to Bea in the kitchen as she carried a load of clean towels upstairs. They'd picked up Flossie yesterday afternoon and taken her on a tour of Aurelia's bookstore, which she was beyond thrilled with. When they showed her Bea's bedroom, she'd told them stories about Aurelia's mother first sleeping in the crib rather than a bassinet by Flossie's bed and how Flossie had snuck out of her bedroom to sleep on the floor in Abigail's room. *I just couldn't be that far away from my baby girl.* When her grandmother learned that although Bea had not one but *two* bedrooms, she had yet to spend a single night in either one, she said Bea was the luckiest little girl in the world to have Aurelia and Ben.

Aurelia knocked on Flossie's door to give her fresh towels.

Flossie peeked out of the guest room, wearing a silk bathrobe and matching slippers. Her silver hair flowed like water, soft and wavy, over her shoulders and down her back. "Come in, bubbelah."

"Happy Mother's Day." She kissed Flossie's cheek and said, "I forgot to put extra towels in your bathroom last night." She set the towels on the nightstand.

"I heard Bea up bright and early. She has lungs of steel, that one. That's good. It means she's strong." Flossie wrapped her hand around Aurelia's arm and said, "How are you this morning, honey?"

Aurelia usually felt a pang of sadness on Mother's Day, but today was different. "I'm good, Grandma. I've got a great guy who has an amazing daughter. You're healthy and here with me, and we're going to spend the day with all the people we love. Life is good right now. Are you doing okay? Is today harder without Grandpa?"

"Grandpa's still with me, honey. I feel him." She put her hand over her heart and tipped her face up toward the ceiling. "He and Abigail are smiling down on us, hoping we'll make the most of today."

"Good. I'm going to head downstairs to help with Bea and breakfast. I'll see you after you're dressed."

"Okay, love," she said as Aurelia left the room.

Aurelia heard Ben singing as she descended the stairs. When she neared the kitchen, she realized he was singing "Perfect" by Ed Sheeran. She tiptoed to the kitchen and peeked in. Ben was dancing with Bea in his arms. His eyes were closed, and Aurelia was surprised he knew every word of the song. She pulled out her phone and began videoing him. She'd thought Bea was the sweetest thing on earth, but this? This was beautiful and tender and so magnificent, words were not enough. She imagined Bea watching the video years from now, knowing how real her daddy's love for her was. Tears threatened as she imagined the video playing on a big screen at Bea's wedding, and she hoped one day she'd be watching Ben dancing and singing with his grandbabies.

Our grandbabies.

Yes, she allowed herself to go there, because that was what she wanted. Ben in her life *forever*.

When he stopped singing, he kissed Bea's cheek and said, "You're *both* perfect, peanut." He turned, spotting Aurelia, and as he closed the distance between them, he said, "You and your mama." He kissed Aurelia and said, "Right, *Mama*?"

Her heart leapt as tears tumbled down her cheek. *Mama. Mama!* It was all she could do to nod.

"Hey there, beautiful." He slid a hand to the nape of her neck, pulling her close as he kissed her. Then he dipped lower and kissed her collarbone. "I had something made for you."

He reached into his pocket and opened his hand, revealing a necklace with three small silver charms. A happy, astonished sound escaped as Aurelia took in the tiny silver charm shaped like an open book with ONCE UPON A TIME engraved on it. Silver heart charms hung on either side of the book. One had *A+B* inscribed on it, the other had only the letter *B*.

"Ben," she said softly. "They're beautiful."

"You're beautiful, Rels." He handed Bea to her and stepped behind her to put the gift around her neck. As he clasped it, he said, "I wanted to give you something to commemorate all the changes in your life."

"Blessings. You guys are blessings in my life," she said, touching the charms.

Ben gazed deeply into her eyes and said, "Once upon a time there were two best friends, a sassy, sexy girl who loved Converse sneakers and was careful with every penny, and an insanely handsome, rich man who adored her. They did everything together except share the truth of their hearts. They joked and cried, ate too much pizza, and sometimes they drank too much. On more than one occasion, the handsome, rich man held the sassy, sexy girl's hair back while she puked." He smiled and said, "And the sassy, sexy girl . . . Well, we won't divulge the details of her cleaning up after his messes. This guy, he wasn't the smartest dude on the block, and he waited too long to let the sassy, sexy girl know how he really felt about her. And one day she moved away—and he was lost without her. And the insanely handsome, rich man realized that without his friend by his side, he wasn't rich at all."

Aurelia smiled through tears, melting inside.

"Then this beautiful baby girl appeared on the guy's doorstep, and his friend, the *smarter* of the two of them, didn't run the other way. The handsome, rich guy knew that staying by his side was the hardest thing that friend had *ever* had to do. She was just starting a new chapter in her life, and she didn't need the chaos of midnight feedings or tracking down women he'd been with. But she stuck to him like glue, and she welcomed the baby girl into her life as if she were her own flesh and blood. And the rich guy fell deeper in love with her and felt richer than he'd ever been."

Her throat thickened as she said, "And she fell deeper in love with him, too."

"I was getting to that," he said, sounding choked up. "Together these two friends worked *really* hard and got *really* exhausted, learning how to take care of the little girl. And the handsome, rich guy knew he was the luckiest man on earth because of the way the sassy, sexy girl is looking at him right now."

Tears slipped down her cheeks. "Oh, *Ben* . . ." she whispered, going up on her toes to kiss him.

"I love you, Aurelia, and I'm so thankful you're mine. I can't wait to see what our next chapter holds."

"I love this, and I love you."

As he lowered his lips to hers, the doorbell rang.

He groaned against her lips and said, "Our timing *suuuucks*."

"I don't know. Our timing might always be a little off, but it is *ours*, and that makes it perfect."

"God, I love you." He kissed her again.

"Want me to get the door while you start breakfast? I'm starved."

"Yeah, thanks." As she walked out of the kitchen, he said, "I'll make your favorite. Ten-inch pancakes!"

"Your daddy is a silly, wonderful, romantic man," she said to Bea as she walked through the living room, touching her beautiful new necklace. "And we are two very lucky girls."

She pulled open the door, and in the space of a second the hair on the back of Aurelia's neck stood on end, and she knew the tall blonde before her, whose teary eyes locked on Bea, was Bea's mother. Aurelia held Bea tighter, tasting bile in her throat.

Please don't be her. Please don't be her. "Yes?"

Eyes on the baby, the woman said, "Is . . . ?" Her lower lip trembled. "Ben Dalton here?"

Her speech was slurred. Aurelia's protective instincts kicked in. She turned away with Bea as she hollered, "Ben! Ben! I need you!"

Ben's phone rang, but the terrified pitch of Aurelia's voice sent him racing from the kitchen. "What's wrong—"

He stopped cold at the sight of the blonde standing on his porch. *Caroline.* His chest constricted, and just as quickly, anger simmered inside him, and his legs propelled him forward. He put an arm around Aurelia's shoulder, guiding her, with Bea in her arms, behind him and said, "Take Bea upstairs, please." He gritted his teeth against the blinding rage clawing up his chest and said, "Caroline," rough and accusatorily.

"I'm sorry," she said, slurring a little.

"Are you *drunk*?"

Tears slid down her cheeks. "I thought I could do it, but I couldn't. I *can't*," she croaked, her words running together.

"How *dare* you come here drunk. You're not getting anywhere near that baby. You *abandoned* her. Anything could have happened to her, for fuck's sake." His words flew fast like bullets. Unable to stifle his rage, he said, "She's a *baby*, Caroline, and you left her like a sack of unwanted trash. You can fight me in court for her."

"Ben, let me explain."

"I don't care why you did it anymore. She's *mine*, and I'll protect her from you if it takes every penny I have."

Sobs broke from her lungs, and she nodded defeatedly. "I'm . . . I'm staying at the inn on Bedford, room 212, if you change your mind."

"I'll have my attorney send you papers there in the morning." He slammed the door, shaking all over. He turned and saw Aurelia, clutching Bea, standing in the circle of Flossie's arms, crying.

CHAPTER TWENTY

BEN PUT HIS arms around Aurelia, Flossie, and Bea and said, "We are *not* losing her, Rels. I've got this."

"She wants her! I heard her say it," Aurelia cried.

Ben put one hand on the baby's back, one on Aurelia's shoulder, and said, "No. It's *not* happening. She endangered her, and she's not getting her back. I'm going to call my attorney."

"This is not any of my business," Flossie said carefully. "But I think everyone needs to take a deep breath. That woman, Caroline, is hurting, too. Giving up a child can't be easy."

"Grandma, are you saying we should give her back?" Aurelia shook her head. "No."

"No, bubbelah. I'm not saying that at all." She took Ben's and Aurelia's hands and said, "Bea belongs here, but it took a lot of courage for that woman to come back and face Ben, and I think he should hear her out, for Bea's sake."

He shook his head, grinding his teeth. "No way. I *can't*. It took *all* of my restraint to keep from saying what I *really* think of her for leaving my daughter on the porch."

"I'm suggesting this *for* your daughter, Benjamin." Flossie placed her hand on Bea's back and said, "What will you tell her? That her mother wanted to see her and you stood in her way? Or perhaps you'll keep that part of her past to yourself?" Her gaze softened, and she said, "That's not who you are." She looked thoughtfully at Aurelia and said, "It's not who *either* of you are. Bea deserves to know the truth."

"I can't even think straight right now. I have to call my attorney." He pressed a kiss to each of their heads and went into his office.

He sank down to the couch with his head in his hands. Anger, frustration, and his love for Bea coalesced in a long, tortured groan. He slammed his eyes shut, Flossie's words playing in his mind like a broken record. What the fuck should he do? Seeing Caroline brought all the hurt and anger to the surface. He couldn't have talked rationally with her if he'd wanted to, but hearing her slurred speech? That was the straw that broke the camel's back, unleashing his rage.

Fuck.

He hated that Aurelia had seen him like that.

He sat up, breathing deeply, and forced himself to focus as he pulled out his phone. He'd missed a call from Mason and quickly listened to the voicemail. *Ben, it's Mason. We got a hit on her credit card this morning in your area. Give me a call when you can.* He called Mason and gave him the lowdown. Then he texted his attorney, apologizing for his rotten timing and asking if he could take an emergency call. Ben's phone rang a few minutes later with a call from him, and he relayed the turn of events. Understanding the urgency of the situation, his attorney agreed to draw up documents for the voluntary termination of parental rights for Caroline to sign and email them over shortly.

Feeling mildly relieved, Ben went to find Aurelia.

Flossie was sitting in the living room playing with Bea. He hadn't noticed her festively long, bright turquoise skirt and black top before. *Damn.* He'd forgotten about brunch.

"Is Aurelia upstairs?" He offered his finger to Bea, who took it, happily waving her arms.

"She is. She needed a moment."

"I'm sorry for losing my cool." Regret ate away at him for ruining her Mother's Day, and what he'd seen as Aurelia's first Mother's Day, too.

"It's okay, sweetheart. Babies have a way of bringing out the best in us, but they also heighten our protective instincts to new, unimaginable levels." Flossie lifted an empathetic though serious gaze to him, and for a moment she just looked at him, as though her words should have deeper meaning.

And they did.

She wasn't just talking about him, or even him and Aurelia. He realized her empathy was also meant for Caroline.

"Things are not always what they seem," Flossie said as she placed her hand over his. "I know my bubbelah, and right now she wants to lock Bea up in a glass case so Caroline can't hurt her again. My heart tells me that you're coming from the same place, and that's a decision only you can make. You're a strong man, Benjamin, and you're a good, kindhearted man. But I respect that you are also a businessman, which I assume makes it easier to separate emotions from some of your decisions. You don't know this, but my husband and I were faced with a similar dilemma when Aurelia's mother died. We knew that Aurelia would have many occasions in her life when she'd need to explain why she was raised by her grandparents, and with each one of them she'd have to revisit the pain of losing the mother she'd never had a chance to know. We could have spared her that by telling her we were her parents." She shrugged, a small smile stretching her lips. "She may never have found out. Or she might have, and then we, the people who loved her most, who wanted nothing but to protect her, would have become liars in her eyes. I'm not saying your situation is the same, or your decisions should mimic ours. I just thought you should know, because whatever decision you make will be Bea's burden to carry for the rest of her life."

He turned his hand over and squeezed hers, his gaze drifting to Bea. "I just want to protect her."

"We all do, and that will *never* change. When she's thirty and falls in love with a wonderful man, you'll still worry over every little thing, but the decisions will be out of your hands. The only question is, will you have given her the foundation she needs to build a solid life, or will an unexpected crack appear, threatening everything she has ever believed to be true?"

Aurelia sat in the rocking chair in Bea's nursery, worrying with her hands. Her mind sprinted even faster down a terrifying road. She closed her eyes, but the visions of a dark forest closing in on her were suffocating. In her mind she saw a fork up ahead and absently pressed both feet hard and flat on the bedroom floor. To her right she saw herself standing with Ben and Bea. The image was crystal clear and light as day. To the left was just her and Ben. Her throat tightened, and she gasped, clutching the arms of the rocking chair. The darkness behind her lids drew her attention straight ahead of her, where she saw a blurry image of Caroline. No matter how much she tried, she couldn't conjure a clear picture of the woman. Either she'd been so blinded by fear she hadn't let her face take hold in her memory or she'd blocked it out of anger. Either way brought just as much pain to the center of her chest, like an empty, gaping hole.

"Rels?"

She heard Ben's voice and searched for him in the darkness, but he was gone. He called her name again, and she felt his hands on hers. "Ben!" Her eyes flew open and she found him kneeling before her. The air rushed from her lungs as she fell into his arms. "Ben, I'm so scared."

"I know, baby. I am too."

"There's no right answer. She's Bea's mother and you're Bea's father. She's not mine, but I feel like she is, and that's *not* supposed to be what this is about."

He drew back, taking her face between his hands. Anger and sadness warred in his stormy eyes as he said, "She's *ours*, Aurelia. Not just mine. *Ours*."

She nodded, but more tears fell. "She's *hers*, too. We can't ignore that."

His jaw clenched, and when he opened his mouth to speak, no words came. His forehead fell to her shoulder as his arms circled her. They clung to each other, shedding tears, swimming against a raging tide as the weight of the morning swamped them.

CHAPTER TWENTY-ONE

LATER THAT AFTERNOON, Ben and Aurelia sat with his family in Willow and Zane's living room, which should have been brimming with smiles and laughter in celebration of Mother's Day. Instead, he held tightly to Aurelia's hand, meeting his family's distraught faces. He'd just told them about Caroline showing up. Thankfully, Derek, Flossie, and Alisha had taken Jonah into another room, and Bodhi and Zane were playing outside with Louie, giving them privacy.

"Oh my God, Ben," Willow said wistfully. "You can't let her take Bea away."

"Did you ask if she wanted to *take* her?" Bridgette asked.

"She abandoned her," Piper snapped. "That woman's not taking her. I've got your back, Ben. You tell me when, and we'll go tell her how it's going to be."

"But you wouldn't even know she existed if not for her," Talia, always the most levelheaded, reminded him. "I think you should hear her out. She's not demanding money, is she?"

Piper glared angrily at Talia. "*Hear her out?* She left the baby on the doorstep. The only thing Ben should *hear out* is his foot kicking her ass out of Sweetwater for good."

"Piper, you're not a mother!" Bridgette snapped. "You can't know why she did it or how she's feeling. I can't imagine how hard it was for her to leave that sweet baby in the first place."

Piper pushed to her feet and seethed, "So you think he should just hand her over?"

"No! I'm not saying—"

"Girls!" Roxie snapped, clutching Bea to her chest. "*Stop*, please. This isn't a matter that can be settled by accusations and assumptions." She turned concerned eyes to Ben and Aurelia and said, "I know you're both hurting, and you're scared, but I'm with Flossie on this one. You said she suggested you talk with Caroline and get the answers before making any rash decisions. Ben, you have more money than you know what to do with, and you're her *father*. Caroline can't take her away without a legal battle. And that's not something I am condoning. I'm just pointing it out. But this isn't about you, Aurelia, or even Caroline."

His mother smiled down at Bea, lovingly stroking her cheek, and said, "This is about this innocent baby girl, where she came from, what her future will hold." Her eyes found Ben's again, and he felt her pain the way he now understood only a parent could feel the pain of their child. "Benny, this is one of the most important decisions you will ever make, and you must remember that it's not about the hurt you feel for your daughter, or how much you want to protect her, or your own heart, or Aurelia's heart. It's about the hurt your daughter will feel if she finds out you kept her from seeing her birth mother."

Guilt strangled Ben, making it hard to breathe, even harder to think clearly. He shifted his attention to his father, the only one who hadn't given his two cents, and said, "Dad? What should I do?"

His father looked around the room at each of his children, who were all sitting on the edge of their seats, except Piper, who was pacing, arms crossed, jaw clenched. Willow sat beside their mother, looking like she was going to cry as she gazed at Bea. Talia was watching Ben, her serious eyes peering out from behind her glasses, imploring him to talk to Caroline. When his father's eyes met Aurelia's, her grip on Ben's hand tightened, and he felt her trembling. Then his father's serious eyes found his, and he saw so many conflicting emotions, it was like looking in a mirror.

"Son," his father said, "do you remember what I said about giving people space to make their own mistakes?"

Unable to form a single word, Ben realized he was holding his breath, and he nodded.

"We raised you to be a good man, and you have excellent judgment. I trust your instincts, and I know you'll make the right decision for all of you."

What the fuck? That wasn't an answer. "Dad—"

His father held up his hand, silencing him, and shook his head.

Piper scoffed. "In other words, you're giving Ben enough rope to hang himself."

"You of all people know that a *rope* can be turned into a lifeline, a sturdy bridge, or a noose," his father said sternly. "Have some faith in your brother."

Piper rolled her eyes and seethed, "I'd rather give that woman a piece of my mind. I have faith in *that*."

That sparked an uproar of angry comments, heartfelt pleas, and accusations. Ben pulled Aurelia closer. He realized he was surrounded by all the people he loved on Mother's Day, a day that should be celebrated. A day he'd wanted to be the most memorable and wonderful for Aurelia. And just a few streets away, Caroline was probably bawling her eyes out alone in an unfamiliar room.

He pressed a kiss to Aurelia's temple as his family battled out his war, and he said, "Rels, can I talk to you privately?"

She nodded, and as they pushed to their feet, his family silenced, all eyes turning to them.

"I want to talk to Aurelia alone for a minute." He led her out of the living room and up the stairs. When they were out of earshot of the others, he sat on a step and pulled her down on his lap. She looked like she was balancing on the edge of a knife, afraid to move.

He kissed her softly, holding her close as he said, "What a cluster-fuck of a Mother's Day, huh?"

She lifted one shoulder.

"I'm sorry, babe. I'm sorry for losing my temper and for the night-mare that we're in."

She swallowed hard. "What do you want to do, Ben?"

"I don't think it's about what I want to do any more than it's about what Caroline wants to do. I can't stop thinking about what you said earlier, about not being able to ignore that she's Bea's mother. You know you've become Bea's mother in *my* eyes, but I feel sick to death because it's Mother's Day and I just slammed the door in the face of our baby's biological mother." He slid his hand to the nape of her neck, as he'd done so often, and touched his forehead to hers, tears burning as he said, "I don't know what's right or wrong, but I know I won't be able to live with that and still look into our little girl's eyes and feel like I'm the father she deserves."

"I know." Her voice was a fraying thread. "I just keep thinking that if my grandparents had lied to me about my mother, it would have totally messed me up. I don't think it would help knowing that they thought they were protecting me. It would feel like a huge betrayal, and I could never fully trust them again. Ben, it's not just that, but look how much our parents affected who we are. If they'd lied to me, it would have made trusting anyone else, even you and your family, much harder, if not impossible. I don't want that for Bea. We're adults. We can weather any storm. But she didn't ask for any of this."

She had taken the words right out of his mouth. "I know, babe. Will you come with me to see her?"

"I want to, to support you, but I think this has to be between you and Caroline. I worry she'll feel ganged up on, and that will put her on the defensive. But if you need me, I will go with you."

His love for her seeped into every crack and crevice of his being, filling spaces he'd never known needed filling. "I will always need *and* want you," he said as he embraced her, soaking in her essence, her love, and her unconditional support. "But I've got this, babe, for all of us."

After spending way too long explaining to a certain sister why he had to see Caroline alone, Ben gave Bea and Aurelia more kisses and tighter hugs than ever before, and then he headed over to the inn. As he made his way to Caroline's room, he tried to prepare what he'd say when he saw her, telling himself not to go off on her again, to count to three before saying a word.

By the time he reached her door, adrenaline had him wide-eyed and breathing hard. *I can do this. Calm. Be fucking calm.* He squared his shoulders and knocked.

The door opened slowly, and he was surprised to see a man standing on the other side. The slim man's head was shaved to a sheen of stubble, matching his scruff. Thick chestnut brows accentuated kind green eyes.

"I'm sorry. I think I have the wrong room," Ben said nervously.

"No. You have the right room, Ben." He had a gentle demeanor and wore a checked dress shirt and jeans. He looked younger than Ben, maybe in his midtwenties. "I'm Brad, a friend of Caroline's." Ben took his proffered hand, and Brad said, "I'm glad you came. Come in, please."

Ben stepped into the room, thrown by the man's friendly greeting after the way Ben had treated Caroline, and was met with an Asian man dressed in all black, standing just a few feet inside the room.

"This is Nelson, my husband," Brad said as Nelson offered his hand and a nod.

"Hi. Ben Dalton," he said, shaking Nelson's hand.

When Nelson stepped aside, Ben's gaze swept over a sofa and armchairs, and just beyond, Caroline, lying on the bed. He hadn't noticed how gaunt she'd looked that morning. Her eyes were red and puffy, her cheeks still damp from tears. She looked embarrassed as she pushed up to a sitting position. He was the one who should be embarrassed after the way he'd treated her.

"Careful, Car," Brad said as he and Nelson went to her.

"I'm okay," she reassured them. Looking sheepishly at Ben, she said, "I didn't expect to see you again."

She spoke slowly, and some of her words ran together, but Ben could tell she wasn't drunk. He wasn't sure what he was dealing with, but it was clear that Caroline was not the same vivacious woman he'd met at the bar all those months ago.

Regret peppered him like machine-gun spray as he said, "I'm sorry for how I treated you—"

"It's okay," she said softly. "I deserve it. Believe me, I've been beating myself up since I left her on your doorstep."

Brad put his hand on her shoulder and said, "Caroline is a good person, Ben."

She smiled at Brad, and then she said, "I'm no better than anyone else, though. But I need you to know, I didn't intend to leave her with a note."

Nelson waved to a chair and said, "You should sit down."

"Thanks, I'm good." Ben remained standing, eyes on Caroline, trying to think past the rush of blood in his ears. "Why did you?"

"I think Nelson's right. You should sit down for this," she said.

Something in her tone made him sit.

She inhaled deeply and blew it out slowly. Then she moved to the chair nearest him. Nelson sat on the love seat, and Brad remained standing. He placed his hand on her shoulder again, and she reached up, putting her hand on his.

"When I realized I was pregnant, I thought about finding you and telling you. But that night we were together, all you talked about was the woman you were in love with, and even though you were trying to forget her, I got the feeling you weren't done with her. I didn't want to mess that up."

"Then why did you track me down? And how did you find me?"

"I had no one else to turn to. I had to find you, and you'd told me the name of your company and that you were from Sweetwater. It took only about three seconds to find you on Google."

Of course . . .

"Ben, I'm glad you came, and I want to tell you everything, but it needs to be in short form. I had some trouble with headaches and fatigue during my pregnancy, mood swings, too. My sense of smell was off, and sometimes I couldn't think clearly. But I was pregnant, so I expected some changes, and my doctor wasn't worried. Two weeks after I gave birth, the headaches worsened, and there were times I could barely function. I went in for tests, and they found an inoperable brain tumor."

A pained sound escaped Ben's lungs. "Caroline . . ." he said, but there were no words to describe the pain and regret consuming him. More importantly, he knew that pain was nothing compared to what the three other people in the room were going through.

Nelson put a hand on Ben's back and said, "It's a lot to take in."

"Yeah," was all Ben could manage. "Why didn't you call me?"

"She didn't tell anyone," Brad said. "I didn't even know about Janie until yesterday."

"I don't have close friends in LA, at least not friends I wanted to burden with this. And I guess I was in denial, trying to care for Janie and prove the doctors wrong. But it was becoming harder to focus, and my headaches were getting worse. I couldn't fool myself any longer. I knew I couldn't care for her, and I also knew it was unfair to think I could just show up and spring her on you, but other than Brad and Nelson, I'm pretty much alone in this world."

Ben tried to process what she'd said, but he was still trying to wrap his head around her fate.

"The morning that I was going to see you," she said, "I had a head-ache so debilitating, I couldn't speak. I was drooling, my vision blurred, and all I kept thinking was that something could have happened to Janie. The headache didn't fully subside, but it eased enough to drive, and that's when I took her to your house. I was so afraid that I'd get hit with another one and not be able to explain, I left the note and waited down the block where I could see the front door. Once I knew you'd found her, I left town. I was heading back to LA, but I had a seizure in the parking lot of the airport. A nurse who was on her way to catch a plane saw me. I got lucky. She knew what to do to make sure I didn't choke. After I came out of it and regained control, which seemed like hours later, she wanted to take me to a hospital, but I convinced her to call Brad, who lives in New York City. He and Nelson have been help-ing me ever since."

"We didn't know any of this," Brad explained. "We didn't know she had a baby, much less left her on your doorstep. We would have been there for her throughout her pregnancy, the birth, helped her care for the baby."

"Her seizures have gotten worse, and yesterday she told us about Janie because she was afraid to drive herself here to see you," Nelson explained.

Ben felt like he'd been gutted—for Caroline, for Bea, and for Brad and Nelson, too.

"I don't want to take her from you, Ben." Tears welled in her eyes. "I'm so sorry to do this to you. I knew you could afford to take care of her, though I wasn't sure you would want her. But when we were together that night, the way you spoke of the woman you were in love with, and your family, I knew in my heart that if Janie had any chance of finding a loving home, it would be with you. I'm so thankful you took her in."

Fighting tears, Ben reached for her hand. "Caroline, I'm so sorry. I'll help in any way I can. Get you the best doctors—"

Tears slipped down her cheeks, and she said, "I'm grateful for your offer, but nothing can be done. I don't have a lot of time left, but I'm glad to know Janie has a chance for a new beginning and that she'll be loved." Sobs stole her voice, and Brad wrapped his arms around her.

"I know, Car," Brad said, giving Ben a look that told of his love for his friend and his grief over losing her.

Nelson pressed a kiss to Caroline's head, and Brad stroked his cheek, giving him a reassuring nod. "Excuse me," Nelson said, and then he went into the bathroom.

"I'm okay. I'm okay. I'm okay," Caroline said, as if she were convincing herself. She wiped her eyes and sat up straighter, as if she practiced schooling her expression daily, and said, "I have medications to help, but I have only a few weeks left. I just want to see Janie one last time, to hold her, kiss her, smell her. I want to apologize to her and tell her how much I love her."

Her trembling voice and damp eyes belied her steely facade. Ben felt his heart crumbling in on itself and said, "Of course. This afternoon?"

A laugh bubbled out of Caroline. She covered her mouth with her hand, but she couldn't hide the elation in her eyes. "I'm so tired. Can we please do it tomorrow morning? Mornings are often better for me."

"Absolutely. You can see her as often as you'd like."

She shook her head, no longer trying to hide the rivers of tears streaming down her cheeks as she said, "Things are going downhill fast. I don't want her to see me at my worst. This will be my final goodbye."

They talked for a long while, and Ben told her about Aurelia and how Bea had brought them together. He learned that Caroline had known Brad in college and had stayed in touch via texts and phone calls the last few years. But she'd been in such deep denial when she'd received her diagnosis, she'd truly believed she could beat her fate.

"Thank you for understanding. I'm looking forward to seeing Janie."

"We call her Bea," Ben said.

"*Bea*. That's beautiful," she said through her tears. "Jane means *gift from God*. She truly is a gift."

Gift from God. Another spear of regret stabbed him for thinking Caroline hadn't even cared enough to pick a meaningful name. "Yes, she is truly a gift, Caroline. Thank you for trusting me enough to bring her to me."

CHAPTER TWENTY-TWO

AURELIA WORRIED HERSELF into a frenzy Sunday night over how she would react when she saw Caroline with Bea. Would she burst into tears for both mother and daughter? She wanted to be open and welcoming and worried she might make things harder for Caroline if her sadness broke free. But from the moment Caroline arrived Monday morning with her friends Brad and Nelson, Aurelia felt a sense of relief and a kinship with her. She was warm and lovely and had a sense of humor despite all she was dealing with, and she approached the day as a gift rather than a goodbye. It was easy to see why Ben would have been attracted to her. She was strong, and she was smart and kind.

Now Aurelia and Ben sat in the living room with Caroline and her friends. Caroline cuddled Bea on the rocker, wearing the most serene expression. She closed her eyes, nuzzling Bea's neck, and when she opened them, her love billowed out. "Nothing smells as good as she does," Caroline said softly.

"Except at three in the morning when she has a messy diaper," Ben said.

They all chuckled.

Caroline rubbed her nose along Bea's cheek and said, "I'll never forget you, sweet Janie, and I hope you'll never forget me." She touched Bea's foot. "The first time I felt you kick, I didn't recognize it for what it was. But you wanted me to know it was you, didn't you? Because you did it again and again. And the first time I held you? I have never known love like my love for you, baby girl."

Aurelia fought tears.

"I will remember every second with you, and everything about you, until my very last breath," Caroline said softly to her daughter. "And I know that you are well loved."

"I'm going to get the bag from the car," Nelson said, and quickly left the room.

Brad and Caroline exchanged a look of understanding. "I'd better go with him." Brad followed him out.

After they left the room, Caroline said, "Nelson doesn't like to cry in front of other people." She nuzzled Bea's cheek again and said, "But we're not going to cry, are we? Because this is a blessed day, a day I'll never forget."

Aurelia leaned against Ben, trying desperately to hold back tears, and whispered, "You did the right thing."

When Ben had returned from their visit yesterday afternoon looking like he'd been through hell and told Aurelia and his family what had transpired, they'd all broken down. Aurelia had cried for Bea and Caroline, for Caroline's friends she hadn't yet met, and even for Ben. She and Ben learned that every fleeting moment counted, and nothing—*nothing*—was meaningless. Ben confided in her and said he felt like he was losing Caroline, too, even though he barely knew her. That had brought more tears, and she understood where he was coming from, because every time they looked at Bea, they'd see Caroline's face and they'd miss her. After taking Flossie home and finally crawling into bed, emotionally spent, Aurelia had realized she'd also been crying for herself and the loss of her own mother.

Caroline looked at them now and said, "Please don't cry. I know the gravity of our situation, but because of you and Ben, my baby girl will have a wonderful life, full of family who loves her. That's what I want to carry with me when I walk out this door, not the image of us all in tears."

"I'm sorry," Aurelia said, trying to force her emotions away. She needed something else to focus on and scrambled for something to do. "Would you mind if I took pictures of you and Bea?"

Caroline smiled. "I would love that. The bag Nelson said he was getting has her baby pictures, birth certificate, and other things I thought you might want."

"Thank you," Ben said.

Aurelia took pictures of Caroline and Bea, and eventually the guys returned with the bag Caroline had mentioned. Caroline snuggled Bea a little longer.

"I've had a wonderful visit, but I should go before I start feeling poorly," Caroline said.

Aurelia's stomach clenched. She had so much respect for the woman she'd thought she'd hate, she ached with sadness that this was all she'd have with her baby. With *their* baby. And that's exactly what Bea felt like now that Aurelia had met Caroline. *Their* baby—the three of them.

"I know you call her Bea, which is beautiful, but will you keep Jane as part of her name?" Caroline asked.

"We were thinking about making it her middle name," Ben said.

"Oh, Ben," Caroline said with a soft laugh. "You might want to consider using Bea as her middle name, even if you call her by it. No girl wants to grow up with the initials *BJ*."

They all smiled, but Caroline was getting ready to leave her baby for the very last time, and the weight of that hung in the air.

"Good point," Ben said. "Jane Bea it is."

Caroline snuggled Bea one last time. "I will always love you," she whispered, and then she handed Bea to Ben.

"She really is a gift, Caroline, and we know she's the most precious thing in the world to you. I promise we will do our best to make sure she never forgets you."

Tears slid from Caroline's eyes as she kissed Ben's cheek and said, "Thank you." She turned to Aurelia and said, "Thank you for loving her. I want you to know that Ben's love for you was what showed me I could trust him with her. You're a lucky woman, and he's just as lucky to have you."

She hugged Aurelia so tight, there was no stopping Aurelia's tears from falling.

"This will sound funny," Aurelia said, "but I think we would have been good friends."

"Me too. Thank you," Caroline said shakily. "For everything."

Later that evening, while Bea slept, Ben and Aurelia went through the bag from Caroline. In addition to Bea's birth certificate and immunization records, they found the blanket in which she must have come home from the hospital, along with a tiny pink beanie and a framed picture of Caroline and Bea. Caroline was sitting in the hospital bed with Bea swaddled in the blanket they'd found in the bag and wearing the pink beanie. She was holding the baby in front of her, and they were nose to nose. Bea was looking at her, and Caroline's eyes were closed, but the love in her smile resonated like an embrace from the photograph.

"Ben," Aurelia said, "look at this picture. She must have had a nurse or someone at the hospital take it for her."

He looked at the picture, and tears glistened in his eyes. He showed her another picture he'd found in the bag. A selfie. Caroline was lying in bed with Bea snuggled beside her. Caroline's eyes were at half-mast, but once again the love in her smile told of her joy despite her fatigue.

Ben took the pictures and Aurelia's hand and led Aurelia into Bea's nursery. They were staying at Ben's tonight, too exhausted to pack up and go back to Harmony Pointe. He set the picture of Bea and Caroline lying in bed on Bea's bookshelf and said, "I think this one should go in her nursery in our apartment."

"*Our* apartment? I like the sound of that so much more than '*my* apartment.'"

He set down the other frame and gathered her in his arms. "There is no more mine or yours, babe. There's only *ours*." He lowered his lips over hers, taking her in a deep, seductive kiss. His hand slid down her back, cupping her bottom as he said, "And right now I'd like to get *our* sweet little ass into bed, so I can love *our* sexy little body into tomorrow."

They stumbled down the hall to the bedroom in a tangle of limbs and hungry kisses, stripping off their clothes—and the sadness of the afternoon. How did he know that *this* was exactly what she needed? His strong arms around her, his love filling her up?

"Just *tomorrow*?" She pouted as he nibbled on her neck.

He pulled her against him, his hard length pressing eagerly, *temptingly*, against her belly. His chest hair tickled her skin as she said, "I was kind of hoping you'd love me into at *least* next week."

"Fuck next week, babe. I want forever." He lifted her onto the bed, coming down over her. "I'm thinking about putting my house on the market."

In his eyes she saw more than the pulsing heat between them, and his words finally registered. "You're *moving*?"

"There's that *y*-word again." He kissed her smiling lips and said, "You need to be near the shop, and Bea and I need to be near you."

"You want to move in over the shop? For good?"

"Actually, I was thinking more along the lines of *for better or for worse*."

Her heart leapt. "Ben . . . ? Are you saying what I think you're saying?"

"Aurelia, baby, I have loved you my whole life, and I will love you long after my last days on this earth. I don't have a ring, and I've never claimed to have good timing, but my love for you is endless. Marry me, Relsy, and I promise I'll give you the world. And I'll try to work on my timing."

"Oh, Ben! It's *our* timing, and it's *perfect*." She hugged him tighter, clinging to him like a monkey to a tree as she kissed his lips, his cheeks, and his lips again.

"Is that a *yes*?"

"Yes!" She couldn't suppress her smile, or the urge to tease him, as she said, "If you make me come once before our baby girl gets up, it's a yes. *Twice*, and it's a *hell yes*."

"Oh, babe," he said, pressing the head of his cock to her entrance. "Don't underestimate your man."

He pushed into her slowly, and she felt every inch of his thick length filling her body with the same intensity with which his love filled her heart, and with a glimmer of promise in his eyes, he asked, "What'll four times get me?"

"Eternity . . ."

EPILOGUE

"I CAN'T BELIEVE it's finally happening," Aurelia said as she looked in the mirror for the hundredth time in the last half hour, fidgeting with the ribbons in her hair, which was pinned up, with a few sexy tendrils framing her face.

"You've worked hard for this, babe, and it's going to be magnificent."

Ben hadn't been able to take his eyes off her all morning as she rushed around their apartment, dressing and preparing for the grand opening of Chapter One. She was adorable, and beautiful, and she was *his*. It had been a month since Ben had proposed, and three weeks since he'd moved into the apartment above the bookstore. Thinking of visits with Flossie, holidays with Ben's big family, and adding to their own family in the future, they decided to hold on to Ben's house in Sweetwater. They'd had to delay the grand opening of the bookstore because of a broken water pipe and then had delayed it again when Caroline passed away. But his beautiful, bighearted fiancée hadn't complained. She'd said if she'd learned one thing over the last several weeks, it was that life was full of unexpected obstacles and celebrations, and their plans needed to be fluid.

Aurelia twirled in her Empire-waist dress.

"You're stunning," he said, stepping behind her. His arms circled her waist, and he pressed a kiss to her shoulder. The charms on the necklace he'd given her shimmered in the lights. "Are you sure you don't want to wear a necklace that's more appropriate for the era?"

She smiled at him in the mirror, touching the silver charms. "I've never taken this off, and I never plan to." She turned in his arms and looked at his frilly shirt and black tailcoat. "Mr. Darcy has nothing on you. Thank you for dressing up."

She'd decided to do a reading from *Pride and Prejudice* for the opening. Everly, Lazarus, and Hollis were also dressing up as their favorite literary characters. Ben and Aurelia had bought the cutest *Alice's Adventures in Wonderland* dress for Bea, who had blessed them with an extra-long nap this morning. She kept them on their toes, making them late in the mornings with dirty diapers or puke on their clothes, but neither of them minded. Jane Bea Dalton was legally his, which meant she was *theirs*, and they adored everything about her.

"Anything for you, Relsy." He ran his hands down her hips and said, "The guys will give me hell for dressing up as Darcy, but you can make up for that later." He put his mouth beside her ear and whispered, "After Bea goes to sleep tonight, maybe we can act out your favorite scene from Charlotte Sterling's latest erotic novel."

She'd loved listening to the tape of Ben reading so much, he'd begun narrating her favorite passages from books and leaving recordings on thumb drives in unexpected places with sexy love notes. She'd found them in the diaper bag, in a cup in the pantry, and in her underwear drawer.

Her eyes sparked with heat, and she said, "Thanks, Ben. Now I'll be thinking about *that* all day."

"Good." He pressed his lips to hers, and then he tilted his head and said, "Do you hear that?"

Her brow wrinkled. "What?"

She followed him out of the bedroom and into the living room. He pulled his phone from his pocket and turned on Lukas Graham's "Love Someone."

♥ ♥ ♥

Aurelia had never heard this song before, and as she listened to the lyrics about opening up her heart and making room for someone she loved, Ben reached for her hand and began slow dancing.

"Ben . . . ?"

He gazed into her eyes, singing about how he pinched himself because he couldn't believe she loved him. Every word found its way into her heart.

"We have more than an hour before anyone will be here," he said as he dipped her over his arm.

When the song ended, he took a step back, and "Born to Be Yours" by Kygo and Imagine Dragons came on. Ben's expression turned sinful, and in the space of a second he morphed from romantic to *holy-fuck* hot, hips thrusting to the beat, eyes locked on her. Adrenaline soared through Aurelia's veins as Ben gyrated to the beat, his shoulders rocking as he strutted closer and dropped his coat to the floor, making her temperature spike. He danced around her, singing about how he'd never known anyone until he knew her and how he was born to be *hers*. She could barely contain herself, grinning like a fool and moving to the beat as he danced seductively around her, leaning in close with every move. He brushed his lips over hers as he grabbed the two sides of his shirt and tore it open, sending buttons flying across the room. She couldn't contain her squeals and bounced on her toes as he sang and stripped, his hips moving so seductively, so manly and confident, she could practically feel his thick thighs pressing against hers.

"You wanted a striptease," he practically growled. "My girl gets what she wants."

"You remembered that from *Claimed by Love*?"

His eyes narrowed. "Yeah, but I don't do other guys' moves."

He grabbed the front of his pants and yanked—*hard*—and the front panel separated from the back, leaving him in a very well-filled-out G-string. She squealed again and covered her gaping jaw as he dragged his slacks over her chest and said, "Stripper pants . . . *Thank you, Derek.*"

"Oh my God!" she whisper-laughed, trying not to wake Bea, but she was cracking up and *so* turned on, there was no hiding it!

She reached for him, and he ground his hard heat against her, lavishing her with dizzying kisses. He tore his mouth away and said, "I was born to be *yours*, baby, and you were born to be *mine—*"

The front door flew open, and Piper barged in, arms flailing, yammering about something with Willow, Bridgette, and Talia on her heels, all talking at once.

"Holy Christ," Ben ground out as he shoved Aurelia in front of him. "What the hell? You're not supposed to be here for another hour!"

The girls turned as if they hadn't noticed them before.

"What the . . . ?" Piper stepped closer and peered around Aurelia, who was giggling and snort-laughing uncontrollably.

Willow spotted the clothes on the floor and said, "Ben's stripping!"

Laughter burst from his sisters' lungs, and they all started talking at once again.

"Ohmygod! I *can't*!" Talia turned away, covering her eyes.

Piper circled Ben and said, "Is that a G-string?"

"Bodhi *so* has to do this!" Bridgette said, laughing hysterically.

"Shh!" he and Aurelia warned, both looking at the bedroom.

The front door flew open again, and Remi ran in yelling, "Hide me!" She ran behind Ben and said, "Those burly apes won't leave me alone! I think Aiden really *did* have me chipped—*Ohmygod!* Ben! You're *naked!*"

His sisters and Aurelia doubled over with laughter. Ben glowered at them all, and Bea wailed.

"I've got her!" Willow ran into the bedroom.

Ben looked at Aurelia, and the laughter in her eyes pushed away his annoyance, even as he noticed Piper videoing the chaotic scene. He didn't care that he was in a G-string, or that Remi was going on about hiding from her bodyguards—or that two enormous men dressed in black suits barreled through the front door and froze as they took in the scene. Ben strode confidently to the table and retrieved the diamond ring he'd hidden beneath an open children's book.

He pulled Aurelia into his arms and focused only on her joyful face. As he slid the two-carat rose-gold ring, with bar-set princess-cut rubies on either side of the center-mounted canary diamond, on her delicate finger, he said, "I love our crappy timing, and I love you, babe. I hope today is everything you have ever dreamed of."

"It's already surpassed my wildest dreams." She went up on her toes to kiss him and said, "*You've* surpassed my wildest dreams. I love you, Ben, and I can't wait to see what forever has in store for us."

A NOTE FROM MELISSA

I hope you enjoyed Ben and Aurelia's journey to coupledom. I always enjoy spending time with the Daltons and their wonderful friends, and I look forward to bringing you more Dalton and Harmony Pointe love stories. Willow, Bridgette, and Talia each have their own book and have found their happily ever afters in the Sugar Lake series, all of which are now available for your binge-reading pleasure.

Be sure to sign up for my newsletter to keep up to date with my new releases and to receive an exclusive short story (www.MelissaFoster.com/ News).

If this is your first Melissa Foster book, you might enjoy the rest of my big-family romance collection, Love in Bloom. Characters from each series make appearances in future books, so you never miss an engagement, wedding, or birth. A complete list of all series titles is included at the start of this book, and downloadable checklists are available on the Reader Goodies page of my website (www.MelissaFoster.com/RG).

Happy reading!

Melissa Foster

ACKNOWLEDGMENTS

Writing a novel is always an emotional experience, and I'm thankful for my friends, family, and fans for pulling me through the ups and downs of my writing life. There are too many of you to name, so please accept my heartfelt gratitude for your inspiration, support, and friendship.

If you'd like sneak peeks into my writing process and to chat with me daily, please join my fan club on Facebook. We talk about our lovable heroes and sassy heroines, and I always try to keep fans abreast of what's going on in our fictional boyfriends' worlds. You never know when you'll end up in one of my books, as several members of my fan club have already discovered (www.Facebook.com/groups/MelissaFosterFans).

Follow my Facebook fan page to keep up with sales and events (www.Facebook.com/MelissaFosterAuthor).

A special thank-you to my amazing editor, Maria Gomez, and the incredible Montlake team for bringing Ben and Aurelia's story to life. As always, heaps of gratitude to my editorial team and, of course, to my very own hunky hero, Les.

ABOUT THE AUTHOR

Photo © 2013 Melanie Anderson

Melissa Foster is a *New York Times* and *USA Today* bestselling and award-winning author of more than eighty books, including *The Real Thing* and *Only for You* (from her Sugar Lake series). Melissa and her books have been featured in *USA Today*, *Hagerstown* magazine, *The Patriot*, and more. Her novel *River of Love* has been optioned for film by Passionflix. Melissa also writes sweet romance under the name Addison Cole. When Melissa isn't writing up a storm, she's living her own happily ever after with her husband and a gaggle of grown children. For more news, information about her books, and to chat with her, visit Melissa at www.MelissaFoster.com.